Blood Tr

BLOOD TIES

Richard Pitman

Hodder & Stoughton

Copyright © Richard Pitman and Joe McNally 1996

First published in Great Britain in 1996
by Hodder and Stoughton
A division of Hodder Headline PLC

The right of Richard Pitman to be identified as the author
of this work has been asserted by him in accordance with the
Copyright, Designs and Patents Act 1988.

10 9 8 7 6 5 4 3 2 1

A CIP catalogue record for this title
is available from the British Library.

ISBN 0 340 62856 1

Typeset by Phoenix Typesetting,
Ilkley, West Yorkshire

Printed and bound in Great Britain by
Mackays of Chatham PLC

Hodder and Stoughton
A division of Hodder Headline PLC
338 Euston Road
London NW1 3BH

ACKNOWLEDGEMENTS

I am extremely grateful to Richard Kent of Helshaw Grange Stud which, among other good stallions, houses the Derby winner, Henbit. Richard was cheerfully and unfailingly helpful and his warm hospitality was much appreciated.

Thanks also to vets Campbell Thompson and John Newcombe for answering questions and unwittingly providing some of the scenes you'll read in the following pages.

One

In the dying days of the old jump season, after the toughest five
months since my comeback, I got a phone call.

'Malloy?'

'Yes.' I didn't recognise the voice.

'You don't know me but you'll get to know my voice.'

I hoped not. It had a sniggering, supercilious tone. I said
nothing.

He said, 'You're riding right through the summer?'

'Who's asking?'

'Just listen. You're riding through the summer.' No longer a
question.

'Maybe.'

'No maybe. You will be.'

Stern now. Commanding. Something in the tone caused a
nervous ripple in my gut.

He said, 'Over the next few months I'm going to call you a
few times – probably on the evening before you ride something fancied. I'll give you riding instructions and you'll stick
to them.'

Trainers gave riding instructions, owners very occasionally,
complete strangers were a new one on me. But I held my
tongue, held my breath.

'You listening, Malloy?'

'Keep talking.'

'I know something about you. You do what you're told or I
give it to Kerman.'

Jean Kerman was a ruthless tabloid journalist specialising in
racing exposés – she'd ruined at least a dozen apparently solid
careers.

I'd been shamed and scorned enough in my life. There was
only one thing left, one secret, and I said a brief intense prayer

1

against his knowing it.

He spoke again.

He didn't know it. The sudden relief cushioned the shock of what he did say. I stayed silent, trying to gather my thoughts.

He said: 'You've gone all quiet and shy, Malloy.'

'Just run it past me again.'

'Don't mess me around! You heard.'

'I just want to be sure I've got everything right.'

There was a pause then he repeated everything in an impatient monotone, like a teacher with a backward kid. 'You and Martin Corish are conning breeders. Town Crier isn't covering the mares you say he is. You're using a cheap ringer and charging the full fee. Now, if that gets out, do you want a point by point lesson on how it will affect your career? Or a written declaration of what it will do to your nice little stud business?'

Just over a year ago I'd invested everything I had in becoming equal partner with Martin Corish in the stud he had started. I didn't have a clue what this guy was talking about but he sounded very convincing. I said, 'I think we'd better meet.'

'I think you'd better get your cheating boots on. I'll be in touch.'

'Listen . . .'

He hung up.

I rang Martin. His secretary-cum-groom was evasive, defensive. She told me he wasn't around.

'When will he be around?'

'Ummm . . . I'm not really sure.'

'Where is he?'

'Maybe if you call this evening . . .'

'Where is he?'

'I'm sorry Mr Malloy, I can't say.'

'Look, don't make me drive all the way down there.'

'I'm sorry. I'm just to say he's uncontactable. That's what I was told.'

'Where's Caroline?'

'Mrs Corish isn't well. She's lying down.' The girl was obviously agitated, her voice rising. It wasn't fair to take out my frustrations on her. There was obviously something wrong at the stud. I told

2

her I'd see her in an hour, clicked the answerphone on, grabbed my jacket and pointed the car towards Wiltshire.

I'd been sucked into enough whirlpools in recent years to sense another one when it was still some way off. I was already feeling the pull of its vortex.

Two

It was dusk when I reached the farm. As I swung the heavy wooden gate open insects hummed in the greenery and swarmed towards my car headlights which illuminated the sign reading: THIS GATE MUST BE KEPT CLOSED AT ALL TIMES. It wasn't unusual for a horse to get loose somewhere on the enclosed three hundred acres. If you could keep them off the roads you stood a good chance of getting them back unharmed.

Further safety measures were obvious on the mile-long driveway; regular speed bumps to force visitors to cut their speed to below twenty miles per hour.

Martin Corish and his wife lived in a big farmhouse close to the stableyard. The house was in darkness as I pulled in by the low wall. I got out. The dusk had deepened. The outlines of mares and their foals in the nearby paddock merged into single shapes. No dogs barked.

Something was wrong.

I stood still, listening. Nothing but the sounds and smells of a warm June night in the country. Insects. Musky flower scents. Quiet whickering from mares. From way across the fields the eerie cry of a vixen. Shut your eyes and you'd bet you weren't within a hundred miles of humanity.

I walked into the yard. Halfway across it I heard a phone ringing. After half a dozen rings a light came on inside the office in the corner of the yard and glowed yellow through the barred window. Along with the moths and their brethren I moved quietly towards it.

The top part of the uncurtained window was open about three inches. I listened to Corish's secretary whose name I couldn't recall. She sounded much more aggressive with this caller than she'd been with me an hour and a half ago.

4

'When? . . . Soon's not good enough. It's been "soon" for the past nine months! . . . Oh, it's different all right! It's worse!'

She was shouting. The other party must have told her to cool down.

'Why should I? . . . I won't wake Caroline! She's out of her head as usual and I can see why she does it! . . . Why should I? Give me one good reason!'

It had to be Corish on the other end and he must have given her a few good reasons because she shut up for a full minute and when she spoke again all the fire had gone out of her. The tone was one of weary resignation.

'But what do I tell Eddie Malloy? . . . But what if he does turn up, Martin, what do I tell him?'

Melodramatic by nature, I was tempted at this point to burst in and grab the phone so he could tell me personally. But I thought I might just learn more by staying put.

She said, 'When? . . . Where? . . . What if he asks for your number? . . . Martin! . . . Martin!'

He must have hung up. The girl did the same then started working methodically through every swear word she knew in a steady monotone, as though reciting tables at school.

I went in. She was sprawled in a swivel chair, long red hair unkempt, blue eyes tired and puffy. When she saw me she gasped and reached towards her groin, pulling frantically at the open zip on her tight beige jodhpurs, trying at the same time to get to her feet and turn her back on me.

In a TV sitcom it might have looked funny but I felt an instant pang of regret and shame, almost as though I'd assaulted her. I didn't even manage to redeem myself by catching her as she collapsed in a dead faint. On the way down her head smacked hard against a metal filing cabinet.

By the time I was on my knees beside her she was already bleeding.

The wound was on her scalp and not dangerously deep. Blood trickled across her temple forming a small pool in her ear. Her pulse was steady, her breathing even.

Making a pillow of my jacket I gently raised her head and eased the makeshift cushion underneath. In the corner of the office was a small sink. As I got up to fetch a wet cloth I noticed the girl's white swollen belly exposed by the gaping fly of her jodhpurs. Red pubic hair curled over the pink waistband of her pants. Looking around for something to cover her, I scooped a purple fleecy jacket from the back of the swivel chair and laid it across her midriff.

While I gently rubbed at the congealing blood on her face, I wished I could remember her name.

I checked her pulse again and was wondering whether I should call an ambulance when her eyes opened and tried to focus on me. I moved away, not wanting to seem threateningly close. I sat on the chair. Her face remained calm. She reached up slowly to feel her head.

'Are you all right?' I asked.

She looked at the sticky blood on her fingers.

'Just a flesh wound,' I said.

Puzzled, she stared at me. 'You hit your head on the cabinet,' I explained. 'My fault for barging in like that and scaring you. I'm sorry.'

She made to get up. I was caught between helping her and saving her embarrassment as the jacket covering her bare middle slipped away. She grabbed at it. I stood up. 'I've got a first-aid kit in the car – won't be a minute,' I said, and went out into the cool darkness.

When I got back she was sitting at the desk sipping water from a cracked cup and sobbing quietly. As I moved towards her, luck drew my eye to the top of a thank-you note on the untidy desktop. 'Dear Fiona . . .'

I said, 'Fiona, look, I'm sorry for scaring you like that. I didn't mean to.'

She wiped at her eyes with the blood-stained cloth I'd been using on her head. Opening the green plastic first-aid box, I handed her a clean dry pad. She took it and carried on wiping.

'Got some good painkillers here,' I offered.

She shook her head slowly.

I spent the next fifteen minutes asking questions. Where was Martin Corish? Where were the rest of the staff? Who was tending the horses? I told her I'd overheard her telephone conversation – where had he called her from? Although tempted, I thought best not to question her about the stallions, Town Crier especially. Martin Corish was the man with the answers but if Fiona knew where he was she wasn't saying. She didn't speak a single word, just sat dabbing at the now dry wound and staring at the desk. Her Snoopy watch read eleven o'clock when I gave up.

Footfalls deliberately heavy on the cobbles, I crossed the moon-lit yard wanting to convince Fiona I'd given up in disgust. I started the car, drove about a few hundred yards then pulled in, jumped out and ran back.

Outside the office once again I listened for the frantic return call to Corish but all was silent. Either she'd made it just after I'd left or she genuinely didn't know where he was. I waited twenty minutes. Nothing.

I was tempted to visit Town Crier's box. I knew the horse well and reckoned it would take a pretty good ringer to fool me. But like a number of stallions he wasn't the friendliest beast in the world towards humans, particularly, I suspected, the kind who intrude in the hours of darkness. I decided to leave it till next morning.

With no clouds to blanket the day's heat it was quickly growing cold. I walked back to the car, wondering where to spend the night.

I sat taking stock. The nearest town with a hotel that would let me in this late was Marlborough, about fifteen miles away. But my credit card was swipe-weary and battle scarred; even a three-star hotel bill would probably finish it off. Basic guesthouses would already be well locked up and I had no friends in the vicinity.

As I sat looking through the windscreen at the stars it became plain that the overnight sleeping arrangements were a choice between kipping in the car or heading back to Corish's hay barn. The prospect brought a smile to my face as I remembered past conversations with people who envied the glamorous life of a professional jockey.

Last season's glamour for me had included a virus-stricken stable, three periods of suspension for 'irresponsible' riding, and a series of damaging falls which had left me with a fractured wrist, a broken collarbone and, most recently, four smashed ribs and a punctured lung. Not to mention severely dented confidence and a badly bruised bank account.

Now, just when I thought it was safe to get back in the saddle, this had to happen. The partnership with Martin Corish was the only real investment I'd ever made. No jockey rides forever and the stud was supposed to provide me with some security when I hung up my boots, a notion I'd entertained often in the past few months. I sighed, fighting off self-pity.

Starting the engine, I decided to find a lay-by and get what sleep I could before returning in the morning. The ignition fired and the buttons on my mobile phone lit up as it beeped into life. Before setting off I went through the motions of ringing home to my answerphone though it had been a while since there'd been any worthwhile messages on it.

Tonight there was one and it drew me back north at speed.

Three

I reached the flat just after 2 a.m. and stopped barely long enough for tea and a banana sandwich. I replayed the message again: 'Eddie, Barney Dolan. If you get this message in time there's a winner waiting for you tomorrow . . . er, that's Wednesday. I heard you passed the doctor and thought I'd give you a nice start back. The bad news is it's up at Perth and it's in the two o'clock. I'll hold off till nine in the morning to hear from you.'

Good old Barney. He was one of a handful of trainers I rode for when it was mutually convenient. My retainer was with Gary Rice whose flat I was sitting in now. Gary owned a string of twenty-two trained by Charles Tunney, a good friend of mine, whose Shropshire yard my flat overlooked. Gary paid me a reasonable retainer to ride his horses, and when the stable had no runners, I was free to take rides elsewhere.

Many of our horses had been down with a virus last season and we'd had just eleven winners – a disastrous total that had shaken Charles's confidence. He'd closed the yard for the normal summer break during which he'd vowed to attend Mass every day to pray for a better season next year.

In the meantime he'd buggered off to Alaska for a month's holiday, leaving his secretary Jean to feed the dogs and keep things ticking over.

Up until this season jump racing had always stopped completely for two months in the summer but the British Horseracing Board had decided to grant a limited number of fixtures to courses wanting to hold meetings during the summer. Most of the top jockeys had said they wouldn't ride at these meetings; eight weeks was little enough break from the daily grind of driving, dieting and the inevitable injuries.

I could have done with the holiday – at least my battered body could have – but my bank balance dictated otherwise. So after an

9

hour's restless sleep I left rural Shropshire in the early hours of Wednesday morning for the long drive to Perth, a course lying so far north it never risked racing during the winter months. Every minute on the road took me further away from where I'd planned to be at first light, the Corish Stud.

My thoughts returned to my mystery caller. If my partner was doing what was claimed, how had the guy found out? And how had he discovered my involvement with Martin Corish? We'd both kept it quiet. And what was the caller's link with Jean Kerman, the tabloid hack, she of the poisonous mind and equally poisonous pen?

And always in my mind was the prospect of his next call. I'd count myself lucky to have twenty rides during the summer but that would be twenty opportunities for the blackmailer to try to influence me. And who was to say he wouldn't carry on right through next season proper? What would I do if he asked me to ride a bent race?

I thought about it.

I didn't know the answer.

I knew what I'd want to do. I'd never pulled a horse in my life. Ethics aside, my belief was that as soon as someone had something on you, you could never be completely free. Even one guilty little secret would always stay fixed to you like a choke-chain – a very long one maybe, but one that you could safely bet would snap you backwards when somebody finally tugged on it then slowly hauled you in, to face either justice or another demand.

As dawn lit the hills of the Scottish borders I was no nearer a solution. The choices were: find Corish and get the truth or track down the blackmailer and deal with him. If Corish proved guilty as charged, then apart from finding out why he'd done it, I'd still have to trace the blackmailer. Until that was achieved I had to face the fact that this Perth ride might have to be my last.

The only way to stay clean was to make sure the blackmailer had no leverage. If I wasn't riding he couldn't influence my performance.

But how many rides could I refuse before trainers stopped asking me?

As the summer morning brightened my future looked darker. That little choke-chain was already around my neck and which-ever way I turned strangulation seemed the only outcome.

It looked like my first decision in the battle, to come scurrying north for one ride, was the wrong one. The day would have been much better spent trying to find Martin Corish. Still, I was committed now and at 8.15 I rang Barney Dolan to thank him for the ride and tell him I'd be at Perth by 11.

'Good man, Eddie. You won't regret it.'

I had a very strong feeling that I would.

Four

Perth Racecourse lies in the beautiful fertile grounds of Scone Palace on the banks of the River Tay. Early mist was still rising from the river on this hot cloudless morning. I was first into the jockeys' room and sat down wearily in the corner, dropping my kitbag and saddle at my feet. I hadn't been here in almost eight years.

It was perfectly quiet inside the antiquated wood-panelled room. Faint sounds of birdsong came through the high open window and I laid back my head and thought of the days when just being in a room like this had brought me nothing but pleasure. Every new changing room, every new course, had been a wondrous adventure to a wide-eyed and breathless teenager, drinking in the history of these old places, sitting on every inch of every bench so I could be sure to have sat where all the champions had sat before me . . . That teenager was long gone. It seemed a lifetime ago.

The sweet pine-scented air had come from an aerosol. Motes seemed to hang in the long sunbeam that warmed my legs. I must have dozed.

I woke feeling slightly stiff. Sitting opposite me, crunching crispbread and sipping black tea, was Keith Allardyce who'd been born in Stirling, 'two doors away from Willie Carson' as he always said. Cheeks full of soggy crispbread, he still managed a wide smile as I stretched awake.

'Tired?'

'It's all right for you locals. Probably just fell out of bed ten minutes ago. I bet you've even had time for a plate of fried haggis before leaving home.'

'Haggis season doesn't start till August. We're not allowed to shoot them till then.'

'Contact the British Horseracing Board,' I said. 'They'll get it brought forward.'

12

Keith swallowed and smiled more widely and we chatted about what had been happening while I'd been laid up these last five weeks. The northern racing fraternity moved in their own separate world from the rest of the UK, or so it seemed to many of us, and the gossip in their circle was 95 percent parochial.

'Have you got a paper?' I asked.

Keith hauled a rolled up copy of the *Sporting Life* from his bag and threw it to me.

'How many in the first race?' I asked as I opened it.

'A few, I think. Your old buddy's got a ride, you'll be pleased to know.' He smiled knowingly.

I looked at him.

'Tranter.'

'Oh, Tranter the Ranter, that's all I need.'

Billy Tranter didn't like me. His antics had earned me two suspensions last season just for trying to keep him a safe distance from me during races. The animosity stemmed from a successful objection I'd made to a winner he rode in a valuable race at Newbury back in November. Nothing personal on my part – Tranter's tiring horse had been leaning on mine on the run-in; it was arguable whether or not it affected the result but I owed it to the owner and trainer to try an objection and it was upheld.

Tranter the Ranter lived up to his nickname that day.

Since then he'd had a go at me half a dozen times during races, using various dirty tricks. I'd responded accordingly in the hope that he'd soon tire of it and lose the taste for revenge but all it did was increase his appetite. My fuse burns very slowly but eventually, for purely practical reasons, I'd laid him out flat and stone cold on the weighing-room floor at Bangor.

Next time we rode against each other he tried to put me through the wing of a fence. Grassing on colleagues is as abhorrent to jockeys as it is to crooks of the old school but after that incident I told Tranter that if he didn't pack it in, I'd make sure he got warned off for a long time. It didn't seem to cool the fire in his eyes one degree. Today would be the first time we'd met again since that conversation.

I scanned the race; twelve runners. Dolan's horse, Cliptie, was down to be ridden by his son Rod who, Dolan had told me this morning, had managed to put himself in hospital for a few days after a crash with the family tractor yesterday evening. The first that people would hear of the jockey change to E. Malloy would be when it was broadcast to the betting shops shortly before racing.

That suited me. It meant the mystery caller wouldn't have the opportunity to ring me and make suggestions.

I left Keith Allardyce to the remains of his calorie-controlled lunch and went out into the sunshine to call the Corish Stud. George, the stud groom, answered the phone but seemed very reluctant to answer questions on the whereabouts of Martin Corish. I got the definite impression he was hiding something.

What the hell was happening down there? I resolved to leave straight after my ride in the first and head back to Wiltshire. When I got there I'd make sure I got some answers. I returned to the weighing room almost wishing the blackmailer would call me back. At least he might have been able to tell me exactly what was going on.

The sun was high as we filed out for the first and my dark colours, black with scarlet crossbelts, held the hot rays, slowly cooking my upper half. Sweat ran from my armpits over the heavy strapping still round my ribs. Eager for a cooling breeze, I cantered to the start a bit more quickly than normal. Cliptie, a neat bay gelding, moved nicely beneath me. Well-balanced and alert, he seemed the perfect type for this tight track.

Circling at the start I watched Billy Tranter with concealed amusement. He'd dismounted and was adjusting his mount's bridle. Tranter's face had been a picture when he walked into the weighing room and saw my head popping through the neck of Cliptie's colours. His smile disappeared as though his facial muscles had been sliced.

Women thought him good-looking which I suppose he was in a gunslingerish sort of way; high cheekbones, narrow deep-set eyes, strong jaw, prairie-coloured hair. He could frame a mean look but at five foot five he was more Alan Ladd than Gary Cooper.

He didn't speak to me, didn't have to. It was obvious that normal hostilities would be resumed as soon as possible.

Tranter remounted a big brute, its coat so black the sun glinted almost blindingly from it at times. It was an outsider in the betting and that made me especially wary. If Tranter felt he wasn't expected to win he would concentrate on doing me as much damage as possible. He kept glancing behind as we walked round at the start, both playing a slow game of cat and mouse before lining up.

Dolan was confident we'd win and had told me to lie fifth or sixth and bring him to lead at the last. Tucking Cliptie away in this sort of field shouldn't prove difficult but if Tranter was determined to be in there scrimmaging with me he'd have plenty of cover from the eyes of the Stewards.

It was a two-mile hurdle and the starter called us in and snapped the tape up quickly, letting us go to race clockwise for almost two circuits. I jumped Cliptie off smartly and led for the first furlong or so. He was keen and I had some trouble easing him back towards midfield. After such a long layoff from riding I felt my shoulder and back muscles stretch and resist as I gently wrestled Cliptie into submission, playing the bit in his mouth as an angler would play a salmon.

After we jumped the second he settled and we swung along nicely six from the front with a horse either side. I peeped under my armpit to see Tranter three lengths behind, moving his horse towards the rails. As we turned into the straight for the first time I heard angry shouts from behind then felt my horse take a heavy bump on the quarters.

I looked round again. Tranter had pushed his way up the inside, forcing at least two others to move out quickly. We'd been caught in the domino effect. But Cliptie seemed undisturbed and galloped on. Through clear goggles Tranter's narrowed eyes were fixed on me. Jaw muscles grimly clenched, he ignored the curses of the others as he continued forcing his way forward.

Kicking Cliptie through a gap, I moved to the wide out-side to keep at least one horse between us and Tranter. It would also give the Stewards a clearer view as we turned to go towards the back straight.

But Tranter reined back to come round the middle horse and move inside just as we came off the bend, at which point he bumped my horse hard, forcing us into the middle of the track.

He followed.

I glared across. 'Tranter, what the . . .'

He bumped us again, then with an exaggerated show of trying to straighten his horse, he forced him on to mine, leaning and boring diagonally across the track towards the river.

'Straighten up, you bastard!' I yelled, but he was half-standing in the stirrups now, pretending to haul at the reins while making sure he was still carrying me off the track. Looking at the bridle, I saw the bit had come right through the horse's mouth and Tranter was effectively without brakes or steering.

We were feet away from the white rails and I tried desperately to haul Cliptie back but Tranter's horse carried us both through in a crackling shower of plastic debris as the rails shattered. Almost immediately we were on the downward slope of the riverbank, travelling too fast for an emergency ejection. I made do with getting my feet out of the irons just before Cliptie burst through the glinting surface of the peaceful, slow-flowing Tay.

The sound of half a ton of galloping thoroughbred hitting deep water was like a bomb blast, shaking me almost as much as the shock of the temperature change and the sudden confusion of my senses. Cliptie's momentum carried me under as he overturned in the water.

Temporary panic. Sucked down by the horse. Very cold. Goggles filling through the tiny airholes. Water swilling darkly. On my back. The sun a watery molten disc above. Terrible memories.

A heavy punch hits my back. Must be Tranter. Mad bastard. I turn, in fear now.

No Tranter but Cliptie, kicking out, beginning to swim. The reins move in the water like a dark skinny eel. I grab at them and pull myself towards Cliptie's strong neck which I clasp in a hug, forcing tiny airbubbles from his coat. Could use some of them. Not much air left in my lungs. But Cliptie's paddling strongly now. Best rely on him.

We break the surface.

Cliptie blows through his nostrils as though applauding himself. I cough and splutter and try to look up. Blinded by the light.

Five

The horses were okay. We'd been lucky enough to miss the rocky shallows and plunge into a deep pool in the river's curve. At the Stewards' Inquiry Tranter looked suitably shocked and penitent. The patrol film 'showed clearly', according to the Stewards, that the loose bridle had caused Tranter's misfortune and therefore mine. Although he swore the bridle had been correctly fitted, they fined the baffled trainer of Tranter's horse £200 for not ensuring his tack had been properly adjusted.

Now I knew why Tranter had been fiddling with the bridle at the start, a point he quickly raised in his defence, claiming it had felt loose and he'd been worried about it.

I was almost certain that he had sabotaged the bridle himself. As I had dried myself and changed before going into the Stewards' Room I'd been revising my opinion of Billy Tranter. I had thought he was nothing more than a bad loser, a small-minded guy who naturally harboured grudges. But if he had deliberately loosened that bridle then he'd endangered himself as well as me. Not to mention two racehorses.

I wondered what I had to do to stop him. I'd tried being tough on the track, I'd decked him at Bangor, I'd threatened to have him warned off. What next? He was rushing to ride in the second race and I was in a hurry to get back to the stud. I had to settle for tugging his sleeve and speaking quietly as we left the Stewards' Room.

'When are you going to stop, Billy? When we're both dead?'

He grinned coldly and triumphantly and I was left unsure as to whether that meant his 'honour' had now been satisfied or if he was already planning the next round.

By the main gate Cliptie's lad was walking the steaming horse in a circle. Cliptie looked bright and refreshed for his cool bath. Barney Dolan, his trainer, looked shell-shocked.

He leant against the fence watching Cliptie, looking through him really, with unblinking eyes. He didn't see me till I stopped beside him. The sun filtering through his loose-weave Panama hat cast a tight pattern on his face, making his booze-reddened nose even darker. The knot of his tie hung six inches below his open sweat-stained shirt collar and a heavy sports jacket was draped across his forearm. On the grass at his feet lay his battered binoculars case.

'You okay?' I asked.

He pulled his mind back to the present and focused slowly on me. He nodded. 'Mmmm.'

'You don't look it.'

He reached in his jacket for cigarettes and matches then dropped the jacket beside the binoculars and lit a cigarette. 'He would have won that, Eddie. Pissed up.'

'I'm sorry.' I didn't want to launch into the full Tranter story. I let him believe it was just bad luck.

He nodded again, slowly, not looking at me, drifting back into the distance. He drew deeply and blew smoke into the hot still air. 'We needed that . . .'

Gently I clasped his arm. 'There'll be another time. I'd love to ride him again.'

'Mmmm.'

More smoke. That faraway look again. I didn't persevere. 'Gimme a call if there's anything,' I said.

He didn't reply.

After an hour's driving I was yawning at regular intervals, and halfway down the A74 I pulled off the road into a wide lorry park, reclined my seat and was asleep within minutes. Less than an hour later I was back on the road. I'd planned to stop off home to shave and change but it meant a significant detour westwards. I was tempted to press on down the M5 towards the stud but time was against me.

My ribs ached too. After my ducking the doctor at Perth had restrapped them but the bandages felt tight. And I was hungry. To hell with it. I decided to go home.

I was back on the road by 8 next morning and reached the

stud just before 10. I parked by the wall of the house as Fiona came out of the yard leading a mare whose bright chestnut foal followed anxiously, tottering on too-long legs like a child in high heels. Fiona didn't acknowledge me as I got out. 'Good morning,' I called after her.

'Morning,' she said without turning round.

'Is Mrs Corish home?'

'Try the back garden.'

Following a side path I came to a gate in a high hedge and went through. The big sandstone house cast a long shadow over the kidney-shaped garden, only the top third of which was in sunshine. Two white plastic patio chairs stood in the centre of the lawn. Another white chair and a matching table had been moved into the sunny spot. On the chair, her back to me, sat Caroline Corish.

She stirred slightly as she heard the metal latch click when the gate swung closed but didn't turn around. I called out, 'Good morning!'

She turned, saw me through her sunglasses but said nothing. I walked towards her across the lawn, noticing the impressions left in the grass by the recently resited table and chair. I lifted another chair and put it down by Caroline's table.

She was wearing cream-coloured calf-length leggings which were stained, and what looked like one of her husband's shirts, blue-striped and open-necked, showing a sunburned V of skin. She was shoeless. Her feet were dirty. Cracked dried blood was visible across the toes of her right foot.

On the soiled tabletop lay a packet of cigarettes, an expensive lighter, a two-thirds-empty bottle of white rum and a litre of cola. She drank from the fat glass in her hand. It wasn't yet 10.30.

Even behind the big dark glasses Caroline looked haggard. Fortyish, she was naturally slim but now looked outright thin. As she raised the glass to drink, her wedding ring slid an inch along her bony finger. I'd known the Corishes a long time and had never really understood what Martin had seen in her. Most times I'd met her she'd found something to whinge about. I'd never much cared for her and found it difficult now to express concern for the fact that she seemed to be drinking herself to death. Not that any sympathy from me would have been welcomed.

I kept it light. 'Sunbathing?' I asked, as I sat down.

'Do make yourself comfortable, won't you?' she said sarcastically.

'How are you?'

'Drunk. Cheers.' She emptied the glass in two long swallows and refilled it, the cola frothing and running over the edge, adding another coloured pattern to the table top.

'What's the celebration?'

She turned petulantly and I was glad I couldn't see her eyes. 'Surviving another night alone in the fucking Ponderosa,' she said, nodding back towards the house.

'Where's Martin?'

'Screwing stablegirls, probably.'

I'd assumed his disappearance was to do with Town Crier but now realised there'd been a marital rift wide as a canyon.

'He's been away for a few days?'

'I couldn't give a toss if he never comes back.' She shook a cigarette from the packet and lit it, killing the scent of the morning flowers with the smoke flaring down her nostrils.

'Caroline, it's important that I speak to Martin soon. Have you any idea where he's gone?'

'Why don't you go and ask that little whore Fiona? Ask her if he plans to be back to hold her hand when she's in labour?'

Oh dear. My thoughts returned to Fiona's loosened jodhpurs and protruding white belly. And her haranguing of Martin on the phone. I guessed he had more problems than just Town Crier.

Back in the yard red-haired Fiona looked almost as rough as Caroline did though considerably plumper. She was yelling at two lads to get some tack cleaned. They wandered slowly out of the yard, chatting as though she didn't exist.

'Glad to hear you've got your voice back,' I said.

She stared at me, still flushed from shouting, but didn't reply. I asked where Martin was and she continued the silent treatment which was really beginning to piss me off. I said, 'Fiona, if you want to have a job this time next week then answer me when I talk to you.'

She half-sneered, 'You can't sack me.'

'Martin's disappeared. I'm applying to have the business assigned one hundred percent to me.'

She looked uncertain. 'You can't. He'll be back to . . .' She stopped herself.

'When? Tomorrow?'

'I'm not to say.'

'Okay, Fiona, pick up your things. I'll pay you a month's wages in lieu of notice and send your cards on.'

I turned and went into the office. She yelled after me: 'You can't! You can't!' I came back carrying a jacket and a shoulder bag. 'These yours?'

She crossed her arms. 'I won't accept them!'

I laid them on the ground. 'Anything else you want to recover from the office?'

She scowled. 'You can't do this!'

I looked at my watch. 'It shouldn't take you longer than fifteen minutes to walk to the main gate. Be off the property in half an hour.' I returned to the office and closed the door. A few minutes later I was going through the contents of the filing cabinet when the door creaked open. Fiona stood there, the sun haloing her carrot hair. Staring at her feet like a little girl, she said, 'Martin will be back in the morning.'

'What time?'

'First thing.'

'Fine. Come in and start explaining how this place has been running.'

She worked confidently through the paperwork showing me the accounts. I learned little either way. I was not enough of a financial gourmet to detect the whiff of cooked books and Fiona probably realised this.

Although I knew where Town Crier was stabled I asked her to take me there to see if that shook her confidence but she led me to the box without hesitation.

In front of me was a long strong bay horse, well ribbed up with straight hocks and good legs, a fine head with large ears and a bold eye. The only marking on him was a touch of white no bigger than a thumbprint on his forehead. I was certain within a minute that this was the genuine Town Crier, and equally certain that physically at least there was not a thing wrong with him.

I asked Fiona when he'd last covered a mare.

'Er . . . a week ago today, I think. Yes, last Friday.'

'Were you there?'

'What?'

'Did you see him covering?'

'No.' She looked puzzled.

'Who was there?'

'Martin.'

'Who else?'

Her brows knitted. 'A couple of the lads, I should think.'

She wasn't being evasive. I dropped the subject and told her I was heading into Marlborough to book a room for the evening. I warned her that if she rushed off to ring Martin she'd better tell him that if he wasn't here first thing in the morning, she'd be out of a job and I'd be out looking for him.

I rang home to my answerphone. No messages.

Driving into Marlborough, the storm that had been threatening for the past couple of days didn't seem far away. The sky was over-cast and hazy, the air humid and sticky, made just about bearable by the breeze that had got up in the past couple of hours.

I found a reasonably priced small hotel, removed my rib strapping, had a cool shower and lay wet and naked on the bed, letting the air from the open window dry me. I thought about Martin Corish. He had been my boyhood hero, champion jockey when I was a teenager. It hadn't been just his brilliant riding that had bewitched me: he was interviewed often on TV and always seemed to have a twinkle in his eye and a joke ready, usually told against himself. He was handsome and always had women trailing after him although I never saw him as anything other than what my father used to call 'a man's man'.

By the time I started riding Martin's career was winding down but, still starry-eyed, I'd made no secret of how much I admired him. Admiration which increased when he accepted me immedi-ately as his equal, both as a man and as a jockey. He made me feel special and it took me a long time to realise that that was how he made most people feel. It wasn't contrived on his part, he was just a charismatic type of guy.

After retiring he'd spent a couple of years in the media before setting up as a trainer, something I felt he'd put off deliberately till the highs of his riding days were much more of a memory. To achieve the same heights as a trainer would have been a tough enough task without carrying the inevitable burden of other people's expectations.

Even after the cooling off period Martin never reached higher than middle rank when he was training, and when that pos-ition started slipping he packed up, unwilling to wait for the humiliation that must have followed over the next couple of years. That's when he set up the stud which had been going for three years when he'd approached me last summer, offering me a fifty-fifty partnership for £200,000.

Now in any normal season I'd be lucky to have a twentieth of that in the bank but I'd just come into some money via an insurance company reward. My share had been a hundred and seventy-five grand. I had ten of my own in the bank and on the strength of that I'd borrowed another fifteen and gone in with Martin. I guess I'd never really lost that desire to impress him, to win his approval.

But if it hadn't made me a millionaire, it hadn't proved disastrous either. I'd managed to make the loan repayments quite comfortably and start rebuilding modest savings from the director's salary the stud paid me. Still, I was a long way from getting my money back.

I lay staring at the ceiling, promising myself I wouldn't succumb to Martin's charm in the morning, wouldn't be calmed down by layers of bullshit. I'd be as hard with him as I had been with Fiona.

I swung my legs off the bed and stood up in front of the full-length mirror fixed to the open wardrobe door. Fresh bruises added to the colourful display on my ribcage, shellbursts of yellow and blue. On my right shinbone a familiar old pink hairless scar ran diagonally through the dark hair; the surgeon's entry for a pin insertion years ago. My muscle definition was still good but there was now a perceptible thickening round the middle and more flesh on the upper thighs. I'd never had a weight problem but I'd noticed last season that a pound or two extra had somehow lodged itself on my frame.

I decided to skip dinner.

After the nine o'clock news I made a final call to my answerphone. The first message was from Barney Dolan, Cliptie's trainer. He wanted to meet me at Worcester tomorrow to discuss something important.

The second call was from the blackmailer: 'I see from the papers you took a little bath up at Perth yesterday. Most amusing. Don't ever accept a ride again after the overnight stage. I'll be in touch.'

Arrogant bastard.

Jockeys declared at the overnight stage were guaranteed to have their names appear alongside their mount in the morning papers and, more importantly for this guy, in the papers on the eve of the racemeeting. If he didn't know where I was riding, he couldn't ask me to stop one.

I was seething as I worked through my diary in search of Barney Dolan's number. He sounded anxious when I explained to him I had no plans to be at Worcester tomorrow. I had no booked rides and, more importantly, I had pressing business elsewhere.

There was a long pause then Barney said, 'Eddie, I've got to see you. I'm in deep trouble. Fierce trouble. I've got to see you tomorrow.'

Six

I was at the stud by 5.30 a.m. just in case Martin had decided to pay a fleeting morning visit. In the paddocks mares and foals were already grazing. Mist rose from the river at the bottom of the low fields and dew lay thick on the front lawn of the big house. The yard was empty of people though equine heads looked inquiringly over box doors and there were a few whinnies at the prospect of an early breakfast.

The office was locked. I sat on the red-leaded window sill and watched the sun rise slowly over the grey pitched roof of the stableblock. The air was fresher. Maybe there'd been a storm in the night. I'd slept like a dead man and wouldn't have heard thunderclaps of biblical proportions.

Just after 7 as the lads arrived on foot and by bike I heard a car coming up the drive and walked out to see if it was Martin. The car had stopped two hundred yards along the road beside the cottage where Fiona lived. I heard her front door close but didn't see who'd gone in. Martin drove a gunmetal grey Rover and the car looked the right shape though the angle of the sun made it hard to distinguish colour.

Just to be safe I got into my car, reversed along the drive and blocked the road behind the car. I'd thought the whine of the fast reverse gear would bring him out to investigate but he stayed inside for almost ten minutes and didn't look at all surprised when he came back out and saw me standing by my car door.

Many ex-jockeys quickly put on weight as they indulge themselves after years of self-deprivation but Martin had never been more than half a stone over his riding weight. Now, standing on the steps of the cottage, he had the appearance of being half a stone under it. His five foot ten looked stretched as day-old chewing gum. His hunched shoulders, curved spine and drooping head made him look like a jockey off one of the old cigarette cards.

He stood there like a prisoner in the dock waiting to be taken down, eyes on the ground as I approached.

I'd spent much of the morning rehearsing angry words for this moment but when I saw his face all I could say was, 'Are you okay?'

Raising his head, he found enough from somewhere for a warm but very tired smile, and once again, maddeningly, I felt somehow privileged. It was almost as if he had only three of those smiles left to get him through the rest of his life and he'd chosen to give me one. He put a hand on my shoulder. 'Come in and have some breakfast.'

I stopped him. 'I'd rather we spoke alone.'

'It's okay, Fiona's just leaving.'

She must have been standing just inside the open door for she appeared on cue, kissed Martin lightly on the cheek and came down the front step where he ruffled her hair like an indulgent father before she walked off in the direction of the yard.

The cottage kitchen was untidy. Dirty clothes lay on the floor by the open door of the washing machine and the sink was full of dishes. Old newspapers and office books were strewn on the big table which had a pine bench on either side. Martin cleared us a space on the table surface. 'Sit down, Eddie. Coffee?'

'You sit down. I'll make the coffee.'

He did so without argument and I found the makings of coffee and toast which he said he didn't want though I made him eat it.

Martin was forty-five. Not only did he still have all his hair but it looked to be growing wild and out of control, thick and greying and alive. Framing his fine-boned unshaven face it made him look more like a refugee or half-crazed artist than one of racing's former heroes. But there was none of the usual crazy fire in his blue eyes which were bloodshot, exhausted-looking, lifeless. If the body had its own hospital they'd have been in intensive care.

When he'd forced down the last mouthful of toast he looked at me and said, 'I'm sorry, Eddie.'

There was no need to start barking questions at him. He went through everything from the beginning, punctuating the story with regular apologies. 'I should have thought more about it, should have called you . . . I just sort of panicked. It had been building up for weeks and weeks and when the guy phoned I just blanked, panicked.'

The blackmailer had contacted him on Monday, claiming he knew that Martin was using a ringer to cover for Town Crier. He suggested that Martin approach me and tell me 'the game was up' and that we'd better co-operate, which meant he would tell me which races not to try in. Martin was told to call me the same day but didn't, and when the blackmailer rang back on Tuesday and again on Wednesday, only to find Martin wasn't around, he'd rung me direct.

I said, 'So he's right in what he says about Town Crier?'

Martin nodded slowly, thick tendrils of hair swinging across his eyes.

'What's wrong with him?'

'He's lost it. Just lost it.'

'Lost what?'

'His fertility.'

We looked at each other.

'Completely?' I asked.

He nodded again. 'Went from an eighty-eight percent success rate to zero.'

'What, just like that? Overnight?'

'Almost. Three or four days maybe.'

Stallion fertility is measured in how many mares each horse gets in foal. Town Crier's had always been consistently high.

'Why didn't you call me?' I asked.

His shoulders tensed, hunching again as he moved awkwardly in his seat. 'I thought he'd come through it, Eddie. I thought it might just be a virus or something.'

I shook my head slowly, rubbing my eyes now as the impact sank home. 'You should have told me.'

'I'm sorry, Eddie, I didn't know how to tell you! What was it going to sound like less than a year after you put every-thing you had into the business? After I had persuaded you to invest all that money? What was I supposed to say: "Look, Eddie, sorry but our major asset has just collapsed, our top player has just drawn stumps?"'

I was angry, avoided his eyes so he wouldn't see it, then got mad at myself for being so protective of him. Almost afraid to ask I finally said, 'What about this ringer stuff, that's not true, is it?' I wasn't even sure why I asked because I knew it had to be true or he wouldn't have run away. Like battling on when you're two fences behind in a steeplechase, you're always hoping for that little miracle, and maybe I thought that Martin had scarpered purely because of the pressure of Town Crier's problem being revealed to the public. Maybe that was all it was.

It wasn't. He'd been using Acapella to cover the Town Crier mares and not telling the breeders. Acapella stood at a thousand pounds, half the fee we charged for Town Crier.

That wound up my sympathy and patience to breaking point. 'Jesus, Martin, they're not even the same colour!'

'Close enough. There's enough bay in Acapella's family. We'll be okay.'

'He's black, for God's sake!'

He just hunched his shoulders again and hung his head. His reasoning was that the colouring wouldn't be a big issue and maybe we would sort Town Crier out for next season. The fact that Acapella was also less likely to sire a horse of the same ability as Town Crier's offspring didn't matter to Martin at the moment. Most were bred for jumping and wouldn't see a racecourse for at least five years from covering date. Again he argued that Town Crier would have overcome his problem long before then so half a dozen or so sub-standard progeny wouldn't damage his reputation too much.

I said, 'And what do we do when the blood samples from the foals are analysed for Weatherbys?'

The Jockey Club's administrators, Weatherbys, operate a checking system to prevent the very thing Martin had been doing. As soon as a thoroughbred foal is born a vet takes a blood sample to be sent there for testing. The sample proves the mating that is down on paper is the one that produced the offspring.

Running nervous fingers through his wild hair, Martin said, 'That won't happen for months. We can sort something out by then.'

'Like what, a miracle?'

'We can say there was a mistake here, or maybe we can get hold of the samples before they get to Weatherbys, or bribe a vet or something.'

I stared at him. 'You're kidding me now, Martin. Tell me you're kidding?'

He clamped his head between his hands and squeezed his eyes shut. 'My head's gone, Eddie. Exploding.'

I wondered what he'd told the staff. For each covering there would have to have been at least one other person present. A mare has to be held steady while the stallion is led up and often helped to enter her. Unwilling mares sometimes have to have hobbles fitted to stop them trying to escape or kicking the stallion, so often there will be three people present at a covering.

'What did you tell the staff?' I asked. 'Would they have known who the mares were booked to?'

He shook his head, still avoiding my eyes, and muttered, 'They thought it was a simple booking to Acapella.'

'And nobody questioned why Town Crier hadn't covered for so long?'

He shook his head again. Something occurred to me. 'What about the insurance? Why don't we just claim on that?' Insurance was available against a stallion's losing fertility and most breeders took sufficient cover.

In a quiet voice he said, 'I didn't take it out.'

'You what? We agreed it! It was part of the budget!'

He shook his head, still unable to look at me. 'Didn't think it was worth it. His fertility rate was . . . was so high.'

I sighed. It was pointless getting any angrier. I tried to figure out what we could do to start repairing things.

I asked, 'What are the vets saying?'

Still gripping his head, he said in a tense voice, 'I took a sample of blood and sperm to a bloke in Ireland, top bloke. The blood's fine. The sperm is a hundred percent sterile.'

'Temporary or permanent?'

'No way of knowing.'

'What about a second opinion?'

'Who from?' There was an edge in his voice now.

'One of the top Newmarket guys.'

'Who'll then know that the Corish Stud has a useless stallion. How long before that gets out to breeders?'

'Martin, how else are we going to solve this? We can't keep it covered up.'

'We've got to keep it covered up, Eddie! Make no mistake about that!' There was some fire back in his eyes now, sparked by desperation. But it was blinding him to logic.

'Martin, we're in a hole, let's stop digging . . . please?'

He rounded on me, slamming his open hands on the tabletop. '*You* stop digging! It's all right for you! If the business goes under you've done a few quid. Fine. You go back to riding, back to where you were a year ago. You're young, you'll be okay! What have I got? Fuck all!'

His fists and jaw muscles clenched and unclenched but he wasn't finished.

'I'll tell you what I've got, Eddie, I'll tell you what I've got coming at me from all points of the fucking compass! Divorce proceedings. My first child who'll be born just after my forty-sixth birthday. No business. No money. Nowhere to live . . . And I'll tell you what else I *don't* have that you don't think of now but by Christ you will when you get to my age – I don't have another ten or fifteen years of youth and energy and hope and commitment to pull the whole damn' thing back together again!'

He was reaching across to me now, arms extended. If I'd been directly in front of him he'd have had me by the lapels. His head was low, chin almost touching the table, and there were tears in his eyes. And I was sorry it had taken that much to make me see why he'd done what he'd done in the past seventy-two hours. And it was that that made me stay around for two more hours comforting him, trying to persuade him we'd come through, that we'd get the blackmailer before he did any damage.

When I finally left, hope was back in Martin's eyes. I managed to hide the despair in mine.

Seven

I drove at speed to Worcester races where I'd agreed to meet Barney Dolan behind the main stand after the second race. Waiting for him I watched the boats on the Severn which flows so close to the track that there has never been a winter when it hasn't flooded the racecourse at least once. Looking at the wide dirty river I was glad Tranter hadn't ridden me into this one.

Barney appeared looking like he'd just come from our last meeting at Perth; same clothes, tie hanging loose at the same length, identical expression, cigarette freshly lit sending smoke trails up through the weave of his hat rim. We shook hands and when he glanced furtively around the way they do in B-movies, I thought it was all a wind up, though he'd sounded pretty desperate on the phone last night.

'Why all the secrecy?' I asked.

'I just don't want us to be seen together. You'll know why in a minute.'

A rowing crew came past sweating and grunting. Barney and I were the only ones behind the stand. I said, 'Barney, if anybody does see us together round here they're absolutely certain to assume we're up to something. Whatever it is you want to talk about, let's do it out front. Okay, people will see us but you're a trainer and I'm a jockey, they're much less likely to suspect something.'

He considered that and must have agreed. He didn't say anything, just turned and led me along the single track. Back among people, we walked past a line of glum bookmakers paying out on the second race and on towards the parade ring which we walked around then came back the same way, travelling the route four or five times while Barney told his tale.

It seemed that my bathing partner at Perth, Cliptie, had been carrying a large amount of money, carefully placed in betting shops around the country. So large that if the horse had known he'd probably have sunk without trace. Most of that money, thirty grand of it, had belonged to one of Barney's owners, Joe Dimokratia, fairly well known as Joey the Greek. And herein lay the crux: Joey the Greek did not know that Barney had used his cash.

Joey was spending the month of June in his home country attending to business interests before flying back to collect from Barney the proceeds of the sale of two of his horses, proceeds which Barney no longer had. Barney made it clear that Joey was not the type of man to take this news with any degree of bonhomie.

If it hadn't been for the pallor of Barney's complexion and the nervous pitch of his voice I would have found the whole thing comical. 'So what do you plan to do?' I asked.

'I've got to get the money before he comes back.'

'And what do you plan to use for stakes, if it's any of my business?'

'I've sold another one of Joey's horses.'

I smiled. 'You're kidding. Without him knowing?'

He nodded, shrugged. 'He can't do any more to me for it if it doesn't come off.'

I read that as 'You can't hang a man twice', and wondered where he'd got the courage from. 'Where do I come in?' I asked.

'I want you to be at Market Rasen next Saturday and to leave yourself free for the second race.'

'I'd hardly've thought I was your good luck charm, Barney.'

'You're trustworthy and reliable, Eddie and you can keep your gob shut. We just got a bad break on Thursday.'

He didn't realise how bad a break and I was tempted to tell him that I thought Tranter had sabotaged that bridle. I just wasn't certain enough that he had. But supposing Tranter rode against me again when Barney's money was down? I settled for telling him that Tranter had a grudge against me and that while Thursday's incident might have been an accident, Barney shouldn't risk putting me up on Cliptie again if Tranter had one in the same race.

'Don't worry about Tranter, I'll sort him out.' He said it in such an offhand manner – almost like, 'forget about the fly, I'll swat it' – it worried me and made me realise just how desperate Barney was. I'd expected him to blow his top and demand more details about Tranter and the Perth race but that faraway look was in his eyes again, though this time it was from single-mindedness. He could see the target a week away and wasn't going to take his eyes off it between now and then.

Clutching his elbow lightly, I stopped and turned him towards me. 'Barney, if I want him sorting out, I'll do it myself.'

'Leave it to me, Eddie.' He made to walk on again. I held him. 'Barney . . . I'll sort it out.'

Barney's big red nose always made him look jolly in a music-hall sort of way but his grey eyes were cold and hard and I wondered how afraid he was of Joey the Greek. He said, 'Eddie, I can't afford another fuck-up.'

'Look, you won't put Tranter off easily, I've been trying to do it all season. Play safe, book somebody else.'

'I want you, Eddie.' He didn't voice it but the look in his eyes said, 'You owe me one.'

'Fine. Let's say I'll ride. Just make sure you've got a stand by in case Tranter turns out to have a mount in the race.'

Barney looked down at me, gripping my shoulders with both hands. 'Eddie, you're the stand by.'

It turned out that Rod, Barney's jockey son, had suffered no accident on Wednesday. The plan from the start was to declare Rod, an inexperienced claiming jockey, as the rider at Perth to discourage the public from betting on Cliptie, thus shortening his price. The last-minute substitution of E. Malloy would have gone pretty much unnoticed in the country's betting shops. If I'd been unavailable to take the ride on Thursday, Barney said he would have withdrawn the horse and held off until I was free.

Now he planned to try the same ruse at Market Rasen next week.

Trouble was, our friendly neighbourhood blackmailer had warned me last night never to take another ride like that. Barney was staring hard at me, stiff with tension, and I saw in his face a reflection of Martin's haggard features. I couldn't tell which was the devil and which the deep blue sea.

At least it gave us something to work to, a deadline. We had exactly one week to find the blackmailer.

Eight

As arranged, Martin came to see me on Sunday afternoon and we walked to the pub for a late lunch. On the way there the storm that had been brewing for days finally broke with a lightning bolt and thunderclap that made you believe in God again. We started to run but were drenched in seconds by a deluge that left us literally gasping for breath, then laughing stupidly, and finally saw us splashing like children through the water that coursed along the road.

By the time we reached the pub it had rained itself out. When the sun reappeared it must have thought all the pipes had burst while it had been away but it set about drying things and we sat at a white table in the beer garden, steaming gently.

Martin drank beer. I sipped mineral water as we waited for sandwiches. We had agreed yesterday that Town Crier had to be officially taken off the market so that we weren't compromised further. Martin was to ring the two breeders with mares booked in and tell them the horse was carrying a slight injury, nothing permanent but the vet thought he'd be off for a couple of weeks. It was close enough to the end of the breeding season for them to be unlikely to request a new date.

'How did they take it?' I asked.

'Mrs Sansome was annoyed and moaned like hell but she's a bit of a cow at the best of times. Parsons was okay about it. I got the impression he might even have been a bit relieved.'

I nodded, watching him. He looked much more positive than yesterday, alive again. I'd persuaded him that things would come right if we worked methodically through them. First priority was identifying the blackmailer and persuading him he'd been misinformed. The second was to find out what was wrong with Town Crier and put it right. And the third was to offer the owners who'd had a 'fraudulent' covering by Acapella a free nomination to Town Crier next year.

This was the one Martin was most nervous about. 'Eddie, couldn't we find some way round that?'

'Like what?'

'I don't know.' He squirmed uncomfortably, shaking water drops from his hair. 'I just don't think we can tell them it was a mistake. How incompetent are we going to look when that gets out?'

'As incompetent as you can get, but I think our honesty in admitting it will go a long way in mitigation. And we'll be much better off admitting it before the blood tests from the foals force our hand.'

'It's not going to be easy, Eddie.'

'Look, it's the least of our worries. We made it bottom of our list yesterday. Let's keep it there until we've sorted out the others. Now who else knew about Town Crier's fertility problem?'

'Nobody.'

'Nobody? You didn't tell a soul?'

He avoided my eyes. He had to be lying. The blackmailer had got it from somebody.

'I told Caroline.'

'Right. When?'

'End of March.'

'Did she know about Fiona at the time?'

He shook his head. More droplets. It turned out Caroline had found them in bed together a few weeks later though Martin said it did nothing more than confirm what she'd been accusing him of for years. 'She almost enjoyed it. Like finding the evidence which would save all the cross-examination in the future.'

'Who else knows?'

'Fiona.' He lowered his gaze.

I sighed. 'Why didn't you just take out an ad in the local paper?'

'Fiona wouldn't breathe a word. I'd bet my life on it.'

'So it must have been Caroline.'

'Couldn't have been.'

I leaned across the table. 'It *must* have been, Martin! You can't have it both ways!'

He threw his hands wide and the waitress bringing the sandwiches had to take evasive action. He apologised and turned on his most charming smile but she'd been looking curiously at us dripping oddities all the way down the path and obviously couldn't wait to get back indoors. Martin paid and she hurried off.

I lifted a thin ham sandwich. Martin continued gesturing. 'Carrie would have absolutely no motive for giving the game away.'

Between bites I said, 'Never heard of "hell hath no fury" and all that?'

'Look, all she cares about is screwing me for as much as she can in the divorce settlement. Why should she risk . . .' he sought the right word '. . . devaluing my only asset? Our only asset?'

He had a point. 'Have you asked her?'

'What, if she's told anyone?'

I nodded.

'That's the last thing I need – for her to know I'm being blackmailed!'

'*We* are being blackmailed.'

'We . . . It's the only reason she's still there. She knows we can't sell the business till Town Crier's back on song, so she'll have to sit and suffer till it's sorted out. Or rather *I'll* have to suffer the constant bloody nagging.'

'Thought you were in the cottage with Fiona?'

'I am but she summons me every day for a bloody progress report.'

He bit fiercely into a sandwich. I said, 'You're going to have to ask her.'

'What do I say?'

'Just ask if she's mentioned it to anybody.'

'And if she has, do you think she's going to tell me?'

'I don't know, but if you don't ask, we won't find out.'

He sipped beer and sulked. I was learning more about him all the time. I said, 'Martin, it's the only card we've got at the moment, you're going to have to play it.'

'I'll speak to her tonight,' he said quietly.

'Don't accept the first thing she says,' I warned.

'Unless it's yes.'

I smiled. 'If it's yes, make sure you get the name of the guy she told.'

'That'll probably cost me another ten grand on the settlement.'

Barney Dolan and Joey the Greek came into my mind. I said to Martin, 'You think you've got worries?'

We moved on to priority two – could Town Crier be cured? Any vet we used would not just have to be good, he'd have to be discreet and totally trustworthy. If word got out about the stallion it was doubtful that we'd ever build up faith in him again.

Town Crier had been just short of top class when racing over a mile and a half on the flat. When breeders are trying to get good jumping stock there aren't that many reliable stallions. As most 'practising' jump horses are geldings there is no stud career waiting after retirement. No matter how talented they've been on the racecourse, the chance to pass that on genetically disappeared, usually in their formative days, with a single snip of the scrotum.

So for ex-flat stallions to establish themselves as good sires of jumping stock normally takes years as their early crops are usually tried on the flat for a couple of seasons at least. If they don't prove successful they're often put over jumps where it may take three or four seasons for their talents to show through. Even then breeders will be cautious and wait a few seasons more just to check if the rest of that stallion's progeny also show talent over hurdles or fences. By the time a jumping stallion does make a name for himself he might be sixteen or seventeen years old – or, more likely, dead.

Town Crier was twelve and could easily have another ten years at stud, covering approximately a hundred mares a season. Multiply that by his fee, which would rise in accordance with the success of his stock, and you could see just what a blow it would be to the stud if we couldn't get him back to full fertility. It was this simplified breakdown of figures and prospects that drained the colour from Martin's face.

I'd spent some time on the phone this morning to an old friend and fellow jockey who also happened to be an excellent vet. His name was Brian Kincaid and I'd arranged to meet him while he was at work in Gloucester next day. Martin was very nervous about it.

'Can't you just give him the samples? He doesn't have to know what stallion they've come from or even the stud.'

'And what's the likelihood of his learning anything more from the samples than your man in Ireland did?'

He had no answer for that.

'He's going to have to examine Town Crier, Martin.'

He clasped his head, fingers pushing out thick wings of almost dry hair, and stared at his feet.

'Martin, listen, I trust this guy. I've known him for years. He's one of the old school.'

He nodded, head still in his hands. 'Okay, okay, Eddie.'

'I'll ring you as soon as I've spoken to him.'

He finished his beer and stood up, his soggy trousers sucking noisily at the chair. 'I'd better get cracking.'

As we walked back to the flat he couldn't resist one more go. 'Couldn't we bring Town Crier to him, tell him it was something else?'

'Then expect him to give us one hundred percent trust?'

He hunched his shoulders again and stuffed his hands moodily in his pockets. We walked the last half-mile in silence.

Nine

Next morning I found Brian Kincaid in a box at a Gloucester stud with his arm so far up a mare's backside his right cheek rested on her buttock. He winked and smiled at me. I nodded. He was watching a small black and white monitor, pointing with his free hand to what looked like a white UFO on the black screen.

'Cyst, I'm afraid,' he said to the man holding up the mare's tail. 'It may look like a seventeen-day-old embryo but it's another cyst.'

The man swore but didn't question his judgement. 'Bad luck,' said Kincaid, withdrawing his arm and a thin cable. The cable was attached at one end to the computer and at the other to an egg-sized rubber ball. He placed the ball in a white bowl on the table, peeled off the long dirty plastic glove, dropped it in the bin and reached over to shake my hand. I took his rather gingerly. The smell of fresh horseshit rose from a black plastic bin beside him and the long rubber apron he wore was heavily soiled with it and with some blood and membraney type stuff thrown in to add colour.

'How're you doing, Eddie? Nice to see you.'

'And you.'

He introduced me to the disgruntled tail-holder, the stud manager, who was anxious to get the next mare in. Kincaid said, 'Just one more to do and we'll have a cup of tea.'

I nodded. 'Sure. No hurry.'

The mare with the cyst was led out of the stall and the rear doors slid open to reveal another mare waiting in the yard with her foal. A lad half-pushed, half-carried her foal in and placed it in the stall beside its mother who walked quietly after them. Kincaid swung the half-doors closed behind her to stop her kicking and a lad held her halter while the stud man pulled her tail aside.

Kincaid bent low, plucking a fresh blue plastic glove from a box of disposables and pulling it on to his right arm which he then eased inside the mare. A few seconds later he drew out eighteen inches of shit which seemed moulded beautifully to the shape of his arm all the way to the crook of his elbow. A deft flick saw the load dumped in the black bin. Two more excavations, carried out while chatting congenially to the tail-holder, saw him happy enough to pick up the scanning bulb and go back in.

His eyes turned in my direction. 'You'll have seen this before, Eddie?'

I nodded. 'Once or twice.' I'd been raised on a stud farm but had never quite come to terms with how casually vets took this part of their job.

Kincaid passed the scanner over the top of the uterus and watched the ultrasound waves paint a picture in the screen which seemed clear to Kincaid and the stud man but looked like it always did to me – abstract.

'Twins,' Kincaid said.

The stud man swore again. Thoroughbred mares showed a high incidence of twins which might at first seem like good news for the breeder. But mares rarely carried two strong healthy twins successfully; if they went their full term they tended to be born weaker than single foals which made them poor investments.

This meant that in almost every case the vet would decide which embryo should be killed in the womb to allow the other to develop fully. The vet simply 'popped' one embryo, squeezed it between his fingers. But a wrong decision by him could prove the most expensive pop in the history of the turf. What if that popped embryo had had the genes to be a Triple Crown winner?

The vets were all in the happy position that nobody would ever know how that embryo would have turned out. They tended to base their decisions on whatever evidence was available from a fourteen- to twenty-day-old blob. Inevitably the smallest or most misshapen one would be popped and then everyone just hoped for the best.

Kincaid withdrew his arm and put on another fresh glove before gently pushing his way along the vaginal tract. No scanner to help now, everything done by feel. The mare shifted uneasily and the lad at her head cooed and comforted her. Her ears and eyes were back, almost as if she sensed what Kincaid was trying to do in there. He spoke quietly to her. 'It's for your own good, old girl . . . there.'

He eased out his arm and said to the stud man, 'I'll have another look at her on Wednesday.' Using clean cotton wool and soapy water he spent a minute thoroughly cleaning the mare's vagina and the surrounding area before she was led quietly out through the sliding doors at the front.

The stud man didn't look too happy. Kincaid put an arm across his shoulders. 'Good days and bad, Stan, good days and bad.'

Stan nodded.

Kincaid said, 'Any chance of a pot of tea?'

Stan wandered off to fetch it. Kincaid smiled and stretched, yawning. 'How goes it, Mr Malloy? What's the big mystery this weather?'

Kincaid was a six-footer and strong-looking. He had to waste hard to ride at ten and a half stone. His natural weight would be over twelve. He only rode as an amateur with maybe forty or so mounts a season, but was one of the best amateurs I'd ever seen and well respected in the weighing room.

In his early-thirties, he was fair-haired and threw quite a distinctive profile with his hooked nose and prominent, slightly upturned chin. The lads called him Mr Punch, often in a puppet-show voice, and he always took it with good humour – but what a ribbing he'd got last year when he married a girl called Judy. He had smiling blue eyes and was very even-tempered. I don't think I'd ever heard him complain but he always had a sympathetic ear for others who wanted a moan.

And like most vets I'd known, Kincaid was a true animal lover. One of the things he'd always claimed had stopped him becoming a professional jockey was the expectation of a number of owners and trainers that the whip be used to maximum effect on their horses. 'No way do I want my living to depend on that, Eddie,' he'd told me once.

He stood now, hands on hips, smiling at me as steam rose from the shit bin between us. 'You look well,' I said.

'Bloody tired.' And he yawned again then took a couple of steps into a gloomy corner and reached out. On top of a box was a shiny platter of sandwiches. Kincaid swung it towards me, resting the edge against his soiled apron. 'Sandwich?'

'No, thanks.'

He lifted one and started munching happily, enjoying my expression. 'God, you'll catch beriberi or something.'

Smiling, he shook his head. 'Beriberi's caused by a thiamine deficiency. Plenty of thiamine in blood and shit.' He waved the platter and I turned away theatrically, helping him enjoy it to the full.

The stud man brought a tray with tea things on it and I took it from him. We headed across the yard to sit on a low wall in the sunshine. Kincaid brought his sandwiches and as I laid down the tea tray he reached for the pot and said, 'Will I be mother?'

I grabbed at it. 'Will you hell! Poison yourself if you like, I prefer tea minus the germs!'

He laughed out loud.

We spent quite a while on that wall; our shadows had shifted noticeably by the time we got up. I outlined the full problem, missing out the ruse Martin had pulled on some breeders. Without being at all patronising Kincaid had talked me through the reproductive system of the stallion in detail but the bottom line was that never before had he heard of such a sudden loss of fertility, not without an obvious physiological cause.

He agreed to come and see Town Crier on Wednesday afternoon.

Back at the flat I checked my answerphone – nothing of consequence. I called Martin and told him when Kincaid was coming. 'Did you get anything out of Caroline?' I asked.

'Dog's abuse.'

'She hasn't told anyone?'

'Definitely not.'

'Do you believe her?'

'I'm inclined to. She went ballistic when I even suggested it.'

'Guilty conscience, maybe?'

'Well . . . I don't think so.'

He questioned me on everything Kincaid had said and I dressed things up a bit.

I mooched around the flat thinking, folding clothes, polishing shoes, pottering absent-mindedly. Early evening I microwaved a low-calorie chicken curry and sat eating by the window, looking down on an empty racing yard.

Normally, Charles would have kept a handful of horses around over the summer but because of the virus they'd all been sent away while every box, every inch of the yard, had been disinfected, sterilised – repeated treatments which left a permanent clinical odour everywhere.

It could be as clean as an operating theatre and there'd still be no guarantee that the horses would stay virus-free. Identifying the strain was often impossible and it was mostly a matter of sit and suffer till horses showed they were regaining form. Even then there was nothing to say the virus wouldn't lie dormant for a while before returning on a second, more vicious raid.

But steam cleaning, disinfecting, vaccinating, at least made trainers feel they were doing something, fighting back. Racing folk tend to be very philosophical about the ups and downs and I was certain Charles would persevere for as long as the stable owner, Gary Rice, was willing to pay the bills. I was due to see Gary soon to discuss a new retainer to ride for him next season.

I finished eating, washed up and sat down quietly with a cup of coffee, my mind still turning things over. As dusk set in I called Martin again and asked him how serious Caroline's drink problem was.

'She never drinks while she's asleep.'

'So it's pretty bad?'

'Morning till night, most days. Very steady though, can shift a couple of bottles before blacking out. I . . .'

'Uhuh?'

'Nothing. Forget it.'

I had the feeling he was about to say that with a bit of luck her liver might give out before she put the financial bite on him. I said, 'Is there any way she could have told someone about Town Crier while she was drunk?'

'Like who?'

'I haven't a clue. It was just a thought. That might be the reason she doesn't remember saying anything.'

He was silent for a few seconds. 'Could be,' he said quietly. 'But how do we find out?'

'Who does she see? Which of her friends would . . .'

'Friends? Eddie, all of Caroline's friends are forty proof and don't talk back.'

'There must be somebody she sees outside of the stud. What about a hairdresser, a local shopkeeper or something?'

'On the odd days she gets to see one of those she manages to be relatively sober which means she'd most probably remember what she'd said. Anyway, she wouldn't discuss stud business outside. Shit, she doesn't *know* much stud business to discuss!'

Except that Town Crier's a dud, I almost said. I left it at that and told Martin I'd see him next day and we could go through the list of breeders whose mares were carrying what they thought were Town Crier foals.

I spent the rest of the evening hoping the blackmailer would call me. Finding him was top of our priority list and I had virtually nothing to go on. I'd copied his last message from the answerphone on to a normal audio tape and played it repeatedly in the hope that something in the voice would trigger my memory.

The accent was London, voice pitch on the high side, suggesting he was fairly young. I had to assume he was quite deeply involved in racing; he knew the full implications of using a ringer at stud and he seemed to have the know how to set up whatever betting coups he was planning on the strength of my riding to his instructions. I resolved to start the process of elimination tomorrow, involving Caroline if necessary.

'Jesus, Martin, you don't mess about.' I was examining the list of 'conned' breeders. On it were two prominent Jockey Club members and the wife of the High Sheriff of Wiltshire.

He shrugged, half-smiled, unsure whether or not to be pleased with himself.

'You'd better start thinking up a good story for when you have to go back and tell them a mistake was made,' I said.

'No problem. So long as Town Crier's okay, that's the main thing. I'll come up with something.'

Martin made tea while I got my portable radio-cassette from the car. We sat at the kitchen table in the cottage playing the blackmailer's tape. Martin concentrated, brow furrowed, right ear inclined towards the sound. He said, 'There's something familiar about the voice.'

Pressing the play button again, I watched him. He looked frustrated. 'I can't say I know it . . .' he gestured with his hands '. . . it's not somebody I *know*, if you know what I mean, but it's familiar, I've definitely heard it.'

'Recently?'

He shook his head, listening again. 'It's like a voice I heard but I don't know the person. Like somebody on TV, a newsreader or something, know what I mean?'

'Sort of.'

His frustration was almost painful to watch and the tip-of-the-tongue element was getting to me too as I silently urged him on. I suddenly missed having my riding whip though it was as well for Martin that it wasn't to hand as there was a strong instinct to give him a couple of cracks to make him 'go through with his effort'. I told him how I felt and he laughed, breaking the tension.

We played that tape till it squeaked, drew up lists of people Martin had met recently, tried to plot Caroline's movements, but came up with nothing. I was anxious to go up to the house and speak to her but Martin asked for one more day to try and pin down the voice. I agreed.

Brian Kincaid was due down next day and Martin offered me the spare room. I refused as politely as I could. The company of the sour-faced Fiona (boy, could Martin pick 'em) and the thought of spending the night in that dismal cottage didn't appeal. Maybe I was just getting too used to my own company. Anyway, I went back to the small hotel in Marlborough where I'd stayed last week.

Skimming through the *Racing Post* I checked the entries for Market Rasen on Saturday. Cliptie, my synchronised swimming partner from Perth, was entered in the second race. Sure enough the jockey's name was given as R. Dolan, Barney's son, and I wondered how the poor kid felt about being used as a stooge in betting coups.

If Barney was to bring this one off and the Corish Stud was to stay out of the weekend scandal sheets then we had four days to pin down the blackmailer.

Ten

On Wednesday Kincaid spent more than an hour with Town Crier, giving him as full an examination as was possible without anaesthetic. Martin anxiously followed him around asking questions which Kincaid handled good-naturedly, without offering any immediate diagnosis. He took away more samples and left in an ill-concealed state of excitement which raised Martin's hopes till I told him Kincaid was just thrilled at being involved, secretly, in such an unusual case. 'It's the scientist in him coming out. If he finds the cure he'll want it named the Kincaid Serum or something.'

Watching the vet's car disappear along the drive, Martin said, 'He can call it the Kincaid Master Triumph Total Genius Cocktail if he wants, so long as he cracks it.'

We went back into the yard. The phone in the office was ringing. Martin hurried over but it stopped as he opened the door. 'Damn!'

He picked up the receiver and dialled a short number, listened and noted something down. He dialled again. 'Billy, you just rang me . . . uhuh . . . yeah, Friday's fine.' He hung up and said to me, 'Blacksmith.'

'Makes a change from blackmail. What did you just do? How did you know it was him that called?'

'Just dialled one four seven one, that tells you the last person who called you.'

'When did that system start? Do you have to apply to have it installed?'

'Don't think so. We didn't. It was Fiona who showed me how to do it. You don't need it anyway, your answerphone's always on.'

'Answerphones don't tell you the number of the last blackmailer to call.'

* * *

46

Thursday morning Barney Dolan rang sounding nervous. I assured him I was okay for Saturday. If we hadn't nailed the blackmailer by Friday night I'd been prepared to tell Barney I couldn't take the ride. It wouldn't have been worth exposing the stud just to do Barney a favour. But now that we had an ideal opportunity to get the guy's actual number next time he called, I was happy to take the ride, knowing that if he didn't call before Saturday he most definitely would on Saturday night, especially if Cliptie won.

Still it was better to catch the guy before then if possible so I intended spending the time between now and then at home, waiting for his next call. I was confident too that Brian Kincaid would come up with something on Town Crier. I smiled at the memory of his engrossed, exultant expression as he'd laid those body fluid and tissue samples in his bag like they were winning lottery tickets.

Priorities one and two were now coming along nicely and if over the weekend I could bail Barney out of trouble with Joey the Greek, it could yet prove a very productive week.

The rest of Thursday and Friday proved quiet, frustrating and boring. In the blackmailer's hall of fame our guy must hold the record for the smallest phone bill. I began wondering if something had happened to him. Maybe blackmail was his stock in trade and one of his other 'clients' had sorted him out.

At noon on Friday I checked the next day's declarations on teletext and my normally buoyant heart sank a little when I saw Tranter's name against one of the runners in Cliptie's race.

I was just about to call Barney Dolan to warn him when the phone rang. The pause before the caller spoke speeded up my heart and stopped my breath for a second.

'Eddie?'

It was Martin. I almost swore at him. He said, 'I think I've got our man.'

'The blackmailer?'

'Yep.'

'He called you?'

'Nope.'

'Come on, Martin!'

'I'm looking at a picture of him.'

* * *

47

Martin arrived at my flat that evening and produced a cutting from a monthly racing magazine called *Bloodstalk*. It was a full-page story about the Corish Stud and what a fine establishment it was. The writer's name was Simon Spindari. There was a head and shoulders picture of him at the top of the page – young, dark-eyed, olive-skinned. Your original Latin lover.

Martin explained that the feature was written as 'Advertorial': the stud had paid the magazine £1,250 and they in turn had written the piece in a very positive light.

Martin said, 'I twigged when I saw the cutting on the office wall. That's where I'd heard the voice before. He came to the stud twice to interview me and I found out this morning he came once when I wasn't there and spent the afternoon with Caroline, boozing.'

'Who told you?'

'Fiona.'

'Why didn't she tell you before this?'

'She said she didn't want me to think she was telling tales on Caroline, trying to turn me against her.'

'Telling tales? A journalist having a few drinks and a chat?'

Martin looked uncomfortable. 'Well . . . Fiona thinks it was maybe more than just a few drinks . . . Which is fair enough, Caroline's got her own life to lead now.'

But I could see that in his mind it wasn't fair enough. The thought of Caroline with someone else hurt him, and maybe he now saw why she might have betrayed him and told the great Spindari about Town Crier and what a bastard her husband was. Maybe she'd been drunk, maybe just vengeful.

'Have you asked Caroline about it?'

'Thought it best not to in case she warned the guy.'

I nodded, thinking. 'Are you sure you're right, sure it's him?'

'Positive.'

'Okay.' I pondered our next move.

Martin watched me. 'What do we do now?' he asked.

'I don't know. It'll take a bit of thinking out.'

'Why don't we just ring him up, tell him we know who he is?'

'Where does that leave us? He's still got information that's damaging to us.'

'He's always going to have that, isn't he? Doesn't matter what we do.'

'Unless we can make him believe Caroline was lying to him.'

'How do we do that?'

I told him what I thought we should do, and when he called me a genius my thoughts went back to the days when he was my idol. His praise still made me ridiculously proud.

Before Martin had sussed the identity of the blackmailer the plan had been for him to come to my place and wait by the phone while I was at Market Rasen. Now he had to make a quick return trip to the stud to put plan B into action.

Before leaving he begged me to ring Kincaid to ask about progress on the Town Crier samples but I told him I'd arranged to meet Brian next day. The vet had one ride at Market Rasen and we'd agreed to have a drink after racing. I assured Martin that if Kincaid got a breakthrough he'd be on the phone quicker than you could say 'sperm count'.

Market Rasen is the damnedest place to get to. It lies in the wilds of Lincolnshire about as far away from the major roads as you can get. It's a welcoming, picturesque little track that gets good crowds but I hate going there. This Saturday morning my mind was taken off the journey with figuring out how I was going to cope with Billy Tranter in the second race, which was tailor-made for more of his villainy.

Cliptie had fourteen opponents and was a twelve to one chance in the betting forecast. If he won, Barney would recover Joey the Greek's cash and more besides. But such a big field on this tight undulating track must have Tranter slavering with anticipation.

The only real chance of staying safe and getting a clear run throughout would lie in trying to lead from the start. But horses are individuals and need riding in different ways. Dolan had told me Cliptie did best when covered up for a late run.

By the time I pulled into the carpark I still hadn't come up with the answer.

The past few days had been cooler and it was grey and overcast with big dark clouds rolling in from the west as I walked towards the weighing room. We could have done with some rain earlier in the week to soften the going though the management had been watering and claimed to have produced perfect ground. I'd managed to convince myself I'd probably be hitting that ground hard at some point between 2.45 and 2.50 and had my doubts about how 'perfect' it would feel then.

But trainers must have been convinced as there were more than ten runners entered in each race, a rare thing these days. This meant the weighing room would be busier than normal, which it was. There were the usual calls of welcome and jocular abuse as I worked my way through valets and jockeys in various stages of undress till I reached my peg.

In every changing room there is an unofficial pecking order based on success and experience and everyone observes it. The top jocks always got the positions closest to heaters, toilets, saunas, etc., then the scale slides to the bottom, the dingy corners where you find the humble conditional jockeys their eye as firmly fixed on that number one peg as it is on a Grand National victory.

The place smelled strongly of leather with taints of sweat and tobacco smoke, liniment, saddle soap, boot polish and hope. And most of us treasured it as the sanctuary it was. No trainers or owners allowed, no matter how rich or how well connected. Valets, jockeys, racecourse officials (who seldom intrude) only. It was our own little Wendy House where the baddies couldn't get us and where most of us hoped we'd never have to grow up.

I'd seen Barney Dolan drink before but I'd never seen him drunk. Not until I walked into the paddock. Sweat beaded his forehead and each cheekbone, as though his plum-red nose was radiating heat. His eyes were badly bloodshot with pupils the size of confetti. He stank of gin and slurred his speech as he tried to give me instructions. I squeezed his arm. 'Cool it. We'll be okay.'

He just nodded stupidly and tears welled but didn't fall as his whole face seemed to freeze with the terror of losing. You could have transferred the picture straight into a Gamblers Anonymous leaflet and captioned it 'Addict at the end of his tether'.

I'd been pretty tense myself for the past hour. Tranter hadn't turned up. I'd sat in the changing room watching constantly, waiting to see his face as he came through the door. I would know by his first look whether he intended to try and do me again today. But he never came and minutes before the deadline a substitute jockey was declared, drawing from my uptight body an involuntary sigh of relief that surprised me.

I knew now I could ride the race without constantly watching my back. I'd been looking forward to giving that good news to Barney Dolan in the paddock but his mind was no longer open for business, closed down for the afternoon by that well-known racecourse firm, Fear & Booze.

The mounting bell sounded. Barney stood rooted. I went over to Cliptie and the lad legged me up. Cliptie flicked an ear and rolled his left eye back towards me as though trying to gauge which little adventure I had in store for him today. I clapped his neck as we walked round. 'Relax, I forgot to bring my swimming trunks.' The blond lad looked up at me and smiled.

As we moved forward in the queue to exit the paddock, I looked towards the carpark to see Billy Tranter running towards the weighing room as furiously as his saddle and kitbag would allow. I whistled loudly through my teeth which wasn't the smartest thing to do as Cliptie jibbed in surprise and jumped sideways, but I caught Tranter's eye and gave him a wide smile and a high wave. I saw his mouth form a curse as he slammed the saddle to the ground and kicked it.

We cantered to the start.

My stupid antics had stirred Cliptie up and he wouldn't settle to walk round. He jogged and skittered and generally worked himself into a lather and I was glad that Dolan wasn't capable of holding up a pair of binoculars. By the time the tape went up Cliptie was in such a sweat I could hear my boots squeak against his sides as I fought to settle him. He fought back, throwing his head around, pulling hard, so determined that he barely took off at the first hurdle then almost tied himself in knots as he hurried to overcome the stumble and resume his headlong gallop.

I hadn't managed to rein him back an ounce as we approached the second and I stopped wrestling and just concentrated on getting him over safely. He jumped it cleanly, eager to get back to fighting me.

If trainers give riding orders most jockeys try to stick to them, even if they think they are wrong. It's better to lose a race you could have won than take your chances and disobey orders. If the horse gets stuffed then at least the blame can't be laid on you. The reverse side of this is the fact that a large number of races are settled by decisions taken during running, and I was about to make one for good or bad.

Cliptie needed holding up for a late run. If he tried to lead all the way he'd run out of puff or enthusiasm and pack it in before the finish. On the other hand he was using so much energy fighting my efforts to settle him he'd have nothing left at the finish anyway. So I stopped pulling against him, sat as still as I could and talked softly, sending messages down the reins to say, 'Okay, you win, no more fighting, I promise. Take it easy now, do your own thing.'

And he understood. The frantic attitude disappeared. The pace didn't ease much, if any, but the gallop became rhythmical, smoother, not so taxing. The less I moved, the more his excellent balance became apparent. We jumped the third. I looked round. We were twenty lengths clear. Five to jump. Just five.

How was Dolan coping with this?

Cliptie held together beautifully over the next two. Never faltered. Three to jump.

Trying to lead all the way is different from any other raceriding tactic. Normally you'll have a calm, settled horse who's a proven stayer, who enjoys being out there on his own, who relishes the battle when others come at him late in the race. But even on those types there's always a little spider of doubt waiting to start unravelling its web. Waiting for that almost imperceptible blip in the stride or breathing, that tiniest of signals that tells you it will be a miracle if you last home.

And it's not just getting home, returning in one piece, puttering into the petrol station on your final whiff of vapour. On a thoroughbred there is a pack after you. A pack of animals. And sometimes you want to win so badly. Not just for you, often for the horse, for your partner, the one who's done everything he can to stay ahead of that pack. Sometimes you can almost feel the primal fear he exudes as he falters. And tries to keep going, to keep living.

The worst feeling of all is the helplessness. There's nothing you can do. That was the feeling I dreaded most and that was what I found myself waiting for as I went to the second last on this horse who was trying to lead throughout for probably the first time in his life.

I forced myself to look round again.

They were coming.

The dark pack closed like some snaking eraser rubbing out the distance between us.

Ten lengths behind. Two to jump. Three furlongs to hold on. Six hundred and sixty yards. How much was each worth in pounds to Barney Dolan?

But Cliptie was holding together. Then, a hundred yards off the hurdle, he went, faltered. The smallest of tremors but one that I knew signified the beginning of the earthquake.

He cleared the jump but didn't get away cleanly, lost his stride. I gathered the reins, sat lower, gently tried to bring him back on an even keel. His breath rasped, ears came back. I talked to him. 'Come on! Stay with it! Not far. One more jump.'

I daren't look back. The simple turning action could easily throw him off balance again. I didn't know how close they were.

Till I heard the hoofbeats.

Approaching the last he was almost exhausted and hit the top, stumbled, but somehow got his legs out in front of him and stayed upright. I was now a passenger. Dead freight. I was convinced that if I started riding a finish Cliptie would go to pieces.

Hoofbeats either side. Loud panting. Then in the periphery of my vision a dark stretching nose each side of Cliptie's quarters, both gaining, reeling us in inch by inch, reaching our breastgirth, jockeys like dervishes, every instinct in me screaming to kick and scrub and push but my brain overruling, forcing me to sit still and impotent, letting Cliptie do everything for both of us. God knows how it must look from the stands.

The winning post seemed eerily still, never coming nearer, the only movement from those other two snorting, sweating, whip-marked animals, their heads at Cliptie's shoulder now, at his throat, his jaw, his nose . . .

Then past him.

And the post.

'Photograph,' the PA blared.

'Photograph.'

Eleven

In 99 percent of close finishes you know if you've won or not.
Normally you'll glance across as you hit the line, but I'd been
so afraid to move for fear of unbalancing Cliptie that I'd kept
staring straight ahead. He pulled himself up very quickly, so
exhausted that I jumped off and led him back towards the
unsaddling enclosure.

A few punters by the horsewalk asked me if I'd held on and
that made me more hopeful; it must have been very close.
Dolan was waiting for me in the enclosure, easily identifiable
as I approached. All the colour had gone from his face though
his nose stayed stubbornly red, making the surrounding skin
look even paler. He swayed gently as though just holding on
for the result before keeling over.

He lumbered across, almost blocking my way as I led the horse
in, and tried to ask silently but the intended quizzical expression
resulted in one slightly tilted eyebrow and crossed eyes. At least
if we'd lost he'd feel no pain till he sobered up. I looked at him
and shrugged. It was almost as if we had a pact of silence. The
lad took Cliptie and I clapped the horse's lathered neck. His sides
heaved and his head hung low.

I watched the two others come into the enclosure; neither
went into the winner's spot. It must be desperately close. the
PA crackled slightly and breaths were automatically held. 'Ladies
and gentlemen, the judge has called for a print before deciding
the outcome of the second race.'

Unless it was a desperately tight finish the judge could usually
nominate the winner from the negative. We'd now have to wait a
few minutes more for a full print to be produced. I went to weigh
in then hurried back out. Beside me Barney stared straight ahead
and kept swaying, rhythmical as a metronome.

After five minutes without an announcement there were already murmurs of 'dead heat' around the enclosure. Finally, the PA crackled again. 'Ladies and gentlemen, the result of the photo finish . . .' the usual dramatic pause (most racecourse announcers are frustrated actors) '. . . the judge has called a dead heat between number three, Cranston Hall, and number seven, Cliptie. The third . . .'

I grabbed Barney's arm. 'Will that do?' Bets on dead heats are settled to half the stake. Cliptie's Starting Price was twelve to one. I didn't know how much Barney had put on. But he smiled stupidly and nodded then said, 'Fixed Tranter, too. Fixed Tranter.'

I smiled back. 'What did you do?'

Comically, he bent over and swung his arm as though releasing a bowling ball. 'Old spud up the arse trick!' he bellowed, which I later found out to mean he'd got someone to block Tranter's car exhaust with a raw potato. Barney swung again in a demented action replay then fell over and lay on his back, cackling at the sky.

I went to find Kincaid but he hadn't arrived which was under-standable since his only ride was in the last. He turned up half an hour later and we took Styrofoam cups of black coffee outside and stood by the empty parade ring during the running of the next race. Kincaid's hooked nose touched the edge of the narrow cup and he had to tilt his head back as he drank. He had no news of any breakthrough on the Town Crier samples and told me that progress would be quicker if we would allow him to contact the Equine Fertility Unit in Newmarket.

The lab had some ultra-sophisticated equipment but much of their work came via the Jockey Club and I was almost as nervous as Martin was about any involvement with them. From the beginning, Kincaid, as I'd known he would, had taken the view that if he asked no questions he'd hear no lies so when I confirmed we wanted the EFU guys left out of it he didn't push the issue, just told me we'd have to be patient.

I watched Kincaid ride in the last, admiring how stylish he managed to look for such a tall man. He rode a brilliant race to catch Tranter's horse on the run in and that made victory all the sweeter for this spectator. Although Kincaid had never given up hope on his horse, Tranter's had been well clear on the run in then started idling so badly that Kincaid caught him in the shadow of the post and won by a neck.

I went back to applaud the winners as they came in. As he rode towards the winner's enclosure Kincaid wasn't smiling, he was grim-faced and obviously very angry. Jumping from the saddle, he forced a smile for the winning connections and managed a few terse words with the trainer before hurrying inside the weighing room. I followed him.

After weighing in he strode into the changing room, dumped his saddle and whip on the bare wooden table and wrenched open the buckle of his helmet strap. The way he tore the helmet off must have hurt his ears and as he turned to face me his fury made him almost unrecognisable. Kincaid was the most laid-back guy you could meet, and if anyone had ever offered to bet me I'd one day see him in such a rage, I'd have lost a lot of money.

I'd been anxious to ask what had happened but as I stopped a few yards from him he moved forward, eyes almost burning through me, and pushed me firmly aside with both hands. I turned to see who his target was and as a scowling Tranter appeared carrying his gear Kincaid took two more well-measured steps, drew back his right arm and unleashed a punch Bruno would've been proud of.

The only sound that came from Tranter was the crunching grind of gristle giving way to a hammerhead of knuckle. His mouth opened, half in surprise, half in protest, but before a word could form he was hurtling backwards, scattering tack and dropping his own gear as he fell. A dozen men, jockeys and valets, stood still, watching. Through the open door an official moved forward inquiringly. Kincaid stepped over Tranter and slammed the door.

No outside observers now.

Grabbing the dazed Tranter, Kincaid hoisted him up and tore at his colours till much of Tranter's back was exposed. Grunting, he lifted him off his feet and half-laid half-threw him down on a long trestle table. Kincaid picked up Tranter's own whip and started thrashing him, high hard strokes across his pale skin. Weals rose in instant red ridges as Tranter, still semi-conscious from the punch, groaned and tried to turn.

We all looked at each other, nobody sure what to do. From time to time scores were settled in the privacy of the changing room. It was usually short and sharp and soon forgotten about but Kincaid was out of control. He started shouting: 'If you ever do anything like that again I'll kill you, you fucking despicable little turd!' He was grunting now with the effort of beating Tranter.

'Brian, enough!' I said, grabbing at his elbow. He wrenched free and raised the whip again. I grabbed the collar of his silks from behind and jerked him back as hard as I could. 'You'll kill him!'

He stared down at me. He was literally red-eyed with rage. I took the chance of reaching up to grip his shoulders. 'Brian, for God's sake, calm down! Calm down!'

He kept staring at me and for a few seconds I thought he'd gone permanently mad. He was panting, and blobs of spittle had appeared at the edges of his mouth.

With a mixture of gentleness and firmness I led him slowly away from a prostrate Tranter as the others watched. They moved aside to let us through. Quietly I said to Colin Blake, 'Get the doctor.'

Blakey moved quickly towards the door as I sat Kincaid down on the bench. He stared straight ahead but his breathing eased and the rigidity seeped from his body till he was half-slumped, elbows on knees, head drooping till he gazed unmoving at the floor.

Two hours later Kincaid's demeanour had changed to one of deep depression. We were in a small country pub looking at glasses of whisky that neither of us had any real thirst for. Kincaid's all out assault had been triggered by Tranter's abuse of his horse after being caught on the post. As they'd pulled up Tranter had steered himself behind Kincaid's mount so that he couldn't be seen from the stands and started hitting his own exhausted horse savagely with his whip around the head and neck. Brian described it graphically. Tranter had lashed across the velvety muzzle and, more painfully, down across the horse's last rib so the whip flap wrapped under the soft part of the belly to bite into the fleshy purse that held his penis. Kincaid said Tranter had given the poor beast at least a dozen vicious strokes before he'd managed to reach him and almost wrench him from the saddle.

But the vet was now totally disgusted by his own behaviour and lack of self-control and no matter how much I tried to reassure him that it was justified, his mood grew blacker. I told him that Tranter had never lost consciousness and that the bewildered doctor had said he didn't think there would be any permanent damage.

Nor was there any real danger of Kincaid's being disciplined. Nobody in the changing room would grass on him and, spiteful as he was, it was highly doubtful that Tranter would either. 'You'll have to watch yourself though,' I warned Kincaid, 'the little bastard won't forget it easily. I speak from experience.'

Twelve

Kincaid and I left the drinks unfinished and went our separate ways. Back at my flat Martin confirmed that the first part of our plan to beat the blackmailer had been carried out. As agreed he persuaded Fiona to call Spindari and warn him that he was being set up.

At first Spindari had denied he knew anything about the blackmail attempt but Fiona told him that Caroline, with Martin's knowledge, had deliberately fed him false information on Town Crier in the hope that Jean Kerman would print the story and leave her newspaper open to a huge libel suit from the Corish Stud.

When Spindari asked what Fiona's interest in it was she'd told him she was pregnant by Martin who had now reneged on his promise to marry her and gone back to his wife. The simplest of motives: revenge.

Martin had spent the evening waiting to see if our plan had worked: if Spindari had decided pursuing things was no longer worth the risk. The blackmailer would be aware by now that I'd ridden a winner at Market Rasen, having accepted exactly the type of ride he'd warned me against. But he hadn't called. It looked like he'd swallowed Fiona's story.

Martin stayed overnight and next day we both travelled to Worcester to visit Kincaid, try and cheer him up. The vet's mood had improved greatly since the previous evening; Judy, his wife, had told him he'd done exactly the right thing and that she'd have thought less of him if he hadn't given Tranter a beating.

As we drank tea, Judy moved around the big kitchen preparing lunch and joining in the general conversation. Martin was growing increasingly impatient to ask questions about Town Crier. Kincaid noticed and suggested that we might like a conducted tour of the facilities.

As soon as we were outside Martin pressed for news of progress on the samples. Kincaid explained he was still waiting for some results on the blood and sperm samples.

'Results from where?' Martin asked nervously.

Kincaid smiled. 'Don't worry, they don't know which stallion the samples are from or why I've asked for the analysis.'

'Who are they?' Martin asked.

'Specialists, Casper and Denbourne, a big lab. Lots of vets use them for analysis.'

'Thoroughbred specialists?'

'Specialist analysts, all animals. Look, the samples should be back by Tuesday at the latest. I'm as anxious as you guys to crack this. I don't like mysteries.'

Martin nodded and ran his fingers through his grey mop, pushing it back to reveal that tell-tale gauntness, as though all the worries in his head were sucking at the skin, stretching it tighter over the fine bone structure.

Kincaid reached out and squeezed his shoulder gently. 'I'll ring you as soon as the results come through.'

Martin nodded. We declined Judy's lunch invitation and went our separate ways; Martin, engrossed in his problems, back south to the stud, and I north-west towards the yard.

The best thing that could be said about the next three days was that Spindari failed to resurface. It looked like we'd beaten the blackmail threat.

Kincaid called me just after 9 on Tuesday morning: the lab could find nothing in the samples to offer a clue as to the cause of the sterility. I waited for him to suggest the next step. He didn't. After half a minute's silence I said, 'Where next?'

'Eddie, can you give me till the end of the week?' He sounded serious, thoughtful.

'Sure. What're you thinking?'

'Ask no questions, Eddie.'

'Brian . . .'

'Eddie, listen, I won't drop you in it, I promise.'

'Okay. Can I make one stipulation?'

'Shoot.'

'No Horseracing Forensic Lab.'

The Horseracing Forensic Lab dealt mostly with security issues – the last thing we needed.

'Fine. I'll call you. Oh, are you at Stratford on Friday?'

'I've got nothing booked but I'll probably be there mooching around. Better than sitting here in this heat looking down on this one-horse yard.'

'Dust in the mouth? Tumbleweeds outside the saloon?'

I smiled. 'Something like that.'

'See you on Friday.'

I had to ring Martin with what was essentially bad news but I decided to dress up the facts a little. I told him the samples had highlighted something that needed more investigation, further tests, and that Kincaid had asked us to hold on till the end of the week.

Martin took this well and quizzed me for details. I told him Kincaid had been talking medical terms and I hadn't really taken things in.

When I saw Kincaid at Stratford on Friday he was looking very positive, optimistic. He told me he definitely expected to have some news for me by Monday morning at the latest. I'd agreed to ask no questions and I held to the deal which wasn't a problem. I was content to wait a few days more. Kincaid had been very upbeat and wasn't the type to raise false hopes.

He was at Stratford for one ride in the last. We stood talking just inside the changing-room door. I suggested we have dinner somewhere before driving home. He smiled ruefully. 'Afraid not, Eddie. I haven't eaten since yesterday morning. Got to do ten eight in the second at Southwell tomorrow.'

'On what?'

'Tubalcain.'

'They must fancy it.'

He nodded, smiling.

'Ex*cuse* me.' A voice from behind us. It was Tranter. We'd been half-blocking the doorway. We both moved aside and there was a sudden yelp. We turned to see Ken Rossington, a valet, clutching his right foot and hopping about in apparent anguish. Kincaid had stood on his toe, and although he was most apologetic Rossington made his usual show of it. One of the changing room's jokers, he'd milk any potential laugh for all it was worth.

Tranter was the only one who wasn't smiling. He pushed past. Kincaid stopped smiling and reddened slightly. Tranter looked in poor shape; bruised eyes, nose still swollen and misshapen.

He sat on the bench. Kincaid followed him and it seemed for a few seconds he was going to approach him; there was an air of conciliation about the vet.

Kincaid took a couple of steps inside, hesitated, then turned and strode out, a trace of anger back in his face. I guessed that maybe he'd intended to make peace but the memory of the little bastard beating that horse had stopped him.

Tranter didn't watch him leave. Unpacking his kitbag, he showed no emotion whatever.

I rode in the second race and the fourth, both unplaced, and hung around till after the fifth on the chance some poor bugger might crock himself and let me in for a ride in the last but they all came back safe and I headed for the exits to beat the crowds. Driving home, I speculated on the chances of Kincaid's coming up with something by the time I saw him at Southwell next day but Kincaid never made Southwell. He never left Stratford alive.

Thirteen

I heard about it next morning as I was driving to Southwell. It was an item tagged on to the end of the news on Radio Five: 'An amateur jockey and prominent vet has been found dead in what is believed to have been an horrific accident at Stratford Racecourse. Mr Brian Kincaid, who was married with a baby daughter, apparently collapsed in a sauna and died of severe hyperthermia. Mr Kincaid's body was not found until early this morning. Racecourse officials say there will be a full inquiry.

'And now the weather . . .'

And now the weather.

I must have imagined it. Nobody could report the death of a close friend of mine and simply say 'And now the weather'. Impossible. A hoax or something. It had to be. I pulled the car over, mounting the grass verge. I was vaguely aware of a lorry thundering past, horn blaring, shaking the car. I sat gripping the wheel, staring straight ahead, replaying the newsclip over and over in my mind.

I don't know how much time passed before I reached for my phone and found the number of Stratford Racecourse in my diary. I asked for the Clerk of the Course. Unavailable. Could they confirm the news report? Not prepared to comment. Where could I get confirmation? Sorry, couldn't help.

I had a friend in Jockey Club Security, Peter McCarthy. We'd helped each other out over the years. I knew he tried to avoid working Saturdays so I rang his home number and held for ten rings before he answered.

'Mac, Eddie Malloy. I just heard a news item that said Brian Kincaid is dead. Is it right?'

'Eddie, yes, I'm sorry. Only heard myself about half an hour ago. You knew Brian quite well, didn't you?'

'What happened?' My mind was now trying to handle the news and formulate sensible questions at the same time.

'The theory is, apparently, that he went into the sauna for a half-hour session after the last race and collapsed in there, by which time everyone had gone home.'

'Collapsed?'

'It seems he'd been wasting quite hard to make the weight on one at Southwell today. Tragic, isn't it?'

My mind overloaded temporarily with doubts, questions, and images of how Brian would have looked after lying in a sauna for hours.

Mac said, 'Eddie, are you all right?'

'Mmmm. Surely . . . surely the sauna cabin has some sort of safety cut off?'

'I don't know, Eddie. There will be a full inquiry.' I simply couldn't think straight. Had to get off the phone. I told McCarthy I'd call him later.

I got out of the car and wandered over to a stone wall hemming black and white cattle into a big field. Resting my hands on the wall, I stared across the field into dark woods, trying to pull my thoughts together.

Brian Kincaid was dead. An accident in a sauna . . .

No way.

Not Brian. He was a highly intelligent man with considerable medical experience. Light-headed from fasting maybe, but he would have been more aware than most of the dangers of losing consciousness in a sauna. At the first sign of dizziness he would have got out, I was certain of it. But he didn't get out, so either somebody knocked him unconscious in the box or else prevented him from escaping.

Logical progression: who?

Logical answer: Billy Tranter.

Turning slowly, I leaned back against the wall, staring upwards. Tranter's bruised and sneering face loomed huge in my mind's eye which projected it even more hugely on to the blue sky.

I tried to close down the emotions and think objectively.

After the chances he took up at Perth and the persistence he'd shown in persecuting me it had occurred to me that Tranter might well have the germ of a psychotic disorder. Whether it could have mutated into psycopathic was another matter. I needed to know more.

I got back in the car and back on the road to Southwell. The last thing I felt like was riding horses but Tranter would be there and I wanted to see him. Watch him. Study his behaviour. Analyse it. That's what the logical side of me wanted to do but the logical side was just a small part. What the rest of me wanted to do was find him guilty without trial and beat him till he died.

The news at noon ran the same item on Brian's death; no further details. Two minutes later my phone rang. It was Martin. 'I just heard on the news, about Kincaid.'

'Uhuh.'

'Tell me it's not true, Eddie?'

'It's true.'

'Ohhh . . . Jesus Christ! What are we, jinxed or something?'

'What are *you* worried about? The samples? Town Crier?' I was just in the mood for an argument. Ready to take my anger out on somebody.

'Eddie, what are we going to do?'

'What are *we* going to do? What the hell's Judy Kincaid going to do? She's got a three-month-old kid with no father! We've got a mangy fucking stallion firing blanks! Whose shoes would you rather be in?'

There was a long pause then Martin said quietly that he would call me back later. I told him to be more damn' respectful to Brian Kincaid's memory when he did.

Memory. God, you'd think he'd been dead years. Yesterday I'd spoken to him. Yesterday. In the corridor in the weighing room. He'd been telling me he was wasting hard for this ride.

And who was behind us when he said it? Who was listening? Who could have made a reasonable assumption that Brian might spend some time in the sauna yesterday afternoon?

Billy Tranter.

I pressed the accelerator to the floor, speeding dangerously, stupidly, towards Southwell.

My temper had cooled by the time I reached the course. The guys in the weighing room weren't as subdued as I'd expected and it made me angry, made me feel like preaching a sermon telling them they ought to be grieving for Brian Kincaid. But the fact that he was an amateur meant that he was never really part of the inner 'brotherhood'. It wasn't a matter of not being accepted, simply that most professional jockeys see each other almost every day in the same way as soldiers in a small elite unit do.

We all know each other's characters and weaknesses and there is an ongoing, unspoken acknowledgement that we share the same dangers daily. Amateur jockeys are tolerated and grudgingly respected if they are good. Brian had been respected but there was little discernible emotion at his death, only shock at the manner of it. There was a lot of speculation about how terrible it must have been and some juvenile nominations of the ways of dying some of them would prefer.

Jim Perkins came in and told everyone he'd spoken to the caretaker at Stratford, the bloke who'd found Brian's body.

'He said it was like a potato crisp,' Perkins said, which silenced everybody. Tranter was in the corner. I watched his face but could detect no emotion whatever. I was sorely tempted to approach him and ask him to account for his movements every minute of yesterday, but had to settle for watching him whenever I could: observing, looking for some flicker of satisfaction when Brian's name was mentioned. But I could see none. And paranoia started creeping in. I imagined him congratulating himself as he cantered to the start, pictured him locking himself in the toilet so he could gloat and have a good laugh.

I resolved to wait in my car after racing and follow Tranter, but as the afternoon wore on realised that would be a foolish thing to do. Pointless. Where did I expect him to head for, the scene of the crime? Or did I think he'd go home and erect a banner saying 'I killed Brian Kincaid'?

Half-disgusted, wholly frustrated, I left after my ride in the fourth and drove to Worcester to see Judy Kincaid. The dread of facing her mounted mile by mile but I felt I had to go there, pay my respects, trot out the standard, 'If there's anything I can do'.

She was in bed under sedation; the baby was sleeping in the arms of her sister who slowly paced the kitchen floor as her husband made coffee for us. All three of us sat for half an hour in that collective daze that descends on the newly bereaved and suspends social conversation, excuses long silences.

They promised to tell Judy I'd come and they thanked me. As we said goodbye I had the strongest of urges to stroke the baby's forehead. I reached out and rested my hand softly on the warm pink skin. A tiny smile flickered on the round sleeping face and I thanked God she wasn't old enough to understand how much she had just lost.

Fourteen

I slept on my thoughts and suspicions and they thrived on the rest and were stronger in the morning. Once again I rang Peter McCarthy, the Jockey Club Security man.

'Eddie, how come I don't hear from you for months then the only time you can find to call me is at weekends?'

It was fairly warm-hearted banter. In the humour market Mac and I usually traded at about the same exchange rate but this morning it was the last thing I felt like and I steered him straight on to Brian's death.

'I know very little about it, Eddie.'

'Well, do yourself a favour and get some sniffing around done.'

'You mean, do *you* a favour?'

'Mac, there's no way that was an accident.'

'How do you know?'

I argued my case for Brian's medical expertise, which Mac accepted as a reasonable foundation, then told him everything that had happened with Tranter.

'You ought to be very careful who you mention this to, Eddie. That's a pretty serious allegation.'

'That's a fact, Mac! I'm not alleging anything. I'm telling you what happened between Tranter and Brian, and I'm telling you that Tranter heard us talking on Friday and could have made a reasonable assumption that Brian was going to be in that sauna.'

'Ah, but . . .'

'Ah, but nothing! You came to the same conclusion I did just then when I laid out the facts.'

'It's obvious the slant you're taking.'

'Because it's the logical bloody slant to take!'

There was a pause and I pictured him shaking his head slowly.

He said, 'I think you'd best wait and see what the inquiry comes up with.'

'Which will be when? Weeks? Months?'

'I don't know. Let's wait and see what the police have to say. The coroner's report may throw up something.'

'Like what? What evidence is going to be left in a desiccated corpse?'

'That's not for us to say, Eddie.'

'Come on, Mac, don't go all superior. The cops have to be persuaded, as from now, to treat this as suspicious.'

'I wish you luck in your persuading.'

'It would be easier with your help and you damn' well know it. And you know that's what I'm asking for.'

He sighed, long and deliberate, straight into the mouthpiece. 'Okay, after the beating last week, did Tranter say he was going to take revenge on Kincaid?'

'Well, I didn't hear him say that . . .'

'Did anyone?'

'I don't know.'

'Can you find out?'

'I can ask around, sure, but . . .'

'Perhaps you could also ask if anyone knows what time Tranter left Stratford on Friday, and were there any witnesses to his leaving, and did anyone know where he was going, and can anyone at his ultimate destination give him a credible alibi?'

That cooled my ire. Mac was being sensible and logical and at the same time chiding me gently for not being the same. He'd just set off a train of simple deduction, a straightforward elimination process that I should have gone through before even picking up the phone to him.

Chastened, I told him I'd press on with it and get back to him soon. I paced around the flat trying to concentrate, trying to unravel my thoughts so I could start again using calm logic rather than anger and emotion.

The flat was uncomfortably hot. The heatwave persisted. I went outside, scrambled over the big five-bar gate and walked up on to the gallops. The sun at my back threw long shadows up the grassy slope. I spent more than an hour roaming the open spaces, spooked a couple of hares, heard skylarks high above and steadily ordered my thoughts.

When I got back I sat down at the phone with my diary and started making calls. The first was to Jim Perkins, the jock who'd spoken to the caretaker at Stratford. The caretaker was a friend and Jim said he thought he'd speak to me quite freely if I called. His name was Charlie Kenton and he answered the phone at the first ring.

'That was quick,' I said.

'I was just about to make a call myself! My hand was on the bloody phone! Didn't half give me a fright. Who is it?'

I introduced myself and said I was a close friend of Brian's. Kenton was more than happy to talk, with the performing instinct of an accomplished gossip. I let him warm up with a gruesome rendition of how he found the body and what he'd told the police. When I got the chance I asked questions.

'How come he wasn't found till next morning?'

Kenton blustered about not being able to be everywhere at one time, that his duties were different on racedays, and that generally it was nothing to do with him that Brian's body had lain in that sauna all night.

'Did nobody see his car left in the carpark?'

'Ah, there, you see! He didn't bring his car. He got a lift with a mate.'

'Who? Which mate.'

'Scotty Fraser, so they tell me.'

'And wasn't he travelling back with Scotty?'

'Apparently not.'

'How did he plan to get home?'

That stumped him. 'Er, I'm not sure on that one.'

I pressed him on whether he himself had been around the weighing room after racing. I was trying to find out if Tranter had been among the last to leave. But Kenton admitted that he'd been on 'traffic duty', which amounted to directing cars out of the public carpark. He gave me no further useful information.

I called Scotty Fraser and was glad in a sad way to find him as depressed about Brian's death as I was. Scotty felt guilty about not giving Brian the promised lift back.

'What happened, did you forget about him?'

'No, I was heading back to the weighing room after the last to meet him and I was told he'd already left.'

'Who told you that?'

'Billy Tranter.'

My second call of the day to McCarthy interrupted a late Sunday lunch. He wasn't pleased.

Scotty Fraser had gone on to explain that he'd called Tranter yesterday morning, demanding to know why he had said Brian had left Stratford. Tranter told him he'd done it to get back at Brian after the beating. He'd overheard Brian mention he was getting a lift home and thought it would be a nice little touch to leave him stranded. I told Mac all this.

'Well, there you are then,' he said smugly.

'Mac, come on! Tranter would say that, wouldn't he? He's hardly going to admit killing him.'

'Equally, if he intended to kill Kincaid, he'd have to be pretty bloody stupid to drop himself in it now the way you're suggesting.'

'Why not? He had to make sure that Fraser didn't go looking for Brian.'

'Perhaps, but he could have done that just as easily by forging a note or something.'

'And who'd have delivered it to Fraser?'

'Wouldn't have been a big problem.'

'Mac, why are you being so negative? How come you can't see the obvious?'

'How come you've got tunnel vision? Tunnel vision trained on Tranter?'

'Because he's the only one I know with motive. And he's crazy.'

'Motive for what? You're seeing demons round every corner, Eddie. At the moment we have nothing more than a very unfortunate accident which, with hindsight, some might say was waiting to happen. We've got a jockey who's probably already malnourished to some extent, already riding at around a stone below his natural weight; he's ridden that day having taken no sustenance at all in the previous twenty-four hours. It's quite probable he's drained and already light-headed then he goes and bakes in a sauna. What price a collapse? You wouldn't get big odds.'

We fenced for another ten minutes and Mac said he'd speak to the police officer in charge and raise the possibility of 'foul play'. I urged him to tell them to have a word with Scotty Fraser.

Then I rang Kenton the caretaker back at Stratford and he said he'd be happy to show me around. We agreed to meet early next morning.

I was at Stratford before 8 a.m. Kenton was holding the main gate open as I came up the drive. I parked just inside, got out and reached to shake hands with the caretaker who wore navy overalls over a blue-checked shirt and brown tie. He was around fifty, wore thick glasses and smelt strongly clinical as though he sipped high-octane mouthwash.

The sauna was situated at the end of a row of showers. Kenton told me it was less than two years old. I went inside the box while he chirped on, pointing to where he'd found Brian and how he'd looked like 'some little alien'. I felt like yelling at him to shut up and get out. Not once had he mentioned Brian's family or expressed sympathy for my loss of a friend. I needed time to look around. I asked him if he'd mind returning to the car and bringing me my mobile phone. He took the keys and hurried off.

Trying to keep an image of Brian's corpse out of my mind, I looked around the sauna box: standard, nothing unusual, two benches either side, one above the other, the coals corralled off in the corner, water bucket on the floor nearby. I pulled the door closed from the inside, feeling an unexpected wave of trepidation as it clicked shut on the ballbearing catch.

I pushed it. It needed a little weight behind it but opened quite easily. I repeated the action then went outside and did the same; opened and closed half a dozen times. The handle was of wood, shaped like a bow, about a foot long. Crouching, I looked closely at it, ran my hands down it. The door itself was of a soft pine. Relatively new, it had its share of dents and grazes though it gave slightly even under the pressure of a fingernail.

Where the bottom of the handle met the door, just on the underside of the curve, a ridge ran across. I traced it with my finger; no deeper than a millimetre, it had quite smooth edges. Facing the door, maybe six feet away, was a solid wall tiled in white glaze. I got on my knees at the door and looked up at the ridge but the light wasn't good.

'May I ask what you are doing?'

I turned slowly to see a fit-looking, well-dressed, white-haired man – the Clerk of the Course, Gilbert Grimond.

'Saying a prayer for Brian Kincaid.' On my knees, it was the first thing that came into my head and it was enough to throw Mr Grimond temporarily. 'Oh,' he said. I didn't think it was the right time to tell him that what I was really doing was trying to figure what had been wedged against that handle to keep Brian Kincaid from escaping. What had been used to cover the end of the instrument so that the ridge it left was soft, barely perceptible.

I decided that the real reason could wait until I'd spoken to McCarthy, told him what I'd found. Bad decision.

Fifteen

McCarthy was in meetings all day Monday. I left several messages for him to ring me as soon as he was free but it was late-evening before he called me at home. He sounded weary at first, giving the impression that I was the final one on his 'to do' list and all he wanted was to tick off my name and get a good night's sleep. When I told him about the doorhandle he wakened up a bit. 'I'd better go up there in the morning and have a look,' he said.

'I'll meet you there.'

'No, that's a bad idea. You're much too close to this without having any real reason to be so. Not to the outside world, at least.'

'Mac . . .'

'Eddie! If there is a case to be investigated here the police are going to be touchy enough about me bringing it to their attention. If they think you're the one behind it all, driving things along, they're only going to make life difficult.'

'But . . .'

'Also, it's just going to look like a vendetta against Tranter. Leave it to me. I've got no axe to grind, and apart from anything else it *is* my job.'

'So you say, but how come you always clock on when the rest of the shift have done the donkey work?'

'The craftsmen always come in after the labourers, Eddie. Like the stallion that finishes the job after the teaser's done the dirty work.'

I smiled. 'The stallion? Getting a bit above yourself, aren't you?' But he was probably right. I'd been involved with various police forces in the last few years and if there was a right way to rub them up I'd yet to find it. I contented myself with the thought that definite evidence was beginning to build – circumstantial maybe but it was early days and the outlook was promising.

In a much more positive mood I made a sandwich and sat down to listen to the radio news, half-hoping for some 'offstage' breakthrough by the police. But there was nothing at all on Brian's death – stale news, filed away and forgotten. I wondered how Judy was holding up, whether she was still under sedation.

The phone rang. Martin, sounding strung out. 'Eddie, I'm sorry about your friend but we've got to do something about this horse!'

'What's the big hurry? The stud season's almost over.'

We got into a long argument about the urgency of solving Town Crier's problem. I got the impression that Martin was just feeling neglected because Town Crier was no longer my priority. I told him if he felt so strongly about solving the problem, he should damn' well solve it himself. He said that was just what he would do and slammed the phone down.

Ten minutes later I called him back and arranged to meet him next day. He promised to be at my flat early and was as good as his word, getting me out of bed. Even allowing that I was unshaven and bleary-eyed, I still looked better than he did. That terrible concentration-camp gauntness and desperation were back in his face. I made coffee. Martin paced the floor, unwilling to sit down.

'What's wrong, Martin?'

'We can't let this slip, Eddie. We've got to sort Town Crier out.'

'I know but there's no big hurry any more, is there? We've got seven months before the start of the new season.'

'We've got nothing like seven months! If the story gets out and we have to submit to tests on him, we're fucked!'

I couldn't understand the sudden desperation. 'Martin, what's happened? Has Spindari been back in touch?'

'No, but . . .'

'So how is the story going to get out?'

He marched right up to me, shoving his face in mine, shades of madness in his bloodshot eyes. 'It could! It just could! And you don't care any more! You don't give a monkey's fuck! What am I supposed to do, eh? Tell me!' Then he broke down in tears, deep racking sobs. He sank to the floor, crying uncontrollably and clinging to my leg like a terrified child.

An hour later, with a pint of coffee inside him, he was calmer. He admitted he'd been drinking far too much and that both

Caroline and Fiona were putting 'unbearable' pressure on him. The bills were mounting, Kincaid was dead, my attention was elsewhere . . . He said he just felt everything was slipping away from him and that if he could only be sure Town Crier was going to be okay then that would give him strength.

I looked at this hero of mine, sitting slumped at my table, beaten by his own doubts and fears. This hero, this man, this child. And I promised I'd make everything better for him.

He suggested we visit Brian Kincaid's partners and try to find out what had happened to the samples Brian had sent off. I didn't think he was in a fit state to meet anyone but he promised he'd be okay. Foolishly, I believed him and set up a meeting that afternoon with John Brogan, the senior partner in Kincaid's surgery.

I found a clean shirt for Martin and persuaded him to have a shower and a shave. Just as he closed the bathroom door the phone rang. It was McCarthy. I looked at my watch: 10.25. I'd assumed he'd be travelling to Stratford as promised but the call was on a clear line, no mobile. I said, 'I thought you were going to Stratford?'

'I'm at Stratford.'

'So what do you think?'

'I think we've got problems.'

'The police might have problems,' I said with some satisfaction, 'not us.'

'We've got problems, Eddie.' A serious tone I should have recognised sooner.

'What's wrong?'

'The sauna's gone.'

'What?'

'Somebody burned it down in the early hours of this morning. And the weighing room with it.'

Sixteen

I was driving almost as fast as my mind was working which wasn't sensible on these country roads. My tyres screeched complaints at each bend. Martin stared straight ahead. He'd just lost the argument about concentrating on Town Crier rather than Brian's death which I was now almost certain was murder. He paid me back by not responding to the questions I threw out as we headed south. Few needed answering but I could have used some murmurs of encouragement now and then.

'I mean, if Tranter's done this where does he stop? He kills Brian, burns down the weighing room to get rid of the evidence, the whole weighing room, mind you . . . I wonder if it was anything to do with McCarthy going there this morning? How could he have found that out?'

I asked Martin to get Mac's number from my diary and dial for me. Silently he did it and handed me the phone. Mac's mobile was switched off. Martin tried the racecourse number. It rang out unanswered. I cursed and returned to one-sided speculation about Tranter and his psychological history, motivation, private life, etc.

Finally, as we sped down the slip road on to the M5, Martin spoke. 'What if it wasn't Tranter?'

'Well, if it wasn't, I wouldn't like to be the cop who's got to solve it. I never knew anybody else who disliked Brian. Who could have a motive besides Tranter?'

'You talk like you and Kincaid were blood brothers or something. I mean, how well did you know the guy? How do you know he wasn't up to all sorts of stuff?'

'Like what?'

'I don't know. Could be anything!'

I was annoyed at Martin, almost angry, but since both he and McCarthy had now said I should be more objective about possible suspects, I kept quiet for the next few heat-hazed miles and con-centrated on trying to come up with an alternative suspect. I failed but it set me wondering if Brian's partners had an opinion on it.

The practice was located on the Worcester/Hereford border and we got there twenty minutes early and waited in a small hot yellow room where an oscillating fan riffled the dog-eared pages of old Sunday supplements.

The meeting was disastrous. Brogan knew nothing of Kincaid's work for us and hadn't the faintest idea where any samples might have been sent to. Martin quickly lost the place completely and started berating Brogan, accusing him of being incompetent, of being in collusion with some unknown enemy . . .

In the end I had to apologise and almost drag him out of there. Back in the car we had a serious argument. Serious but pointless. His sole focus was Town Crier's fertility problem and he was obviously willing to batter and bludgeon his way through all obstacles in his attempt to find a solution. He saw no reason to make allowances for other people.

'You simply can't go around behaving like you did in there!' I said. 'Brogan owes us nothing. He'd've been well within his rights to have slung you out of there bodily!'

'Eddie, what you don't understand is we don't have the time for anything else! Hear that? *We!* You're in this with me but you're too fucking busy being nice to people! You're only interested in every-one thinking you're a nice guy! We're bleeding to death, man!'

We travelled in silence for the last hour and as soon as we reached my place Martin got straight into his car and roared off without saying a word. Back in the flat I wondered what to do next, where to start looking.

What a bloody mess.

I got some whisky and added about half a hangover's worth to two inches of water.

I sat at the window and sipped methodically at the scotch, waiting for it to seep under the door marked 'Inspiration' in my brain and open it from the inside.

I was still sitting there come evening, on my second large scotch and water, watching the moon come up before the sun had gone down. I'd spoken to McCarthy. He'd told no one why he was going to Stratford so unless the caretaker had twigged that I suspected foul play, and he'd blabbed to someone, then either the timing of the burning was coincidental or it lent even more credence to the murder theory.

Mac had told me the police were waiting for the Fire Department's forensic report so he'd reserve his opinion till that came through.

I tried to figure out how I could learn more about Tranter's movements on Friday evening but the only people likely to know were his friends, if he had any. If he did then they'd probably know exactly what he thought of me which wasn't going to make them too co-operative.

Another hour of pondering brought no ideas though Martin's mind had obviously been at work on the drive home. Just as I was falling into bed he called me with a ruse of his own.

By noon next day Martin had compiled a list of the labs that could possibly carry out the analysis required on the Town Crier samples. We'd agreed to split it and call them posing as a partner from Brian's practice – further deception. I took three numbers and left Martin with four and a warning not to lose his temper if any of them were unco-operative.

Forty minutes later I had scored a blue line through all of mine: negative. Brian was waiting for one to call back which they did within the next hour: nothing. None of them had received samples from Brian or his practice. Martin lost his temper again and started slagging Brian off, saying he'd done nothing with them, claiming he'd been stringing us along. I knew Martin was under severe pressure but couldn't listen to another tirade. I hung up on him and left the phone off the hook for ten minutes.

It was hot and I was hungry. And back at square one there wasn't too much to eat but plenty to chew on. I wasn't too depressed. The death of a close friend balances your perspectives if it does nothing else. The stud was important to me financially but otherwise, if it went under, I could live with it. I'd had my share of hardship in the past and always got through.

Martin would probably crack up but the way he'd been acting recently had been draining my sympathy levels and even if we came out of it okay in the end I knew our partnership would never be the same. Idols with feet of clay, indeed.

I found some salad in the fridge and boiled a piece of fish. Under 300 calories and it would keep me going till evening. I had to do ten stone at Uttoxeter tomorrow which meant losing at least three pounds. A five-mile run this afternoon would help and maybe a sauna tomorrow morning. The thought shook me and I knew I'd never sit in a sauna again in my life without thinking of Brian Kincaid through every sweating minute.

After lunch I cleaned up around the flat then changed into my running gear, pulling on two extra sweaters. As I was lacing up my trainers the phone rang. It was McCarthy. He said, 'Still want me to tell the police about Tranter?'

He was notorious for trying to tease, for not coming to the point.

'What do you know, Mac?'

'I know that Tranter left Stratford pretty soon after racing finished on Friday.'

'Maybe he did but there was nothing to stop him turning round and coming back.'

'Oh, yes, there was. He didn't have a car.'

I waited. Mac said, 'About five miles from the course a Mercedes 600 ran into the back of Tranter's car at traffic lights. His car had to be towed away and the Merc driver took him home.'

'Who told you all this – Tranter?'

'No, one of the Stewards who was acting at Stratford for 'twas he who was driving said Merc.'

'So how come we haven't heard this juicy piece of gossip on the grapevine?'

'Because our rather embarrassed Steward asked Tranter to keep it quiet, and Tranter, knowing which side his bread is low-calorie-spreaded, has done exactly that.'

'So who told you?'

'The crasher. The Steward.'

'Who is . . . ?'

'Not for publication, Eddie.'

'Fine.' I was miffed but not yet convinced. Tranter could have hit Brian on the head before leaving, I supposed, but could he have wedged that door closed, confident that nobody would have discovered it?

'Also,' Mac said, 'to put the proverbial tin lid on your theory, Tranter was in Ireland when the weighing room at Stratford burned down. If you still think Brian Kincaid was murdered, Eddie, you'd better find yourself another suspect.'

Seventeen

A bluish haze hung over the vast parklands as I ran along an old cart track and I somehow felt the air I was sucking in was this same blue, smoggy air. What the hell must it be like in the cities?

The sweating had started even before I'd broken into a jog and now, beneath the layers of clothing, under the tight-cuffed plastic body suit, I could feel and hear the sponginess under my arms as they pumped out a steady rhythm. I was thinking more clearly and had spent the first three miles wondering who could tell me more about Brian Kincaid. I was certain he hadn't lied about sending the samples to a lab and yet none had them. Before leaving the flat I'd even taken the chance of checking with the Equine Fertility Unit at Newmarket, the one I'd made Brian promise he wouldn't use. They had nothing.

That was the first piece of the puzzle. The second was that Brian had been murdered, I was sure of that. And the third was that Tranter no longer seemed a suspect.

So what had Brian Kincaid done to make somebody kill him?

It was pointless returning to his professional partners, Martin's behaviour had blown any potential trust there. But who else had Brian associated with? The best bet would be to go back and speak to Judy. I owed her a call anyway but visiting after a bereavement was never easy, least of all when your motive wasn't purely one of sympathy.

Back at the flat I had a cool shower, fighting the strong temptation to lay my head back and drink from the gushing jets. Any intake of liquid would counteract the sweating I'd just done. I rinsed my mouth with a strong mouthwash, got dressed and dialled Judy's number. Her sister Amanda answered and told me Judy was with the police in Worcester.

'Couldn't they have come to see her?'

81

'They did, yesterday. She wants to know more so now she's gone to Worcester Police Station to see the chap from Warwick.'

Brain's death had happened in Warwickshire so they'd be in charge of the investigation. Her sister told me Judy had become much stronger when she learned that Brian's death was being treated as suspicious. 'She badly needs someone to blame for taking him away. Now she's got the bit between her teeth, she wants to do everything she can to find out who was responsible.' I told Amanda I'd like to help if I could and she said Judy would be in that evening and she was sure she'd appreciate a visit.

I reached the house just after seven. Judy, in pressed tan slacks and a cream blouse, welcomed me. Slim, with cropped fair hair, she was tall, almost gangly, and wore no make-up. Her cheeks always carried a reddish bloom; a true country girl. Her grey-blue eyes were defiant though still showed signs of weeping.

She led me through the house to a big garden where Amanda was rocking the baby in a small shaded cradle-cum-hammock. Amanda's husband Dave was barbecuing meat which sizzled temptingly and smelt delicious, making me regret that I was wasting hard for Uttoxeter tomorrow.

We sat out there till dusk when marauding insects made things uncomfortable. What I'd expected to be a bit of an ordeal turned out to be enjoyable, uplifting even. We spent a long time talking about Brian, recounting stories, remembering funny things, laughing freely, even Judy whose eyes sparkled at times with memories. If anyone had happened upon us they'd have assumed we were discussing a dear friend long dead but it had been less than a week since his murder – a word, understandably, still forbidden.

I worked the conversation around to Brian's other friends and associates and by the time I left I had the names of three people who'd been fairly close to him. Judy told me he'd thought highly enough of them to maybe confide in them, talk about any worries. I promised to have a word and to see what I could find out from the lads in the weighing room as I moved around the country.

Judy said, 'I'd try Alex Dunn first. Brian loved Alex, he was Brian's mentor. "The best vet in the world", Brian called him. Used to call him it to his face, too, and Alex always blushed.' She smiled again then the smile disappeared and concern took its place. She said, 'God, I wonder if Alex knows . . . He and Brian had spoken half a dozen times in the week before . . . but Alex hasn't called since.'

That alerted me though I tried to show nothing more than a casual interest. 'Have they always stayed in close touch?'

Judy, still distracted, shook her head slowly. 'I don't think so. It must have been Christmas when they last spoke. Until lately, that is.' She turned her head towards me. 'Brian said Alex was helping him out with a little problem.'

I had an idea the problem might have been Town Crier but didn't want to press much further. Still trying to be cool I said, 'Maybe Alex has been away or something and missed the news in the papers. I'll make him my first call tomorrow.'

'Would you?' said Judy, looking relieved. 'That's very kind.'

'Not at all. I'll call you after I've spoken to him.'

I said my goodbyes and drove home through the darkness, still smelling barbecued beef and listening to my stomach rumbling.

Several theories had occurred to me on the journey and after sleeping on them I decided that a phone call to Alex Dunn might not be the smartest way to play things. Dunn's practice was in Newmarket and although I'd heard his name we'd never met. I rang a friend down there on the pretext of looking for a good vet I could recommend to someone.

Without prompting he mentioned Dunn. 'Got a reputation as a bit of a nutty professor, likes experimenting, does a bit of homeopathic horse stuff if you can believe that, but he gets results. Works on his own in a little place at Six Mile Bottom. Lives alone, doesn't smoke or drink, but bets like a lunatic.'

He gave me a couple more names. We hung up and I called Martin and told him I had an idea where the samples might be, though I didn't elaborate. He wanted more info but the last thing I needed was him racing off to Newmarket to grab Alex Dunn by the lapels.

He said, 'So what are you going to do?'

'I'm going to try and see this guy as soon as possible but it'll have to be tomorrow at the earliest. I'm riding at Uttoxeter tonight.'

'Give me his name, I'll go and see him.'

'No, Martin, leave it to me. I'll call you as soon as I know something.'

He argued his case, lost his temper again, and this time he slammed the phone down on me.

I saw Tranter at Uttoxeter. He ignored me, even during the race we contested and which I won. My other two rides were unplaced, but with earnings for the evening of almost £700 I wasn't too unhappy and drove home eagerly anticipating to-morrow's trip to Newmarket.

They were racing there and I learned from the racecourse office that Alex Dunn was attending in an official capacity. There was no break in the weather and as I steered slowly along the drive approaching the racecourse, heat haze distorted the images of cars and pedestrians ahead.

Just after the first race I spotted McCarthy. He was walking towards the stables at right angles to me, his chubby face trying to sweat itself cool. I hadn't seen Mac for a while. Looked like he'd put most of his weight back on. His wife tried to keep him on a sensible diet and when he'd been pitching for promotion last year he'd followed it, but when he got pipped for the big job he'd let himself slip again. Pushing seventeen stones now by the look of him.

He didn't see me till I was almost by his shoulder and when he did his scowl didn't change.

'Hi,' I said. 'Hot, eh?'

'What are you doing here?'

'Nice to be made welcome at the headquarters of racing.'

He stopped and turned towards me, mopping his brow with a handkerchief. From the front I could see a definite tinge of grey in the dark hair at his temples. He said, 'You don't like flat racing, Eddie, what are you up to?'

'Same as I was last time we spoke. I'm trying to find out who killed Brian Kincaid.'

'Leave it to the proper authorities.'

'What exactly are the proper authorities doing about it?'

Mac glanced around. At six foot two his vision covered a wide sweep. He didn't care to be seen talking to me. We'd been in a few scrapes together though he'd always come out of it well enough. He said, 'Look, I've got to speak to one of the stable security staff. Can we meet somewhere quiet during the next race?'

The bars would be fairly empty while a race was on but flat races seldom lasted longer than a few minutes. I suggested I wander towards the stables in ten minutes' time and meet him there which was fairly remote from the main crowd. He agreed. I asked him where I'd find Alex Dunn.

'Why do you want him?'

'I'll tell you in ten minutes.'

Mac said if Dunn wasn't out on the course he usually watched the racing from the owners and trainers stand. He told me I couldn't miss him – six foot six and very thin with white hair.

I recognised him immediately from the description. He was in the stand. On the steps behind him was a noticeable gap; few would have a decent view over his head topped by a Panama hat. I watched him throughout the mile race that was in progress: elbows out holding binoculars steady, a rolled up newspaper in his right fist fixed like a pathfinder to the binoculars which moved slowly as the commentary built, the crowd murmur grew to a rumble, the approaching hoofbeats drummed louder . . .

Then they were past the post.

The noise died. Dunn's binoculars came down but he looked like he was still staring into the far distance, giving the distinct impression that what he was watching was a large wager disappearing over the horizon.

Slowly he pushed the newspaper into the jacket pocket of his light brown suit then gripped the crush barrier in front of him with both hands and almost slumped forward. My inclination was to give him time to compose himself but my instinct told me to move in while his defences were low. He stayed put like a skinny breakwater as the crowd moved around him and the stand emptied. Within a couple of minutes he was alone.

I came at him head on up the steps, smiling. 'Mr Dunn?'

He nodded slowly, wondering if he should know me, brows meeting as he searched for a name. 'Eddie Malloy.' I said, holding out my hand. 'I am a friend . . . I mean I was a friend of Brian Kincaid.'

There was an immediate change in his brown eyes. He swallowed dryly then held out his hand. He looked to be in his late-fifties though the hat hid most of his hair which was Aspirin white and would, I guessed, make him appear considerably older.

'You knew Brian?' I said.

He nodded, still struggling for normality but showing no surprise at my change of tense. I decided to go for it right away but the PA system announcing the SP drowned out my next words. I repeated them. 'The samples you were helping Brian with, they were from one of my horses.'

He was already quite pale but that spooked him, driving what remained of the colour from his bony face. At the same time his whole body recoiled a few inches as though I'd raised a hand to hit him. Poker player he wasn't.

Taking off his hat, he ran skeletal fingers through his thin hair, put the hat back on and said, 'Which samples?'

He was trying.

I stared at him. 'The samples from my stallion. The semen, blood, biopsies.'

He looked at his watch, hand shaking slightly, and said, 'I'm very sorry but I'm actually on duty today.'

'I can wait. We can meet after racing.'

'I have a number of appointments.'

'We need to talk, Mr Dunn. I'm sure you know why.'

He looked at me like I was the bailiff at his door. I thought for a few seconds he was going to start crying. He said, 'Perhaps you could come and see me at home?'

'Fine. This evening? Six-thirty?'

He just nodded slowly, still watching me like I was the snake, he the rabbit.

He gave me his address and phone number when I pressed him then I left and went to meet McCarthy.

He was still inside the racecourse stables. I waited, walked around by the gate, watching my shadow. I was pretty keyed up. Dunn had behaved as though he'd murdered Brian himself. Surely his behaviour couldn't simply be put down to his secret involvement with the samples analysis. I smiled. Maybe there'd be a bonus in this yet. Maybe Dunn could still crack Town Crier's problem. Maybe he'd already cracked it.

McCarthy came waddling towards me and we moved over into the shade of the stable buildings. He told me the autopsy on Brian had shown up a long thin bruise on the scalp above the right temple which could have been caused by a 'blow from a third party' or from a fall. The fire that destroyed the weighing room had started, they reckoned, as a grass fire outside after the weeks without rain. What they couldn't say was whether the grass fire had been arson.

'Come on, Mac, at three in the morning? It's hardly going to be spontaneous combustion.'

'They're still looking at it, Eddie. I'll keep you in touch. Now why did you want to see Alex Dunn?'

'Why, are you interested in him too?'

'Should I be?'

'Are we going to spend the rest of the afternoon swapping questions?'

'Would you like to?'

We both smiled. Mac said he wasn't particularly interested in Dunn, and since I was nervous about the Town Crier samples I played it as cool as I could and told him that Brian and Alex Dunn had been close friends and I'd just wondered if Dunn could give me a lead.

'And did he?'

I tried to look disappointed. 'Nah, nothing. He's still in shock too from Brian's death.

'I didn't know they were good friends.'

'Well, old friends. Judy Kincaid told me they didn't see much of each other but they were in touch recently. Just a shot in the dark.' I was keen to move McCarthy off the subject now in case he sent the police to talk to Dunn. The vet would probably drop down dead at the sight of a warrant card.

Mac said, 'So, what next?'

I sighed. 'I don't know. Any suggestions?'

He put a hand on my shoulder. 'Yes, go home and hang up your pipe and deerstalker. Let the police handle it. You're getting too old for all this amateur sleuthing stuff.'

I smiled. 'And what does that make you?' Mac was at least ten years older than I was.

'I'm a professional sleuth.'

I raised a mischievous eyebrow but resisted saying, 'Oh, yeah?'

He promised to keep me informed of police progress and I wandered off trying to convey an air of resignation though it was important not to overplay it. Mac knew me quite well and quitter wasn't a caption he'd have placed under my mugshot.

I had a sandwich in a pub then rang Martin to tell him I'd set up a meeting and was hopeful of having something more solid for him by tonight or tomorrow morning.

Alex Dunn's place wasn't easy to find. I had to get directions from a garage attendant and got there just before 6.30. An old bungalow with flaked cream masonry and mustard-coloured door and sills, it lay down a narrow road facing acres of deep woods. There was no car in the drive and if Dunn was at home he wasn't answering the front door. I went around the back along paths bordered by colourful but neglected plants and shrubs.

The house looked much bigger from this side. I tried the door of the long porch. It was open. I went in and knocked on the half-glassed door inside. Nothing. Complete silence. I went back to the car and waited. An hour later Dunn still hadn't showed and I began to grow angry with myself for so easily accepting his suggestion of meeting here.

If he had no intention of keeping the date, I had little intention of breaking it. Starting the engine I cruised slowly along till I found a track going into the woods. I turned in and drove till I could no longer see the bungalow for trees.

I got out, taking with me the waterproof I always carried, and headed back through the woods towards the house, stopping twenty yards in and settling on the ground where I could see without, I hoped, being seen.

Come darkness I was still there. Not even a car had passed. The only sounds came from nocturnal creatures on the prowl. I decided to join them and just after 11 returned to the back door of Dunn's place and broke in. Angry that he hadn't turned up, and even more convinced he had something serious to hide, I didn't bother creeping around in the darkness but switched on the lights in each room I checked.

If he came home now I was prepared to argue my case for being here and pay for the broken door pane, but otherwise my conscience was clear.

The biggest room in the house had been converted into a lab which, unlike the rest of the property, was clean and tidy to the point of obsessiveness; to the point where I tried to replace each phial, each box, back in its exact spot. I spent more than an hour checking cupboards and shelves searching for anything marked with Town Crier's or Brian Kincaid's name. There was nothing.

I tried a door in the corner of the lab. It was locked. I went back out to the hall. Hanging empty behind the front door were several coat hangers. Taking a wire one and bending it as I walked, I returned to the door in the lab and within a minute had picked the lock.

There was nothing inside but piles of cardboard boxes marked with huge letters: GUTERSON'S GLOVES. Hauling the top one down I eased back the already open flaps. Nothing but blue plastic arm-length gloves for use in veterinary examinations.

I moved next to the office and raked through filing cabinets, drawers, and a Rolodex telephone list where I found Brian's office number which looked to have been written some time ago, with his home number added untidily at an angle below.

Beneath the big wooden desk I found a box file of copy invoices going back more than a year. Under the bright desk lamp I worked through them till I saw a name I recognised, a name that brought me to a breath-holding stop, my finger unmoving on the page, just as the man himself would have done had he appeared in front of me – Edward F. Malloy: my father.

I felt faint as his figure loomed huge in my mind. I'd spent many years trying to erase his memory, succeeding only after psychiatric help, and now he was back, unintentionally, uninvited, but with almost the same shattering impact of the worst days of my life. I felt I had to get out of the room.

Eighteen

I stood outside, leaning against the corner of the house, the dry old paint flaking under my hand. Staring up at the full clear moon, I recalled the disciplines of old and made myself breathe deeply, hearing the breaths, focusing on them, trying to use them to clean my mind again, to erase that picture before the well-remembered anxiety attack set in.

But I was out of practice and the image of my father stayed stubbornly where it was. I resigned myself to the anxiety attack but it didn't come. And I stood there for God knows how long, wondering if finally, at the age of thirty, I was capable of coping with thoughts of the past.

I went back inside, sat down and looked again at my father's name which, in my mind, took up the whole page. I stayed there staring till the impact lessened, till the name diminished and took its proper place on the page above the address: a stud in Newmarket. Someone had told me years ago that they'd moved here. And then I thought of my mother too and the dread drained out of me and sadness seeped in.

Eventually I pulled myself together enough to start wondering how long my father had been a client of Alex Dunn's. The invoice was marked 'Quarterly as agreed' and was for £1,050. It was dated 30 March. I skipped back and found one other dated the end of December. Both, unusually, were marked 'Professional Services'. Most invoices in Dunn's file carried details of the work carried out, like scanning, cyst removal, etc.

What was Dunn doing for my father that had already taken six months and looked to be ongoing? Why were the details of it not shown? I took a note of the address and phone number of my father's stud then checked the rooms in the rest of the house, not terribly sure what I expected to find in them.

On an old sideboard in the sitting room was an almost full bottle of whisky. The temptation to pour a large glass was considerable but I settled for promising myself one as soon as I got home.

The broken-paned door ground noisily over the glass as I pulled it close behind me. I wondered if Dunn would report the break-in to the police but doubted he would. There was nothing missing after all though if he needed clues as to the culprit I was sure he'd still find the echoes of my childhood bouncing around his dark little office.

I'd brought no overnight bag but I was certain I'd pin Dunn down next day at Newmarket races so I drove back into town and found a hotel where the receptionist didn't seem at all surprised at a baggageless traveller who, at pushing 11.30, still hadn't found himself a room.

Next morning, Saturday, I called the number Dunn had given me as his home telephone. No answer. I tried several times without success.

Faced with a few hours to kill before racing started I found the piece of paper with the address of my father's stud and asked the hotel porter for directions. I drove the short distance there with increasing doubts as to my purpose and, when I reached it, parked fifty yards past the entrance gate, switched off the engine and sat in silence.

The car windows were fully down but it was still uncomfortably hot in the sun. Turning in my seat, I watched the gate. Trees and bushes shielded the house from the road. I just kept staring at the gate, hoping for I don't know what. This was the home of my parents, a home I had never known.

We'd come to England from Ireland when I was seven and I'd spent the next nine years on a farm in Cumbria. My father kept horses and had dabbled in breeding even then. It had always been his ambition to own a proper stud farm.

Well, now he did though it looked to be a small operation. I watched the gate, wondering what I would do if my father suddenly appeared, or my mother. And my first thought was that I would duck out of sight. Would they recognise me if they did see me? I looked in the rear-view mirror. Had I changed much in the fourteen years since I'd left home?

In looks, maybe not much; inside me, immense changes. Forty years was what it felt like in my head, not fourteen. I started the car again and pulled slowly away.

Dunn didn't turn up at Newmarket races. I was tempted to ask McCarthy to find out if he'd phoned the racecourse with some excuse but I didn't want him to know how keen I was to speak to Dunn. I drove back to the bungalow. It was deserted, the broken glass still on the floor in the back porch.

Where the hell had he gone and why had he panicked so soon? I went back inside and spent more than an hour going through the copy invoices again, making notes of the names and addresses of all his clients then getting their phone numbers from his Rolodex.

On the long drive home I spent most of the time trying to figure out what it was I'd said that had scared Alex Dunn so much. I'd only raised two issues: Brian's death and the samples from Town Crier. Which one had set him off? And what exactly was Dunn working on for my father?

A possible link came to mind. Tenuous but worth exploring.

As soon as I got back to the flat I lifted the *Directory of the Turf* from the bottom shelf of the small oak bookcase and started skimming through the stallion ads, checking the stud names below the glossy colour pictures. The Keelkerry Stud, named after my father's home town, had a quarter-page ad dominated by the picture of a bay stallion named Heraklion whose career highlights, and those of his offspring, were listed in bold type. Three other Keelkerry stallions were advertised but by name only.

I rang Martin and told him what had happened in the past twenty-four hours. Dunn's sudden disappearance cheered him immensely – he was convinced the vet must know something about the Town Crier samples and equally sure that we'd soon find Dunn. I asked Martin to call the Keelkerry Stud posing as a breeder who wanted to send a mare for a very late covering.

'Why don't you call?'

'We don't get on. I haven't spoken to my father in years.'

Martin said, 'They'll think I'm mad calling this late, the season's virtually over.'

'Act a bit eccentric then. Tell them you made a last-minute decision.'

I explained how I wanted him to go about it: to ask advice on which stallion to use then maybe name two or three from the ad and see what the reaction was.

Ten minutes later Martin called back, excitement in his voice. 'No Heraklion!'

'Who did you speak to?'

'I think it must have been your mother.'

'What did she say?'

'She didn't question me at first, seemed anxious to have the chance of some unexpected revenue. She did a bloody good selling job on every stallion but Heraklion. When I suggested him she said he'd been retired for the season and I said, "Oh, still hasn't recovered from his problem then?" which threw her more than a bit. I told her some friends of mine had tried to book mares to him early in the season and the horse had been on the easy list. She rallied then, I'll say that for her, said he'd been suffering from a complex fracture of the off hind after being kicked by a mare. "Just an accident," she said, "inherently sound, you know, and we're sure he'll be back to his best next season."'

So, two smallish studs who'd lost their best stallion. Maybe Heraklion had been kicked but the stud's mysterious link with Alex Dunn who was also connected, albeit indirectly, with our stud made it too much for mere coincidence. Martin told me my mother had almost desperately tried to sell him a covering from one of the other stallions. Business must be pretty bad. I felt a strong pang of remorse for having deceived her.

Martin was set on finding Dunn, determined to go and stake out his place if necessary, and I knew by his voice he wouldn't be argued out of it this time. Not that I couldn't have used some help but I didn't think Martin could keep a cool head. But he promised to stay calm and be guided by me so I gave him Dunn's address, warning him that he wasn't to pounce.

'If he turns up, try and follow him. We'll learn more that way.'

'Sure,' he said. 'Don't worry.'

'Stay in touch with me on my mobile. I'll probably be back in Newmarket tomorrow anyway so let's meet.'

We set a time and place, and when Martin hung up I resisted the strong urge to replace the handset because I knew I'd find it hard to pick it back up again and do what I knew I now had to which was to call my mother.

I dialled and tried to steel myself for the voice I'd last heard when little more than a child.

It rang seven times then a voice said, 'Keelkerry Stud.' It was my father. The voice had changed; less volume, weaker, as though the edges had worn away. I couldn't bring myself to speak. 'Hello!' he said. 'Hello!' And that impatience, that pent up anger I remembered so well, was still there now. I felt my top lip film over with sweat. My mouth dried up. I replaced the receiver quietly, as though he might be able to tell it was me and call me to account for it. I lowered myself slowly on to the chair by the window and sat staring out, seeing nothing. My throat tightened and I swallowed repeatedly, pumping out silent tears.

Nineteen

The following day I packed an overnight bag and headed back to Newmarket, determined to go and speak to my parents. I wasn't a child any more and I wasn't going to let my father return me to that state. I was a grown man with a legitimate interest in my father's association with Alex Dunn, and I was damn' well going to ask some questions.

That was the theory at least but much as I disciplined my brain, my emotions continued to mutiny. A few times I looked at the speedo and found it registering well below my normal speed from subconscious dread of reaching my destination.

Martin called me just after 9. He complained of being cold and stiff after sitting in the woods for half the night waiting fruitlessly for Dunn to come home. I offered to meet him for lunch in town but he told me to come to Dunn's place, said he wouldn't move from it till the vet appeared.

I was in Newmarket before 10 and on the approach to the Keelkerry Stud my stomach tightened nervously, causing me to shift in my seat. I pulled into the side of the road about a hundred yards before the gate, determined not to drive past this time. I'd get out here and walk across, go through the gate and straight to the front door of the house. No hesitation. No stopping.

I switched off the engine and checked my face in the mirror. As I reached for the door handle a light blue Vauxhall Estate coming towards me slowed and indicated then turned and nosed up to the gate. The driver was so tall he had trouble getting out of the car. It was Alex Dunn. He opened the gate, drove through, then closed it behind him before driving towards the house just fifty or sixty yards up the driveway which was screened by a high hedge.

I got out and ran across the road to the hedge, making my way along the outside. The stud stood alone in open land on this quiet road. The only witnesses to my skulking would be passing motorists and I doubted they'd be interested.

Staying close to the hedge, I heard Dunn switch off the engine. A car door slammed. I hoped my father might be there to meet him. Perhaps they'd start talking in the yard. No. Just faint footsteps on gravel then another door closing. No knock. No greeting. It sounded as if Dunn had simply walked right into the house.

I looked across at my car on the verge and the sunlight glinted on a side window, almost blinding me. I couldn't leave it there much longer. If anyone in the stud saw it they might become suspicious.

I'd have to drive about half a mile round a long steady bend before the car could be parked out of sight. I ran back across to it, did an unhurried U-turn and headed back down the road. On foot again I came at the stud from a different angle, cutting across open land to try and see how far back the trees and hedges ran. They seemed to border the whole property in a looping semi-circle. A couple of furlongs down from the house and stables they thinned out enough for me to peer through and see eight fenced off paddocks with maybe a dozen horses grazing quietly in the sunshine. All were in open view of the buildings. Once through the trees and on to the property there was no decent cover.

I'd hoped to get inside, get close to whatever horse Dunn was visiting and eavesdrop on his conversation with my father or the groom or whoever. But unless I could get through the thick hedges close to the stables themselves then it would mean trying to cross a tract of open ground which would leave me exposed. If I was to face my parents again it wasn't going to be as an intruder.

I spent the next half-hour circling the perimeter of the property but couldn't find a safe way in so settled for returning to the hedge close to where Dunn's car was parked. Maybe I'd hear something as he left.

But he didn't leave. At dusk his car was still there. I'd had my mobile switched off in case someone rang just as Dunn came out. As darkness fell I walked what I considered to be a safe distance away and called Martin. He was still outside Dunn's place, hungry and frustrated, and when I told him where I was and why, pretty damned angry too. 'Why the fuck didn't you call me? You knew Dunn was there, you could have saved me hanging around this shithole any longer!'

'I thought he'd leave at any time and maybe head back your way.'

'Well, he didn't, did he?'

We were both silent for a long moment then Martin said, 'Did you say he's been there since this morning?'

'Around ten he arrived.'

'Fuck me, that's one long consultation! I wouldn't like your old man's vet's bill.'

'I think he might be paying in kind.'

'Huh?'

'Dunn might be staying there. He's been doing some unspecified work for my father for the past six months or so.' I told him about the invoices I'd found, mysteriously short on detail. Martin arrived at the stud within twenty minutes and we watched together till the last light went out in the house just after 11. So Dunn was staying there.

We were tired and very hungry and I suspected I also looked as scruffy as Martin did with his heavy stubble and soiled clothes. Earlier in the evening I'd taken the precaution of ringing the hotel I'd stayed in previously and booking a twin room. We made our way back to it, persuaded a bored young girl to fix some sandwiches, downed a large scotch each and trudged wearily to bed after booking a 6 a.m. alarm call.

In the morning Martin was going in to collar Alex Dunn.

We were back outside the Keelkerry Stud by 6.30 a.m. in case Dunn upped stakes early but his car was still in the drive. Martin and I spent a couple of hours dissecting what we'd learned, theorising, but simply didn't have enough evidence to come to any logical conclusion.

At 8.40 Martin pulled away towards the stud and parked outside the gate. From a short distance I watched him go in.

Twenty-five minutes later he reappeared and drove off, as agreed, in the opposite direction from where I was stationed. I hurried the few hundred yards back to my car and drove past the stud and out of sight again about half a mile along the road where I turned quickly and came past the stud once more. Just as I slowed to stop and turn back again Dunn's blue estate overtook me at speed and I accelerated smoothly, following him.

I stayed well back until approaching the edge of Newmarket town where I had to close up for fear of losing him. But he didn't know the type of car I drove and so long as it wasn't Martin's car behind him I didn't think he'd be suspicious. He slowed considerably going down the Bury Road as strings of racehorses were crossing at regular points on their way to and from the gallops. Near the bottom of the road close to the town centre Dunn took a right, and just as I turned off the main road behind him I saw his tailgate disappear in another right turn into one of the big racing yards.

I parked behind a white delivery van and phoned Martin. 'How did it go?' I asked.

'He's rattled all right! He knows something. I told him if he didn't come up with the samples and the results by this time tomorrow, I'd bring the police in.'

'Did you speak to him alone? Was my father there?'

'Just Dunn. He was actually coming down the drive as I was walking up. He kept trying to get away, said he had an important appointment, tried the same thing with me that he did with you: "Come and see me at home this evening."' Martin put on a whingeing voice.

I said, 'Well, he's now reached his important appointment. I'm outside one of the big yards in the town. Think it's worth keeping a tail on him?'

'No, no way. He's too scared to do anything now. He said he'll definitely meet us at his house tomorrow morning. Ten o'clock.'

'Do you believe him?'

'Eddie, he'll be there.'

He wasn't. Next day we were there before 9.30 and waited till 11. Dunn had been back. The broken pane in the door had been replaced, the glass shards swept up. I broke the new one and we went inside. The house had been cleared, very effectively. There wasn't so much as a thermometer left in the lab, a pen in the office or a sock in a bedroom drawer. Dunn had moved out. Each empty room seemed to deal Martin an almost physical blow. By the time we'd finished the tour he looked stunned, defeated, and sounded that way too when he spoke. 'What do we do now, Eddie?'

'We find out where he's gone.'

'How?'

I looked at him, the tired eyes, the downcast expression, the beaten dog look, and I realised how much he was pissing me off. Martin was fine if things were going well; otherwise he either blew his top completely or whined and moaned, expecting somebody else to get him out of trouble. 'We'll find him,' I said coldly, and walked out and along the path to the front gate.

Martin followed. 'But, Eddie, I can't spend any more time here just now. I've got stuff to do, we've got a business to run.'

'Go back and run it then.' *What's left of it,* I thought.

'Just for a few days, then I'll come back and help you.'

Yeah, when I've found Dunn, you'll come back and play the tough guy.

'Fine,' I said.

I watched him drive away and wondered how he could so quickly become disheartened. My own resolve had been strengthened by Dunn's disappearance. You didn't flee your home and workplace overnight just because of a few mysterious samples. Dunn was involved in something serious. And how close was he to the Keelkerry Stud? To my parents? Could they be implicated?

I headed for their stud, a cold determination in me crushing the emotions of the past few days. I parked at the gate and marched up the drive. The house was of yellow stone, big deep windows, climbing plants around the door where my gaze was fixed. The white door, coming closer as though a movie camera lens was tightening in on it. I was aware of the sounds of gravel crunching but seemed somehow removed from the notion that it could be my feet making the noise. All I was aware of was my unblinking gaze fixed on that door.

I reached it.

Pressed the bell.

Waited.

It opened slowly. My father stood there. Still taller than me but age showing now: thinning grey hair, hollow cheeks, loose skin on his face, his throat. Shoulders drooping, hair growing from his ears, eyebrows getting bushy – and hatred in his eyes. No, not hatred, scorn. His jaw muscles clenched and he slammed the door shut so hard I felt a mild shockwave on my face.

I didn't move. Stayed there, back straight, head high, and was proud of myself for it. And I reached for the bell again and I pressed it and I held it and I could hear it inside hammering like a fire alarm. The ringing went on for more than a minute before the door opened again. My mother. Older, smaller, softer, kinder-looking, the way I remembered her from my infant days. Her hair shorter but still a rich auburn which now looked so out of place framing the pale skin, the pale, pale skin. Still no hint of shame on her face as she looked at me. I'd never known her speak a word against my father for his treatment of me. But there had never been any hatred in her either. Sadness, yes. Despair, maybe, but at least she'd never hated me for what had happened.

'Eddie,' she said quietly, and stepped aside, pulling the door fully open. I didn't trust myself to say the word 'Mum', just accepted the silent invitation to go inside.

She led me along the hall, her slightly splay-footed walk exactly as I remembered it, to a small cluttered office with one chair, a typist's swivel chair. No cosy sitting rooms; this was to be a short formal discussion so far as my mother was concerned. She said she'd bring another chair for herself and politely offered me tea. I declined, unwilling to accept the little gestures that moved me into the same bracket as any business caller at the stud, that helped her forget she'd carried me inside her for nine months, nursed me, loved me once, her first-born.

She came back with a light pine chair, closed the door behind her and sat down opposite me, open-faced, pleasant, receptive. And, setting my emotions aside for the first time when thinking of her, I wondered what kind of woman this was. How could she not be moved enough to show some feelings? How could she stand so rigidly by her man to the exclusion of everything else on the planet? Had she never in her life questioned that loyalty? Still closely involved in racing, she must have known about my troubles over the past eight or nine years. Had there never been a twinge of regret, an ounce of longing to come and comfort me?

Here she sat waiting for me to state my business. No: 'How have you been, son?' No: 'Good to see you after all these years.'

She said, 'Edward's out in the yard.' A cue to start talking, reassurance we wouldn't be disturbed by the man she could no longer even bring herself to refer to as my father.

I said, 'How have you been, Mum?'

'We're all right.'

We. The Siamese marriage.

'My father looks very strained.'

She blinked at the word 'father'. 'Edward has . . . this has come as a bit of a shock to him.'

'It would after fourteen years.'

She nodded, blinked again. Some emotion there now. I said, 'Aren't you going to ask how *I've* been?'

'You look fine.'

'I'm well practised in looking fine, Mum, at making it look like I'm solid and sane throughout.'

She looked at me, determined not to be drawn in. 'Why did you come here, Eddie?'

'After all this time, you mean? You forgot to tag that on to the end of your question, Mum.'

She stiffened slightly in her chair. 'If you've just come to open old wounds . . .'

I leaned towards her, elbows on my knees, hands clasped in what I realised was almost anguish. I'd promised myself I wouldn't react like this but I couldn't help it. I said, 'Open old wounds? Mine never closed, Mum! It bleeds and it weeps every day of my bloody life and it keeps people away from me! It festers . . . it . . . it infects any relationship I try to have!'

'Eddie . . .' Her pale face flushed. She wasn't coping any more, not with this adult, this son who was no longer a child.

I said, 'Wasn't there any remorse? Ever? Even in the early days?'

She stood up, held on to the chairback, tears rising. 'Please go,' she said.

I shook my head. 'No, I'm not going.' And I felt suddenly filled with this power, this knowledge that I could stay if I wanted, that neither of my parents was a threat to me any longer. I could stay and take revenge, dish out some torment, pay them back.

Then just as suddenly the notion seemed vile, abhorrent, shameful. I stood up, calmed myself, and in a quiet voice said, 'I'm not going until I find out what Alex Dunn's been doing for the Keelkerry Stud.'

Twenty

About an hour later, when I left, my mother came to the door and watched me till I was through the gate. Driving back towards Newmarket town I tried to come to terms with my feelings; a strange mixture of personal achievement, self-renewal, a growth in stature that felt almost physical, and a wish that I had come years ago and said my piece.

But there was also a feeling of being used. When she'd latched on to the fact that I could actually help my father, my mother had become quite enthusiastic. She'd admitted that Heraklion, their top stallion, had indeed suffered a similar loss of fertility to Town Crier and at around the same time. Faced with a ruined business, my father had asked Alex Dunn to do what he could. It seemed Dunn was an old friend and had offered his services for the comparatively small retainer of £350 a month, hence the invoices in his office.

She told me Dunn had been sworn to secrecy and that was why he'd panicked when I had confronted him at the races. I told her it had to be more than that but she said she had no reason to doubt him. Had Dunn actually come up with a potential cure yet for Heraklion? The answer was no but he kept saying he thought he was getting close to it.

The bottom line was that if my father knew I was involved he wouldn't accept my help. My mother accepted it on his behalf on the condition that he wasn't to be told. Whether or not the business was saved, my father must never be allowed to get the impression I'd done anything for him. My mother's side of the bargain was that she would try and find out where Dunn had disappeared to this time. He and my father were quite close friends, it seemed, and my mother thought she should be able to get information from my father without arousing too much suspicion. She had my home and mobile phone numbers though

I drove away from the house under no illusions. As soon as this was over the phone numbers would be burned and I would once again become the invisible member of the Malloy family.

That prospect didn't bother me too much anymore. For the last couple of days I'd harboured a fantasy that I would appear on my white steed after fourteen years and save the Malloy business, drag my parents back from the brink, finally winning the approval I'd craved all my life. But the last couple of hours had brought home to me that although there would always be an instinctive, emotional link to them, a vague longing, they were both people in their own right – and as people rather than parents I cared little for either of them.

Dunn's story of being rattled by my fairly innocent questions didn't stand up. Vacating his house overnight, lock, stock and stethoscope, smacked rather of abject fear. I wondered if he'd had anything to do with Brian Kincaid's death. I wondered too how many other small studs were harbouring infertile stallions. How many of these cases had Dunn been working on? Well, I was in the best place to find out. Newmarket was virtually nothing but a racing community and redolent with jealousy and bitchiness. A few days spent in the pubs and hotels and I would harvest whatever was on the grapevine.

I couldn't afford to go on staying at the hotel I'd been using so I found a bed and breakfast place for two nights, got my mobile phone out and booked a place on the gossip train, first stop Francis Loss, racing manager to Sheikh Ahmad Saad.

F. Loss was an old friend, known since his riding days as Candy. Sharp and well-educated, he'd landed himself a brilliant job with one of the most prominent Arab racehorse owners and breeders in the world. His job was to offer advice to the Sheikh on every aspect of his thoroughbred operation, from buying foals to setting fees at the two major studs he owned. Candy had his finger on the pulse more often than a junior doctor in the NHS – if there was something afoot with local stallions, he'd know about it.

I didn't say on the phone what it was about. Candy agreed to meet me for half an hour. He was flying to the Middle East later that night. We met at 7 in a hotel in town and I felt distinctly underdressed as I watched him approach in about a grand's worth of clothes and footwear. About five foot eight, late-thirties, he'd kept the slim athletic shape he'd had when riding. He smiled as he shook my hand. Good teeth and tan, dark brown eyes and shiny chestnut hair which, most of the time, successfully hid his only physical blemish: a port wine stain behind his left ear, the shape of Italy on a map.

I bought him a mineral water and we did the long-time-no-see routine for a few minutes. Candy had never got above himself. People always found him the same way, open and friendly, but I thought I detected an air of wariness. I knew I'd have to be careful. Gossip conduits are two-way and I needed to get what I could without giving too much in return. We talked about Brian then I dropped in a few inconsequential subjects to move Candy away from any notion that Brian's death was one of the reasons I'd asked him along.

I said, 'Listen, you know I do a little bit of amateurish nosing around from time to time?'

He smiled. 'Not quite so amateurish over the last year or two from what I hear.'

I returned his smile. 'You know me, modesty forbids and all that. I've got a guy who's offered me a few quid to try and help him out. He owns a smallish stud which ain't gonna be a stud much longer unless he discovers what's gone wrong with his best stallion.'

I thought I saw a sudden spark in Candy's eyes but it lasted a millisecond and I couldn't be sure it wasn't my imagination. He sipped his drink and looked interested. I said, 'The horse completely lost its fertility just at the start of the season. He's had vets in testing everything except its IQ but they're stumped. If he doesn't get it sorted out before next season he's finished.'

'Which stallion?'

'Sorry, Candy, I can't say. The guy's managed to keep it a secret from most breeders, or at least he thinks he has. I know you'll think I've got a cheek asking you for something and not offering much from my side but I'm trying to do my best for him and his business.'

'So what are you asking me, Eddie?'

I shrugged. 'Just if you've heard anything on the grapevine about anyone else who's got the same problem?' I was taking the chance that Candy wouldn't know about my own involvement in the Corish Stud, something I'd never publicised.

'Stallions have fluctuations in fertility.'

'We're talking more decimation than fluctuation here, I'm afraid. From eighty-eight percent to zilch as quick as you could say, "no foal no fee".'

He fingered the port wine stain under his hair and looked thoughtful. 'So why did he bring you in? Does he think the horse has been got at?'

'As I said, he's desperate.'

'Do you think the horse was got at?'

'I don't know. What would the motive be? How would you do it so the vets couldn't detect it?'

He shook his head slowly, fingered his tanned chin. I said, 'So you haven't heard of any other stallions in the same boat?'

He continued thoughtful, staring at the tabletop, and said, 'No . . . no.'

I sighed and sipped some scotch. He said, 'Sorry, Eddie.'

'Not your fault.'

'What's your next move?'

I almost started shooting off about Alex Dunn disappearing but something in my brain slipped the safety catch on for some reason and I settled simply for saying that I had heard Dunn was a bit of a specialist in fertility and that I was hoping to track him down. 'Any idea where I could find him?'

'Sorry, Eddie, I've heard the guy's name but I don't know much about him except that he's a bit of a quack. I wouldn't set too much store on this "specialist" stuff.' Candy seemed anxious to finish the conversation. He said, 'It's an interesting one. I'll sniff around a bit myself over the next week or so, see if I can find anything out.'

'Good. That'd be great, Candy.'

'No problem. Maybe you could keep me in touch with progress from your end?'

'Sure. Sure I will.'

'Fine. Give me a ring any time.'

I smiled. 'They've got phones in Lear jets now, have they?'

He stood up, smiling, and finished his drink. 'It's not all a bowl of cherries, Eddie, as the saying goes.'

'No, strawberries and cream, more like.'

He laughed. 'See you. Keep in touch on this.'

'Will do.'

He turned and left. A few seconds later I followed quietly and watched him in the carpark. He got into a Range Rover and immediately made a phone call. I had a hunch Candy knew more than he was saying.

I rang Martin, gave him some work to do to take his mind off things. 'I want you to ring round as many studs as you can and give them that story about a late booking. Make a list of who's willing and any stallions they try to steer you away from.'

'What about my phone bill?'

'*Our* phone bill,' I reminded him. 'Come on, Martin, twenty-four hours ago it was death or glory to get to the bottom of this. Now you can't even be bothered making a few calls?'

He grunted something and hung up. I called McCarthy.

'Mac, did you know Alex Dunn's moved out of his house?'

'It's not the sort of thing I get wildly curious about, Eddie.'

'I know, but if you could find out his new address you'd be doing me a favour.'

'Why? I thought you'd spoken to him and he said he didn't know anything about Brian Kincaid's death?'

'That's right, but as I said to you he was in pretty deep shock at the time and I just wondered if maybe, once he'd had time to think, something might have come to him.'

'Like what?'

'I don't know, Mac, but I'd really like to speak to him again.'

'Eddie, tell me what this is really about?'

'I've told you, it's a quiet time for me. I'll be lucky to get ten rides in the next month and I don't mind filling my days in trying to make sense of Brian's death.'

'And I've told you, leave it to the coroner, let him try and make some sense of it!'

'Mac, come on! I don't like doing this but you owe me one. More than one.'

'You don't like doing it? You're *always* doing it! I should have kept notes! Traded bloody IOUs!'

I smiled. 'Your hysterics are coming on again, Mac, careful!'

'I'll ring you back.'

'When?'

'As soon as I know something.'

'Soon, Mac, please! On my mobile. I'm in Newmarket for a few days.'

That brought him up short. 'Newmarket? What for?'

'I've just told you, I want to speak to Alex Dunn.'

'Eddie, you'd better not be working for Compton Breslin.' He sounded genuinely annoyed. Breslin was a big bookmaker, based in Newmarket, who covered most of the southern courses.

'What would I be doing for Breslin?'

'Don't be so bloody disingenuous.'

'Me? I don't know the meaning of the word!' Which was the literal truth but I didn't need to ask anything else. Dunn was obviously a serious gambler. I wondered how much he owed Breslin.

Mac said, 'I'll tell you this now, Eddie, if you're working for Breslin I want nothing more to do with you.'

'Mac, you've got my word on it.'

'Okay. Fine. Goodnight.'

He hung up. The smile was still on my face. I loved these little jousts with McCarthy.

It wasn't yet 8.30 and I knew there were two evening racemeetings on. Breslin's credit office would still be open. I'd never met the guy but I'd seen him on the racecourse. He was renowned as a proper bookmaker of the old school, one who'd back his own opinion and lay big bets. He paid promptly and expected the same from his clients. I rang his office. He answered the phone personally. I said that we might have a common interest in Alex Dunn and he agreed to meet me in a local Chinese restaurant at 9.45.

Twenty-one

Breslin was your stereotypical big fat bookmaker: jewellery, checked suit, torpedo cigar, slick hair, Chaplin moustache. He looked like he'd just stepped off a Blackpool postcard. He was watching my face as he lumbered towards me and sat down in a jingle of watch chains and bracelets. He smiled at me. 'Bet you thought this was my showman's gear, strictly for the racecourse?'

'Well, I did, actually.'

His smile grew wider, moustache spreading slightly like curtains preparing to open. 'You're always on show in my business,' he said, looking down at the big checked waistcoat. 'The more prosperous you look, the more people want to take money off you. And the more they try, the more I get to keep.'

I nodded, smiling. He glanced around and beckoned a waiter over. 'Anyway,' he said, 'that's my excuse for going around dressed like one of the Marx Brothers. At night, alone in my room, I slip on my Versace which has seen nothing but lamplight and a long wardrobe mirror. Sad, isn't it?'

I smiled. I liked Breslin. He ordered the best wine and half a dozen courses like he was listing runners in a race. The waiter didn't seem at all surprised and I guessed this was a regular haunt. He said, 'Got to keep the waistline up to Industry Standards. Dirty work but some bugger's got to do it.'

We got talking about Dunn. 'You're looking for him?' Breslin asked.

'I'd quite like to speak to him.'

'Been a bad boy, has he?'

'Not that I know of. I just think he might be able to help me out.'

'Got a veterinary problem?'

'More of a personal one, really. Well, on behalf of a friend.' I mentioned Brian Kincaid and gave him the same spiel I'd given McCarthy.

'I can give you his address,' Breslin said.

'The bungalow out at Six Mile Bottom?'

'You've got it?'

I nodded. 'But it's no good.' I told him about the moonlight flit.

He laughed. 'Well, bugger me, maybe he's going to welch this time.'

'Does he owe much?'

He shrugged his big shoulders. 'About seven grand. It's not the end of the world.'

He wasn't showing off, he genuinely didn't seem that concerned about it though he said, sure, he'd like to know where Dunn turned up if I managed to find him. In exchange he told me a few details about Dunn's gambling habits. One titbit was to prove very useful.

Thankfully, Breslin brushed aside my offer to pay the bill and we parted on good terms. Always a better audience than a performer, I'd enjoyed his company. He gave me his card and we made mutual promises to stay in touch.

My first stop next morning was a newsagent's shop where I picked up a little tourist booklet about Newmarket, Headquarters of British Racing. Inside was a map listing the names of all the training yards along with the trainers currently inhabiting them. Breslin had told me that a significant number of Alex Dunn's bets in the last eighteen months to two years had been on horses trained by William Capshaw, one of the town's most successful trainers.

I found Capshaw's yard location on the map and just to double check I walked down the Bury Road and past the yard itself. It was the same one Dunn had made a run for after Martin had confronted him. I thought it unwise to pass the yard gates again and took a different route back to the High Street.

So Dunn was getting information from Capshaw's yard. In exchange for what? Veterinary services? I didn't recall seeing Capshaw's name among Dunn's copy invoices though maybe that was the deal, no cash would change hands. I went to a small cafe, ordered coffee and got out Dunn's client list: no sign of Capshaw's name.

Maybe Dunn was holed up at Capshaw's place. If so would he be stupid enough to have his car somewhere close by? It was worth risking another walk past, more slowly this time. My mobile rang, shattering the peace in the sunny little cafe and bringing condemning looks from three elderly ladies. It was Martin. I went outside. Following my hint of the other day he'd rung thirty-seven studs. Seven of them had given him reasons for suspicion and put him back aboard the rollercoaster on the optimism wave again. I didn't want him back with me and managed to persuade him to look much more closely at the studs involved. I asked him to plot their locations on a map, find out their histories, who was running them, their background, if they'd had maybe the same employee through their hands, etc. – enough work to keep him in Wiltshire for a few days and out of my hair.

On the off chance I'd been spotted walking past Capshaw's yard I decided to delay another stroll in that direction until this afternoon. It occurred to me that if I watched the yard from a safe distance around lunchtime maybe I'd see some of Capshaw's lads heading for the pub. If I could have been certain none would recognise me it would have been easy to strike up a conversation over a drink and try and find out if the vet was a temporary lodger. But one or two of the lads might know me and start spreading the wrong kind of stories around the town.

I decided to stick to lone observation, at least until the end of the day, and found a carpark close enough to Capshaw's place to let me watch, unobtrusively, one of the exit roads from the yard. I had no view of the yard itself and if Dunn came out of it and turned right I'd miss him completely but better to cover half the options in relative safety than all of them in an exposed position.

In the car, with the windows rolled right down for air, I settled back with a copy of the *Sporting Life* which would offer extra camouflage if necessary.

I wondered how Dunn was running his business. Would he be having his calls automatically transferred to wherever he now was? I rang his number. Answerphone. That meant he would have to play it back . . . He could do that remotely, didn't have to go back there.

As the 11.30 news summary came on the radio my mobile rang. A voice I didn't recognise said, 'Alex Dunn is at his house

110

at Six Mile Bottom right now.' The caller immediately rang off. I started the car and headed for Dunn's place, wondering who my informant was. Maybe Breslin had put the word out. Quick work if he had.

I pulled up, blocking Dunn's driveway in case he made a run for it, but his car wasn't there. Either I'd been hoaxed or I'd just missed him. I went through the green cast iron gates to the back of the bungalow. As I turned at the end of the wall I stopped short. Two men were sitting on an old garden bench. Both wore expensive dark suits and lounged lazily, faces tilted to the sun, smiling though I couldn't see their eyes behind wide sunglasses.

The one closest to me stood up and came towards me, smiling and holding out his hand. 'Mr Malloy, how kind of you to drop in.' Bewildered, I shook his hand, waiting for him to introduce himself. He didn't. His friend was standing now, smoothing out imaginary wrinkles on the front of his trousers. They were both mid-twenties, fit and hard-looking, tall as University oarsmen.

I said to the one who'd greeted me, 'You called me?'

'That's right. I understand you're seeking advice.'

'Information. I've got all the advice I need at the moment.'

He was still smiling. It annoyed me that I couldn't see his eyes. The high sun made it worse as I squinted up at his face. He said, 'The wrong kind of advice, Mr Malloy. It's good reliable advice you need, and luckily that is our specialist business. Come and sit down.' He put a hand lightly on my elbow. I eased it away. 'No, thanks.'

'Fine. I give the same high-calibre advice standing up.'

'Which is?'

'Drop what you're involved in and go back home. Go back to riding horses.'

'Who do you work for?'

'We're a charitable organisation dedicated to keeping people out of hospitals.'

'You're threatening me?'

The smile faded. Stern-mouthed now he said, 'I'm offering you genuine professional advice. You won't realise how valuable it is unless you don't take it, then you'll reflect on this conversation with a bit more circumspection.'

An educated hit man. He took off his sunglasses, exposing blue eyes which looked very sincere. He said, 'It is very important to me that you leave Newmarket within the hour and that you stay away from the town and the people who live here. It is vitally important to me that you stop asking questions.'

He was serious. I didn't know what to say or how to take it. 'Do you understand how important it is to me?' he pressed.

'If you tell me why, it might just drive the message home.'

A flicker of anger in his cold eyes. He made a conscious effort to regain the calm expression and that was when I knew how potentially dangerous he could be. I thought it best to call it quits for the time being.

They both came out on to the road and watched me till my car was out of sight. Curiouser and curiouser. No heavy stuff but they'd looked the part all right and I was in no doubt the gloves would be off next time. Where had Dunn got these two from? The guy spent all his money gambling, what was he paying them with?

And why had things accelerated so quickly?

Twenty-two

By the time I got back to town I'd decided to pack up and leave immediately. Dunn would have his spies out and would think I'd fled. Maybe he'd go back to his own place then and it would be a nice surprise for him when I turned up there in a couple of days. At my digs I made a show of throwing my things in my bag, leaving it unzipped as I hurried out to my car and scooted along the High Street and out of town at a pace that would have drawn attention. Hamming it up, I know but if it brought Dunn out quicker I could forgive myself.

I drove back to my own flat for a change of clothes. It was late-afternoon. The yard was still as quiet as it had been since the end of May. It would be another month before the horses were back. Melancholy place, a racing yard without thoroughbreds.

I thought about Charles Tunney, the trainer who occupied the yard. The man who'd buggered off to Alaska for a month after watching some TV series about a town there. Impulsive man, Charles. I smiled, thinking about him.

Charles and the stable lads were my only regular contacts, a big bantering family without emotional obligations. I missed them all.

I'd planned to stay away from Newmarket for a couple of days in the hope Dunn would think I'd given up but I couldn't face another day in the flat. I packed enough clothes for a week and headed east again, stopping only to fill up at a petrol station and buy some groceries.

The closer I came to Newmarket, the darker the sky grew as layers of cloud rolled across the sun. The first heavy drops fell as I pulled up in front of Dunn's bungalow, blocking the drive again. The empty drive. I went down the path, heels clicking loudly on the flagstones, and round the back.

Nobody on the garden bench. Nobody in the house. The second glass pane I'd broken hadn't been repaired nor the mess cleaned up. On the trip across I'd decided on a plan of attack. Anxious to get started I returned to the car and drove to the clearing in the woods I'd used last week. I took my kitbag, locked the car and walked back to Dunn's house where I unpacked the bag then cleared away the broken glass. Eventually, Mohammed would come to the mountain. When he did, I'd be on the summit, waiting.

I listened to the messages on Dunn's answerphone; all were from customers and had been left that morning so he was emptying his machine regularly. Next time he did I'd try Martin's trick of dialling the recall code to see where Dunn had called from. I used the phone to call McCarthy on his mobile. He didn't sound delighted when he heard my voice. 'Did you find Alex Dunn?' he asked.

'Nope, that's why I'm calling. I need to see you, Mac.'

'That means you want a favour.'

'Have any of the "favours" you've done me in the past worked against you? You've always come up smelling of roses.'

'Mostly because you dropped me in deep manure to begin with.'

'Heeyyy! Where have you been sharpening your wit?'

'On the horns of all the dilemmas you've left me in.'

'Touché, Mac. First two rounds to you.'

I could almost feel his smug smile down the phone. I said, 'Where are you going today?'

'Got a meeting in London. A long one.'

'Want to come here afterwards for dinner?'

'Where's "here"?'

'Newmarket.'

'No, thanks. I promised Jean I'd take her out.'

'Where are you tomorrow?'

'Sandown.'

'Can you spare me half an hour there?'

'I suppose so.'

'I'll get there before racing. Want to meet by the parade ring?'

'No. Meet me in the carpark an hour before the first. I get nervous talking to you on course.'

'Okay. I'll see you in the carpark.'

'Eddie, I'll stay in my car. Come and find me.'

'Sure.' Very wary.

I didn't particularly want to leave Dunn's bungalow in case he came back but I thought it was time to start building in a few alternatives. I'd have to tell Mac more than I'd originally planned to but not enough to compromise his position in Jockey Club Security.

Next I rang Martin who was barely halfway through the task of assimilating all the information on the suspect studs. The staff histories were proving much the toughest as I'd known they would. I left him to it.

I found three tea bags lying on an otherwise bare shelf in Dunn's kitchen and made a mug of strong black tea which I sipped as I dialled Compton Breslin's office number. A girl told me he was betting at Yarmouth. She gave me his mobile number. His cheery voice brought back an immediate picture of him in his loud suit. I asked him for a list of all Dunn's bets this season. He promised it would be ready for close of business next day. I told him I'd collect it.

I sat by the silent phone for a while then paced around the living room. Looking out of the front window I saw the glint of the sun reflected from deep in the woods and realised I hadn't driven the car far enough into the trees. I was reluctant to go back out in case Dunn called to empty the answerphone then someone else called immediately after him, wiping out his recall number.

I thought about it. I'd need to be desperately unlucky for that to happen. It was just after 12.25. There was every chance Dunn would be having lunch. Deciding to chance it, I hurried out into the woods and ran towards the car. I couldn't have been gone more than ten minutes but when I returned the flashing light on the answerphone had stopped.

It had been emptied. I grabbed the handset from the cradle before another call could come through and dialled 1471. I jotted down the number given by the recorded voice, even said thank you to the lady. Dunn must still be in Newmarket; that was the STD code.

My impulse was to dial it immediately but that might prove counter-productive. If Dunn realised I'd tracked him down he'd probably take off again, sending me rapidly back to square one. It would be much better if I could find out the address the number belonged to. Mac should be able to get that. I rang his mobile again: switched off. I tried him every fifteen minutes until 6 then gave up. Tomorrow would have to do.

Twenty-three

I spent ten minutes wandering around the Sandown carpark looking for Mac then I saw his big silver Rover come in off the road and along the drive. He bypassed the turn into the officials' carpark and backed into a space against the fence. I walked over the opened the passenger door to see Mac's big belly touching the steering wheel.

He was red, flustered, and trying not to look it. 'Sorry I'm a bit late, Eddie. The traffic's deplorable.'

'Don't worry. No hurry. Not on my side anyway.'

'Well, I don't exactly have all day. What was it you wanted to talk about?'

'Alex Dunn.'

'Again?'

I told him about Dunn's disappearance, about the two hard men I'd run into at his house, about how anxious Dunn was to discourage me from finding him. I was still playing it around Brian Kincaid's death, not mentioning anything about the stallions.

Mac said, 'So you think Dunn's involved in Kincaid's death?'

'I don't know. But I do know that a simple question from me sent him into a panic that was bad enough for him to up stakes and leave his home and business.'

'How do you know you were the catalyst?'

This was where things got tricky. I didn't want to bring Martin's name into it at all, let alone tell Mac it was the confrontation with him that had been the real cue for Dunn's vanishing act. I busked along, trying to convince Mac that the pure shock on Dunn's face when I'd first approached him at the races told me that he had to be deeply worried.

I was trying to choose my words carefully. The thing that had really scared Dunn, I felt, was my mention of the samples Brian had sent him. But Mac, understandably, believed I thought Dunn was directly implicated in Brian's death.

He shifted heavily in his seat so he was looking straight at me. 'You'd best be very careful, Eddie. You can't make accusations on hunches.'

'Come on, Mac, it's more than a hunch, you've known me long enough to know that.'

'The same as your first suspect in Kincaid's death was more than a hunch? Tranter, he of the cast-iron alibi?'

He had me there. 'Okay, fair enough, Mac. That was a mistake. We all make them.'

He sighed. 'So what do you want me to do?'

I looked at him. 'Mac, don't make it sound like it's all for me. You guys should be investigating Dunn's disappearance.'

'What disappearance? He's let the racecourses who normally use him know that he's unavailable until further notice. If we "investigated" every vet, doctor or starter who decided to take a few weeks off work, we'd never get anything done.'

'You know it's more than that, Mac! Dunn is up to something. I'm tipping you off, trying to make sure you're not left with large helpings of egg on your face.'

'Very philanthropic of you.'

A frown I knew well gathered on Mac's face. This was the poker hand where he had to decide whether to fold and let me get on with it or draw some more cards and stay in. I knew he'd be worried about coming in too late if this did blow up into something big. Not much point in the Jockey Club Security Department having their finger on the pulse of a dead case.

He said, 'Okay, Eddie, let me see what I can find out.'

'Maybe you could start with this phone number?' I said, giving him the recall number used by Dunn to clear his answerphone. Mac promised to ring me when he had something then asked me to get out of the car 'as unobtrusively as possible'.

I did and he drove away to take up his customary spot in the officials' carpark. I'd half-toyed with the idea of going into the racecourse for a couple of hours just to see if I could pick anything up but I decided against it. Until I'd pinned Dunn down it was important to make him believe I'd been scared off.

Back inside my own car I'd just started the engine when I noticed a familiar figure step out of a big black Mercedes parked off to the right about six rows in front of me. It was old Iron Fist in a Velvet Glove himself, the guy who'd warned me off at Dunn's bungalow a couple of days back. I switched off the engine and sat still. Iron Fist set off towards the stands. I let him get up the steps and through the main doors before I started to get out to follow him. Just as I did so the driver's door of the black Merc opened and out stepped another man I knew, another man I'd seen recently: Sheik Ahmad Saad's racing manager, Mr F. Loss. Candy.

I stayed in my car, waiting to see if anyone else would come out of the Merc, but Candy locked it up and headed towards the stands, striding out boldly in his perfectly cut pinstripe suit.

I settled back in the seat, lightly drumming on the steering wheel, trying like hell not to jump to conclusions. What was Candy's connection with the hitman? Did they know each other 'professionally' or had Candy simply, and perfectly innocently, offered him a lift to the races? If so, why had they sat so long in the car? Why had they gone into the racecourse separately?

What should I do next?

Before I could make any connection I had to find out who this guy was. Maybe Mac would know him by sight. It was just a matter of getting Mac within safe viewing distance of Iron Fist which might not be too difficult. Today's crowd wouldn't be that big and it was still half an hour before the first race.

I locked the car and headed for the entrance.

Wending my way through the parked cars I came upon a racecourse photographer I knew unloading his gear. I had an idea and asked Charlie Harris to let me borrow one of his cameras with a zoom lens, promising to let him have it back by first race time. He told me it was a spare and that I could keep it all day if I needed to.

It took less than ten minutes to find Iron Fist. He was by the parade-ring rail with his equally tall friend from Dunn's place. Two for the price of one. I climbed the steps to the balcony overlooking the parade ring. Three horses were being led around and as each of them approached the pair, who were deep in conversation, I raised the camera and took a few shots; more than I'd intended with the first burst as the rapid motordrive reacted to my heavy finger and fired off a salvo. I shot the whole film then found Charlie Harris by the unsaddling enclosure and returned the camera.

Esher High Street is just a few minutes' walk from Sandown Racecourse. I doubted I'd find a one-hour-development place but not only did I find one, the girl insisted she could produce standard size prints within ten minutes if I wanted to wait. My intention had been to get eight by six prints to give Mac a clearer picture but I could get those done later. I settled for six by fours.

My luck had been good and I didn't want to push it by going back into the racecourse. I couldn't be sure that the two hard men, or maybe Candy if he was involved with them, hadn't already seen me. I sat in my car and dialled Mac's mobile number. It rang eight times before he answered.

'Mac, can you spare a few minutes to come back out to the carpark?'

'When?'

'Now. It's important. Just two minutes.' I gave him the approximate location of my car and shortly afterwards watched his grey-suited bulk pick its way towards me.

Mac settled into the passenger seat, his dark wavy hair brushing the roof. I showed him the pictures, told him I'd just taken them. 'Recognise them?'

He stared, brushed his finger over a slight flaw on one of the prints. 'No.'

He didn't seem totally sure. 'You've never seen them before?' I asked.

'Can't be certain I've never seen them before but I definitely don't know them.'

'Think you could find anything out?'

He nodded thoughtfully. 'Maybe.'

I turned to face him. 'Mac,' he looked at me, 'can you still make the telephone number top priority? This was just an unexpected bonus today. What I really need is the address that call was made from.'

'Okay, Eddie, I'll try and get it for later today.'

'Good. Thanks. Can you call me when you do?'

'Where will you be?'

'Back in Newmarket, just call me on my mobile.'

'Okay.'

He left. I was glad he hadn't drawn it all out with the usual whys and wherefores. I drove south west back to Dunn's place, stopping off at Compton Breslin's office to pick up a Private & Confidential envelope and the last three seasons' formbooks as promised. Heavy skies still hung over Six Mile Bottom, particularly dark and sombre above the woods opposite Dunn's bungalow.

No lights flashing on the answerphone. I dialled 1471 again just to reassure myself and found it was the same number as this morning. In the dim kitchen I shifted the table and a chair close to the window, not wanting to alert any potential visitors by having a light switched on. I plugged in the charger for my mobile and left the phone slotted into it. Armed with a cup of coffee, pens and a thick notepad, I settled down to try and find some definite strategy in Alex Dunn's betting habits.

The computer printout listed 2,418 bets in the space of 123 weeks with total stakes of £482,115. Almost half a million.

It worked out at an average of just under £200 per bet. Dunn's losses in the period were £98,777. And 23 pence.

Breslin's customer monitoring was very efficient. He'd put a note in telling me that his profit margin on Dunn's bets, just over 20 percent, was slightly worse than average for Breslin since he normally expected a gross profit margin, on all business, of around 22 percent. Breslin also apologised for being unable to provide a more detailed analysis of Dunn's bets. The printout showed every horse he had backed but there was no trainer or jockey information, something Breslin said was being built into his new computer programme.

Almost all the bets had been struck on course which meant betting tax wouldn't be deducted. Comparatively few had been placed by phone. I stared at the list of horses' names feeling somewhat like a commentator studying for the Charge of the Light Brigade. I'd sat down to this with considerable optimism but now it looked as if it would take days rather than hours.

I sighed, sipped tepid coffee and set up list headings on my pad: Owner, Trainer, Jockey, Date and Racecourse. Then, starting with Dunn's very first bet, I opened the relevant formbook.

By the time McCarthy rang I was working by a flashlight lodged between two books.

'Mac! Any news?'

'Yes, though I'm not sure it's what you want to hear. The telephone number you gave me is from a public callbox in Newmarket.'

'Public or in a pub or something?'

'In the street, the High Street.'

'Where exactly?'

'Well, I don't know exactly but there can't be many, it's hardly Sunset Boulevard down there.'

'Can you find out exactly where it is?'

He sighed. 'It'll have to be tomorrow.'

'Morning?'

'I'll do my best.'

'What about Butch Cassidy and The Sundance Kid?'

'Nothing, I'm afraid. I've showed the pictures to my own people. Nobody can put a name to either though some mentioned seeing them around the racecourses recently.'

'How recently?'

'The last three or four months is the best guess.'

'Mac, could you put a man on one of them for a few days?'

That sigh again, louder this time. 'Eddie, it's very difficult.'

'I know it is but I need a favour. I'm sure it'll be worth your while finding out who these guys are.'

'Leave it with me.'

'Till when?'

'Please don't push me, Eddie.'

'I'm in a pushy mood.'

'Are you ever any other way?'

I smiled. 'Where are you tomorrow?' I asked.

'Back at Sandown. Aren't you riding at Market Rasen?'

'Not unless there's a message on my answerphone, promising me a winner. I'll still be here in Newmarket. Will you call me in the morning?'

'Okay.'

'And Mac, look out for those guys again tomorrow. I'll be interested to know if they turn up and more interested to know if either of them is seen in the company of Francis Loss.'

'Why?'

'I saw one of them getting out of Loss's car at Sandown today.'

'So?'

'Just a thought. No big deal but if either of them is seen with Loss again, I'd like to know.'

'Leave it with me.'

'Okay. Call me tomorrow.'

Twenty-four

Just after 9 p.m. the mobile rang.

'Hello?'

'Mr Malloy, it's Alex Dunn.'

The last person I'd expected. Odd, too, to feel I was sitting in his house.

I stayed silent. He said, 'Do you still want information about your stallion?'

'I want to know what's wrong with him.'

'I can tell you that. Meet me tomorrow at noon at your father's place.'

'Are you there now?'

'No, but I'll be there at noon tomorrow, I promise.'

'You've promised before.'

'I know. I'm sorry.'

There was something wrong. Dunn's heart didn't quite seem to be in what he was saying.

'Why this time?' I asked. 'What's changed your mind?'

'Today. I . . . look, I'll tell you tomorrow.'

I still had doubts but there was little to lose. 'Okay. I'll be there.'

'Good. I'll see you then.'

He hung up. I considered ringing my mother, hesitated, put down the receiver and picked it up again. Dialled. The answerphone at the stud clicked on, my mother sounding all proper. I didn't leave a message.

I decided it was best not to let Martin know that I was meeting Dunn next day. I didn't want him to go blundering in, scaring him, and there was also something in me that doubted Dunn would actually turn up and I didn't want another scene with my partner if that happened.

I was there at 11.45. Dunn's blue estate was in the drive. There was no sign of any other vehicle. I wondered where my father's car was.

I went to the house first and rang the bell. No answer. I waited a minute then pushed through the creaky gate into the yard.

Something not right.

A row of empty boxes. Last time I'd been here all six had been occupied. Now the doors stood open.

I resisted calling Dunn's name and moved forward slowly, quietly.

I thought I heard a groan coming from the box in the corner and someone moving in the straw. I glanced behind me as a car passed on the road, the sound fading quickly into the distance. I walked towards the open box, stopped outside and listened. Nothing.

I looked round again then took a step inside. The double doors were unevenly opened, the gap throwing an oddly shaped wedge of sunlight against the back wall of the box, highlighting the dust motes like tiny stars above the straw landscape.

I heard a sudden noise from behind me and turned but someone pushed a wide hood down over my head. Light material. Like cotton handkerchiefs sewn together, the sun still bright through the material as I was spun round, as something was clamped across my nose and mouth, sweet-smelling but sharp, recognisable even as consciousness left me. Ether.

The same hot burning sun greeted me when I opened my eyes. Blue sky. No clouds. I was staring up at it without having to bend my head back. Couldn't understand it. Blinking wildly, screwing my eyes up against it as consciousness returned, senses came back. And I could feel something very familiar beneath me, feel it and smell it. A horse. Warm, reassuring.

But skitty. Whinnying lightly. Shuffling.

Couldn't see the horse. Wasn't astride it. But fixed there. Tied on backbone to backbone. Wrists bound under the neck, ankles roped under the stifle. Thought it must be a dream, an after effect of the ether. I tried to get up, almost wrenching my wrists out of their sockets. Tried my legs: the same. They'd been forced down across the animal's ribcage, fastened under her belly, fixing me like a hog on a spit except that nothing had been shoved in one end and out of the other. Not yet.

The sun was hot on my body. I raised my head. I was naked.
Nearly laughed.

Tied to a horse. Naked.

I'd heard of King Midas in reverse. Now Lady Godiva in
reverse.

No blonde hair to cover my modesty. Nothing. Funny.

What was happening? What the hell was Dunn doing to me?

As my head began to clear of ether I heard a sound that blew
away all my comical notions: the unmistakable snort of stallion.
Off to my left, not underneath me.

He neighed excitedly and tramped the ground and I realised
that I was tied securely to a mare in season.

My head was the only part of me with freedom of movement.
I turned it, trying to see exactly where he was. The first pass
reminded me of the shark in 'Jaws'. His head glided past, mouth
open, eyes wide, ears pricked. Black he was.

I swallowed, prayed for my head to clear properly so I could
do something.

The mare moved nervously beneath me. I could hear her ears
flick. I realised her spine was noticeably dipped. An old hand, her
back curved with age and the strain of bearing numerous foals.
God only knew what was going through her mind.

The black stallion came alongside, rubbed himself against her,
jamming my right leg. The mare tried to move away. Somebody
said, 'Whoah!' quietly and held her steady.

'Dunn!' I called out. 'Dunn! Is that you?'

No answer.

'You crazy bastard! Get me off this!'

The stallion came in again, nipped my bare calf, snorted,
rubbed again. I could feel no bridle. I raised my head. No one
was holding him. No one controlling him!

I pulled with hands and feet but the rope bit tight and the
mare whinnied and reared up, giving me a brief rollercoaster
view of the big black stallion as he prepared to mount her. They
held her steady then suddenly he was up, his huge dark head
and wild mane blotting out the sun. I yelped in fear as his front
legs clasped mine hard to the side of the mare and his big open
brown-toothed mouth bore down on me.

But he slipped off.

Then he was up again, more anxious now, eyes wide and

white, staring madly at this strange intruder, this naked helpless chaperone. Then he was in her and on me, grunting, slobbering and biting at her neck, catching my left arm, biting me. I wanted to cry out in pain and fear but didn't want to enrage him so I lay there, eyes closed in terror, feeling the rhythmical pump of his loins, thinking of the times I'd sat astride others of his breed beating just as rhythmically and maybe just as frighteningly with my whip.

I curved my own spine desperately downwards, trying to follow the line of the mare's, trying to get some of the weight of the stallion off me as he bore down on my pelvis. Sweat lubricated our backbones, allowing me to slip that vital few inches lower as the stallion's own sweat rubbed into a froth covering my genitals and thighs. The side of his open mouth painted saliva on my arm as his head rose and fell and I could hear his teeth grate against the hair on her neck and I prayed he wouldn't take my arm in his mouth.

Suddenly the mare neighed loudly and moved as voices urged her forward. The stallion raised his head and almost screamed as he tottered after her, struggling to keep his long penis inside. Suddenly I saw what I thought was a pitchfork arc upwards, the metal tines hitting the stallion in the mouth. He squealed and backed off and I lost sight of him as the mare trotted away, bouncing and bending my spine. She moved in a straight line and I realised she was still being led. Raising my head again, I saw us approach the gate in the corner of the sandy quadrangle we'd been locked into. The gate was open. The escape route was there. I sighed long and loud.

But the mare was pulled up short before the gate and my bonds were quickly cut. I was dragged to the ground, landing hard on a sharp stone which bit into my buttock.

Then the mare was away through the gate.

And the gate swung closed.

And I rolled over to find myself alone with a half a ton of dark wrathful thoroughbred. He stood foursquare by the gate staring after the departing mare, his loud neighing almost a roar, his huge penis pulsing and swinging, pushing through the bars of the gate as he suddenly reared.

As quietly as possible I began moving away at a crouch, anxious to stay below his line of vision. All around me was a high panelled fence, sheer and unscalable. The stallion blocked the only exit route.

He reared again, pawing the air then catching the top bars of the wooden gate with his hooves as he came down. I'd moved away into the far corner. The fading sound of the mare's hooves finally went out of human earshot and a few seconds later he turned and came straight towards me as if he'd known exactly where I was all the time.

Big black head down, thick neck straight out, eyes rolling wildly, ears laid back, his shoulder muscles bunched and flexed as he came at me in a determined swinging trot. I sprang to my feet, painfully aware of my nakedness, blood running down my bitten forearm as my hands automatically covered my genitals. His open mouth twisted sideways, dripping blood where the pitchfork had pierced him, and the sun caught silver strands of saliva spanning those monstrous teeth.

I glanced around for a weapon: nothing, not even a lollipop stick, lay in the loose dirt.

The dirt.

I bent and scooped a double handful as, teeth snapping, he bore down on me. I threw the dirt as hard as I could towards his eyes and saw most go in his mouth, but it slowed him long enough for me to race past him, deliberately brushing his shoulder so he would have to make a full turn to come after me.

I heard him splutter and cough as I sprinted for the gate about thirty yards away. Then his hooves grinding as he spun, and his angry roar. My bare feet pounded the small stones but I wasn't aware of any pain as the strongest surge of adrenalin I'd known for years carried me towards that gate, hoping and praying that whoever had put me in here wouldn't suddenly reappear to cut off my escape.

I could hear the stallion's hoofbeats now, swore I could feel his breath on my neck, but I was within springing distance of that gate and boy did I spring, my outstretched hands catching the top bar with perfect timing, helping me vault over to land on my back and roll in the dirt, praying once again that the bastard wouldn't try to follow me.

He didn't. And I lay laughing with relief and saying, 'Jesus! Jesus!' giggling nervously and uncontrollably as I thought how ridiculous I must look.

Only his head was over the gate and he stared at me, snorting in rage and frustration. Smiling I said to him, 'It wasn't me that put her off. Maybe it's your technique.' I got to my feet, very relieved, still smiling but feeling some sympathy for the stallion. 'You've got to treat them better. Bottle of bubbly. Some nice flowers. Try that next time.'

Then the elation ebbed suddenly as I realised that whoever had doped and tied me was probably still around. I stood still and listened but could hear nothing but the stallion breathing loud and pawing the ground.

Where were my clothes?

Moving stealthily outdoors on bare feet isn't easy but I made a reasonable attempt at it, nursing my injured arm as I went in the direction the mare had been led. I found her, unperturbed and alone in a box. I rubbed her nose and she drew away, staring disdainfully at me.

I said, 'I didn't mean to break up the party, honestly.'

I skirted the buildings checking the other boxes, the feed room and the barn where I picked up a shining hand scythe which still had the price label stuck to the handle.

Nobody. No more horses. Working my way back to where I'd started, I returned to the open box where I'd been grabbed. I remembered thinking there'd been someone inside it. Holding the scythe loosely in my right hand, I pushed the bottom door of the box fully open and saw the straw behind it. Then I pushed the top door. It was gloomy inside but I couldn't hear so much as a breath. Cautiously I went in.

My clothes were on the floor beside the long thin white-headed corpse of Alex Dunn. His body was still quite warm but there was no pulse. He lay on his side in the foetal position, his face frozen in a painful grimace. There was nothing I could do for him and I felt a powerful urge to get dressed and get my wound attended to. The last thing I reached for was my shirt. Lying on the straw beneath it was a large brown envelope.

My name was written on the front in broad black marker. Opening it carefully, I moved towards the light as I drew out a handful of typewritten notes. I stood in the sunshine but had never felt colder as I read those pages. They listed the most painful, shameful episode of my life. Baring and freezing my soul in a few hundred words of harsh detail. I closed my eyes, raised my face to the sun, tried to find some hope, some miracle that would let me look again at the papers and find something different.

There was no accompanying note, no blackmail threat. None was needed. What I held were photocopies.

Someone somewhere had the originals.

Twenty-five

In four separate interviews with the police over the next forty-eight hours it was made obvious that they were highly sceptical about my story, especially with regard to the stallion and mare. If it had happened, they said, then Dunn had been trying to take some crazy revenge on me before committing suicide. The vet had left a typewritten suicide note claiming I'd been hounding him over gambling debts. Still unable to disclose the real reason, I insisted that all I'd been seeking from him had been information on our late mutual friend, Brian Kincaid.

When the news of Dunn's death broke my parents reappeared to be grilled by the CID. It seemed that Dunn had called and offered them a two-day break in a Welsh holiday cottage he owned. He'd volunteered to move in and look after the horses while they were away.

In the days after Dunn's death I frequently found myself swamped by anger. Rage at my mother and father and the police and Dunn; anger at him more for dying than anything else, dying and removing my one solid lead to this whole bloody complicated mess. What the hell was going on? Who was behind all this? What was behind it? Much more than the gambling problems of a racecourse vet, I was certain.

Then there was the dire prospect of the blackmail call when it finally came, the task of convincing these people who held the originals of the photocopied documents that I'd do whatever they wanted to keep this quiet. And all the time the fury was building in me, bolstering the cold determination to find them and deal with them, pay them back.

It had been three days since Dunn died and I'd left the flat only briefly to buy fresh dressings for my bitten arm though the wound wasn't deep and would heal quickly. The papers

I'd found were locked away in a small metal filing box. I'd expected a call by now from the blackmailers. None had come. They were making me sweat.

I'd like to have established a definite link between Dunn and Capshaw the trainer but I simply hadn't had the time to cross-reference all Dunn's betting records with the formbook to check Breslin's suspicion that an unusually high percentage of bets had been on Capshaw-trained horses.

Now I had all the time it took for the blackmailers to get in touch. Hours or days. I'd be as well filling that time by working on the printouts. I sat working long into the night, stopping occasionally to look at the silent phone, never expecting there to be a cut off point, even at three in the morning, when they might not call.

They didn't. I woke stiff and uncomfortable to the sunshine through my window, my head on one of the thick printouts, the heat from the still-burning desklamp warm on my right cheek.

I put the kettle on then dragged the phone as close to the bathroom door as possible and stepped in the shower, ready to jump out as soon as the phone rang.

Wet-haired and chewing toast, I returned to the desk to review the previous evening's work. It was obvious now that a high percentage of Dunn's bets had indeed been on Capshaw-trained horses. The first place Dunn had made for that morning when we'd given him a fright at my father's stud had been Capshaw's. There had to be a link. Capshaw had to be involved.

The one person who'd known Dunn well seemed to be my father. Well enough, I was almost certain, to have been the one to have told him the truth about what had happened all those years ago. And Dunn had told the blackmailers and they had killed him. I'd yet to learn how he'd died. The cops had refused to release the cause of death, pending further enquiries. I needed to talk to my father.

I called the stud. My mother answered, sounding very strained, still shocked.

'Mother, it's Eddie. Are you all right? You sound quite . . .'

'I'm fine.' Tension now too at the sound of my voice.

'I need to see you both.'

'Edward is ill, he's not seeing anybody.'

'I think he'll be seeing me all right.'

'He's not at all well.'

'I'm afraid he's going to feel even worse, Mum, when he sees what I've got. Please prepare him for a shock – another shock, I suppose I should say. And you too.'

'Wait until things are better, Eddie.'

The first time she'd said my name for years. A strange feeling, like a drowning man staring hopelessly up at the deck of a liner only to see a hand stretching down towards him. I was silent for a moment. Then, more softly, I said, 'Things aren't going to get better, Mum, I'm sorry. Not until we sort this out.'

'Please . . .'

Her voice, cracking now, almost made my cry. 'You'll understand when you see this, Mum, you will. I'll be there this evening. I'll try for around seven.'

I heard the shortest of sobs before she hung up.

When I arrived my mother was watching from the window as I closed the gate and drove towards the house. She stood very still, arms folded, eyes cast down, not looking at me as I approached the door. Then she moved away and I heard her footsteps in the hall. She opened the door. I looked at her weary, unsmiling face, tired and old but not yet defeated. That touch of iron was still in her eyes, a quality I now realised had always been there even though, as a kid, I'd never recognised it for what it was.

'Hello,' she said quietly and pulled the door wide to let me in.

'Hello, Mum.'

Still no smile.

This time she led me into a large drawing room, tastefully furnished but sadly unlived in. A lonely old table and two easy chairs, a cold empty fireplace, two horse and jockey paintings facing one another from opposite walls as though they'd been waiting years for this race that would never start.

I stood awkwardly in the middle of the room. My mother looked up at me. 'Would you like some tea?'

I smiled. 'No, thanks.'

She gestured towards a chair. 'Please sit down.'

I did and the fat cushion sank down, leaving my arms on the rests almost at shoulder level. She moved silently in old blue shoes and perched on the hard edge of the chair opposite, waiting. Waiting to see what was in the bulging brown envelope I'd brought. I placed it on my knee.

'Where's my father?'

'He's ill. He has to stay in bed.' Her eyes were calm but determined. I said, 'He's got to see this, Mum.'

Mum. Again. I watched for her reaction to the word. None. She reached out, her bony arm emerging slowly from the sleeve of her beige cardigan, her wrinkled work-worn hand. I placed the envelope gently between her fingers. She opened it and drew out the papers. I sank back slowly in the chair and watched her as she read, her hand steady as she turned the pages, eyes still set hard, the only sign of emotion the occasional movement of her jaw muscles.

She put the papers back in the envelope and offered it to me. 'Why did you do it?'

'What?'

'This. After all this time.

'It wasn't me. I found these in one of your boxes the other day, close to Alex Dunn's body.'

'Who wrote it?' Anger rising now.

'That's what I'm trying to find out. That's why Father's got to see it.'

She shook her head. 'No. It will kill him.'

'It'll kill him even quicker if the press get hold of it.'

She sat rigid, staring straight ahead, defying the welling tears to rise any higher. Determination to protect him, something that had served her all her life, was no longer going to be enough and she knew it. I edged forward in the big chair and said quietly, 'Did Father tell Alex Dunn this?'

She shook her head, not looking at me.

'Are you sure?'

No answer. Tears winning the fight now, glistening in her eyes, softening them, slipping out slowly, seeking the widest wrinkle in her cheek. And I knew he must have told Dunn, and I knew she knew. And Dunn had told whoever was behind all this, maybe not intentionally but he'd told them, betrayed my father, condemned himself.

'Where is he?' I asked softly.

'Upstairs. In bed.'

I rose. 'I'll go up.'

'No.' She got to her feet. 'I'll take it up. You wait . . . Please, wait.'

She took the envelope from my hands and left the room. I sat down again, hearing her feet on the creaking stairs, a door opening then dull voices punctuated by silence. And my mind slipped slowly back through the years to the dark evenings when I'd lie in bed and hear those same voices rise from around the big kitchen range, making me smile with delicious anticipation as I listened to them discuss plans for all the years ahead.

All the years.

The horses, the children – me and my brother and sister – the big stud farm we'd build, the biggest in Newmarket. The champions we'd breed. The fun we'd have. All the years. All the dreams.

Then the world caved in. The darkness came.

Sitting here in this strange big house I wished I had tears left for it. But that allocation had been used up a long time ago. That part of my heart was shrivelled and dry.

I became aware of my mother standing in the doorway to my left. I hadn't heard her come back. 'He'll see you,' she said.

An audience bestowed by the mighty one, the withholder of happiness. I followed her up the stairs.

The room was dull, curtains drawn. The papers lay under a lamp on a round bedside table. His gold-framed glasses were on the top page, reflecting a coin of light on to an empty glass stained inside with a rim of white powder. The bed was high, wide. He had sunk into the middle of it, the horizontal position removing the superiority he'd always found in his height.

I went and stood by the bed, my mother behind me. He stared straight up at the dark ceiling, the gloom too deep to let me see the true shade of his pallor, but his cheeks were hollow, his eyes dull. I tried to find some sorrow for him inside me but that had gone the same way as the tears.

'Hello, Father.'

His jaw clenched.

He's biting back the hatred, I thought.

I waited. After a minute or more he said, 'Who wrote that?'

I watched him. Demanding still. In a moment it would be a command. 'Who wrote it?!' There was fire enough in his voice. I didn't answer. He kept staring upwards. I heard my mother shuffle uncomfortably behind me. I said to him, 'Look at me.'

He flinched noticeably though I'd spoken quietly. The jaw clenched again.

'Look at me,' I said.

All three of us waited. Just the sounds of our breathing. Slowly his jaw relaxed and he turned his head on the pillow till his eyes met mine. A challenge from his strong son. It couldn't be declined. I hunkered down level with him and looked long into his eyes. He never blinked. 'Who wrote that?' he repeated.

'You wrote it, Dad.'

Anger flared in his face. I raised a finger to my lips to hush him. The anger softened to surprise. 'You wrote it when you told Alex Dunn everything, just as surely as if you'd sat down at the typewriter yourself.'

His head rolled back, breaking eye contact. 'He was the only person I ever told,' he said, voice shaky. 'It helped me . . . to tell.'

Look where it's got you now.

He closed his eyes, squeezed them tight shut. Mother moved forward and reached to take his hand, squeezing it twice then interlocking her fingers with his. I looked up at her. She stared down at him, her eyes showing love and hurt, her jaw and mouth steely with determination.

Slowly I stood up and moved to the end of the bed where I could look at them both. I said, 'We might be able to stop this getting to the papers. I've got to find the person who wrote it and left it there. Whoever it was will call soon.'

My mother looked at me. I said, 'He'll call one of us.'

She said, 'What do you want me to do if he rings here?'

'Just listen to what he says. Write it down. Try to hear if there's anything in the background that might help us pinpoint where he's calling from. You know, like trains or heavy traffic.'

I watched her face as she accepted this new role, her brain making yet another adjustment in a lifetime of coping. 'Should I ask him anything?'

I half-smiled, trying to ease the tension. 'You can ask him who he is and why he's doing this but I doubt you'll get an answer.'

She nodded thoughtfully and looked at my father whose eyes were closed again. I said, 'Dad, are you awake?'

At the sound of the word 'Dad', he seemed almost to stop breathing for a moment then, eyes still closed, he nodded slightly. 'You trusted Alex Dunn?'

Mother said, 'He was a very old friend.'

'So what would have made him betray you like that?'

She shook her head slowly. My father frowned angrily. I said, 'Who did Dunn associate with? Somebody must have had a hold over him.'

Mother looked at Father and he seemed to sense her gaze on him. He opened his eyes slightly but looked at her as he answered. 'He did a lot of work for Capshaw, didn't he?'

Mother nodded as she reached again for his hand and squeezed it.

'Dad . . .' Slowly he brought his head round to look at me. 'What sort of work?'

'Just standard vet stuff as far as I know.'

'And what was he doing for you?'

Mother said, 'He was trying to find out what was wrong with Heraklion.'

'Did he say he knew of any other stallion suffering the same ailment?' I asked.

Mother looked at Father. He said, 'It baffled him. I'd never known him so annoyed or frustrated.'

I changed tack. 'Did he strike you as the type to commit suicide?'

Looking at the ceiling again, Father said, 'He could get pretty down when the horses weren't running for him. He gambled a bit.'

'So I've heard. But would he have killed himself?'

He shook his head quite vigorously. 'Not that way, he wouldn't.'

'What way?' The police had been withholding the cause of death.

Father looked at me. 'One of the CID men told me he injected himself with quite a large dose of prostaglandin.'

I flinched involuntarily. I knew prostaglandin was used regularly on mares to abort them, to clean out the uterus. God only knew what it would do to a human being.

The ridiculous scenario of a TV game show came to mind. 'We

asked one hundred people their favourite methods of committing suicide.' I'd bet injecting prostaglandin wouldn't be one of them.

'What sort of death would that have been?' I asked my father.

He looked at Mother, wondering whether the conversation was getting too morbid. She responded by nodding encouragement. He stared at the ceiling again and said, 'It would have been agonising, I'd have thought, but you'd be best asking an expert.'

Mother said to me, 'Do you think Alex may have been killed?'

'It's a possibility.'

Father turned again to Mother, forlorn hope in his eyes. 'But maybe he *did* commit suicide. Maybe he wrote everything out, knowing we'd find it when we came back, before the police or anybody. That means nobody else would know about us.'

I felt a momentary anger as he excluded me from this potential get-out. But he was only following the habits of a lifetime. And anyway, I knew Dunn hadn't left those papers, there were too many other things going on. My parents didn't know about all the peripheral stuff yet and I didn't feel it was safe to tell them.

My father looked at me, animosity back in his eyes. 'You've brought this on us. Why couldn't you just have left Alex alone? What does it matter to you if he owed some bookie money?'

'It's nothing to do with that.'

'That's what the note said.'

My mother, too, was staring accusingly at me now.

'I wasn't chasing Dunn for gambling debts,' I said. 'He was involved in something serious . . . criminal.'

'Rubbish!' my father cried, then went into a coughing fit. Mother glared at me and fussed over him. I left the room quietly and waited for her downstairs. Ten minutes later she came into the room. 'Is he all right?' I asked.

She nodded then sat down across from me, looking serious. She said, 'If Alex Dunn was involved with something criminal, is it possible those papers . . . that, that story . . . was meant to frighten you off?'

'It's probable.'

She clasped her fingers and moved uncomfortably. 'Well, couldn't you just do what they want and not . . . interfere any more?'

I stared at her. She met my gaze. I said, 'Do you want these people, this person, to hold it over us for the rest of our lives?'

She shrugged, opened her palms. 'I just thought . . .'

'Mum, it won't work. We can't live that way.'

She lowered her eyes, stared at the floor.

I sat forward. 'The best I can do is promise that I'll keep a very low profile. I'll try and make them believe they've scared me off, try and convince them that it's worked.'

She looked at me again. 'But how will we know if they believe that?'

'I think that they won't call unless they decide I need another lesson. If the blackmail call doesn't come, it means they think I've dropped out.'

She nodded, still unhappy but knowing from the look in my eyes that I wouldn't change my mind. She said, 'Promise me you'll try hard?'

'To find them or to convince them I've given up?'

'Given up.'

'I'll try. I promise.'

I stayed with her another half-hour or so, prodding gently for more information on Alex Dunn but learning little. He was an excellent vet and a terrible punter. He had never married and had no family that she knew of. But, said Mother, he was a nice man.

Well, he'd got in with the wrong people and I had to find out who those people were. The only immediate link I had was the trainer, Capshaw. It might take a while to find out all I needed to about him so it would be best if I was based not too far from Newmarket though I wouldn't want to be in the town itself. All part of keeping a low profile. Mother came to see me out. I explained that I needed to be fairly close at hand for the next couple of weeks. She tilted her head to look up into my eyes, knowing what I was really asking, knowing that it was the first concrete thing I had ever asked for since those dreadful days when what I'd begged for hadn't been in her power to grant.

'I'll speak to your father tonight. Perhaps you could call me tomorrow.' I nodded, smiling. Her neck was still arched and I felt a strong urge to kiss her gently on her upturned cheek. But I thought better of it.

We stood by the door. I noticed how quiet the yard was. 'Where are the horses?' I asked.

'Gone,' she said flatly. 'We just can't cope for the moment. We've sent them to various people we know.'

People we know. No use for the word 'friends'.

She stayed at the door, watching me cast a long shadow in the beam of the security light as I walked to the car. That night I slept in a small hotel, closing my eyes with a strange mixture of fear and hope in my heart.

Twenty-six

Next morning's *Sporting Life* told me William Capshaw had two runners at Ascot. Not all trainers appeared at the races when their horses were running but Ascot was a sufficiently prestigious course for most to make a special effort.

Even if Capshaw wasn't there, I'd get a chance to see Candy again. Sheikh Ahmad Saad had six horses entered at Ascot and his Racing Manager would be bound to be there. I wondered if Candy might just happen to bump into the same hard man I'd seen him with at Sandown, one of the guys who'd warned me off at Dunn's place.

If that had been coincidence and the guys were nothing to do with Candy, I couldn't now risk talking to him. I just didn't know who I could trust. The more I considered it, the more I convinced myself that the papers I'd found with Dunn had been meant as a silent warning. So long as I kept my nose out of things no blackmail call would be needed. The day the call finally came would be the day I'd know I'd been rumbled.

It would be impossible for me to watch both Candy and Capshaw so I arranged for Martin to meet me in the carpark and to bring two cameras. Before getting heavily into booze, Caroline had been a photography buff and Martin arrived with two bags full of gear and started unloading them.

Bearing in mind my intention to keep a low profile, I was fairly confident that few of the flat-racing community would recognise me, especially in 'civvies'. But I didn't want to bring attention to myself or to Martin.

I said, 'Martin, for God's sake! We're supposed to be moving around unobtrusively, taking a few discreet pictures. All we need is a camera each with a reasonable telephoto lens.'

'Okay, okay!' He spent a few minutes choosing and fitting

lenses then gave me four rolls of film. 'If you need any more, give me a shout.'

'I won't. It's best if we don't speak to each other once we're through the gates.'

He agreed and we arranged to meet later. The plan was that we would take turn about following Capshaw and Candy at what we hoped was a safe distance.

Capshaw had a runner in the first. I took up an early position by the parade-ring rails watching the horses go round until owners and trainers filtered in. Capshaw was with two men and two women, smiling at them, fielding excited questions from all sides, stoking their enthusiasm and hope.

He was a small man, dark and quite dapper in a well-tailored navy suit, white shirt and patterned tie. The tallest man in the party pointed to the ground and Capshaw smiled and bent over to tie his shoelace. As he straightened he mouthed the words 'Good luck' and the party giggled, a slim dark girl nervously patting his arm. I checked the racecard: the owner's name was K. Semple. I wondered which of them it was. Raising the camera, I shot a few frames.

Their horse ran well before fading to finish fourth. All seemed delighted. I tracked Capshaw as best I could over the next hour though he disappeared from time to time into places like the owners' and trainers' bar where I couldn't follow. The only sign that all was not well with him came when he was alone. In company he was animated, smiling. It was a good act. As soon as his companions turned away Capshaw's face took on the expression of a very troubled man.

Sheikh Ahmad Saad's horse won the fourth and I moved towards the winner's enclosure to watch them have their usual post-race discussion. Martin stood against the opposite rail and I watched him take a few pictures then nodded to indicate that I'd take over.

The Sheikh's Racing Manager, Candy Loss, looking tanned, fit and elegant was, as usual, among the entourage. He also looked worried. The race they'd just won was hardly top class but I'd have thought it would have produced a smile. I looked at the rest of the party – mostly glum faces. The Sheikh himself had a smile of sorts, grim and fixed, below his dark moustache.

Here was a small band of people on a fine sunny day at

one of the world's biggest racecourses. Their horse had just won and their oil wells back East were pumping out more cash than they could ever spend – and all they could manage was an interesting variety of frowns. God help them if they ever ended up on the streets.

I followed Candy for twenty minutes or so on the off chance he'd bump into one of the hard men who'd warned me off from Dunn's place. I'd spent some time thinking about that. If Dunn had had the clout to recruit those guys and he was as afraid of me as he'd claimed in the suicide note, why hadn't he simply sent them back to teach me a proper lesson? Or had they been the ones who'd doped me and tied me to the mare?

Whoever had done that must have known Dunn was dead in that box. Could they also have killed him?

Even discounting the chosen method of death, it struck me that Dunn was an unlikely suicide candidate. Part of the nature of the compulsive gambler is the constant belief that something will turn up, that tomorrow will be the day fortunes change, that it's just a matter of time. Hopelessness tends to be a temporary condition with them.

Also, why kill himself at my father's place, and why with prostaglandin? I was certain Dunn would have had access to many more types of drugs that would have offered a more peaceful passing.

I thought back to my first meeting with him and recalled how shocked he'd looked when I'd mentioned Brian and the lab samples. He knew something crucial about one or both of those matters and now he was dead. Did the burden of the knowledge he'd had make him kill himself or was he murdered to keep him quiet?

All this was turning over in my mind while I followed Candy around at what I hoped was a safe distance. He spoke to two of the trainers the Sheikh employed and various other dogsbodies but the heavies didn't appear.

Martin and I swapped quarry again for the next race then once again for the last where Capshaw trained the winner. I went to the winner's enclosure to watch them coming back in. Capshaw looked much relieved and I wondered if his owners had had a serious bet. They looked pleased enough. There were four of them around the sweating chestnut, patting and kissing the horse and posing for pictures while Capshaw spoke to the press.

I noted Martin in the corner, still snapping away.

Checking the racecard, I noticed that the winner was owned by Guterson's Gloves Ltd, and that the race had also been sponsored by them. It was always nice to win your own money back. The company's name rang a bell with me though it took me a few minutes to recall why: Guterson's had been the name on the boxes of plastic gloves stored in the locked cupboard in Dunn's bungalow.

Nepotism rules, okay. Guterson had a horse in training with Capshaw, Dunn is tied in with Capshaw, Dunn had to buy Guterson's gloves. Neat.

I stayed around for the presentation which was made by Mr Bob Guterson, large, grey-suited, completely bald and smiling widely, to his own Marketing Manager at Guterson's Gloves. Guterson certainly had a grasp of monopolies.

When we met again in the carpark neither Martin nor I could claim to have photographed anything which looked nefarious but he said he'd get the films developed and I said I'd ask Mac to go through them with me to see if he could spot any dodgy characters.

I rang my mother. She told me Father was no better but that I could stay in the spare room for a few weeks if I would try not to disturb him. I promised and hung up the phone, allowing myself the tiniest smile as I sensed another small repair in that long-shredded umbilical cord. I realised that the invitation had only been motivated by their terror of disclosure and that was not the way I'd have wanted it. But there was a subconscious bitter-sweetness there I could almost taste.

I changed routes and headed north to pick up as much stuff as I could from the flat. If my stay in Newmarket turned out to be an extended one, I didn't want to be travelling back and forth.

I reached Shropshire just after eight. The yard was as quiet as a Benedictine coffee morning and I hurried upstairs to empty my wardrobe and grab a few books and tapes. The light was flashing on my answerphone though, as always, I'd emptied it remotely that morning.

One message from a trainer, Ken McGilvary, offering me two rides at Exeter next day. I thought about it as I stuffed extra toiletries into a plastic bag. I hadn't ridden for a while and was missing it quite badly. Also I could do with a break from all the sneaking around and, more to the point, if I was seen to be back riding again so soon the people who wanted me out of the stallion case would be reassured that I'd downed tools and returned to normal life.

That decided it. I called Ken and accepted. He told me at least one would win and that I should arrange to have a good bet. Jockeys aren't allowed to gamble but many place bets through a third party. Personally I avoid it. I find owners and trainers just about the worst tipsters in the land. They are optimists by nature. I'm a pessimist and have seldom been proved wrong.

I was at my parents' place for 10.30. My mother let me in and managed a strained smile as she led me along the hall towards the back of the house, the sound of snoring from my father's room growing louder then fading as we passed.

The big bed made the room seem small. Fresh flowers on a chest of drawers by the window scented the air. The patterned wallpaper looked tobacco brown in the dim light and the room gave the same impression as the others in the house: that of a steady decay.

Still the sheets were clean, the quilt thick and the pillows deep. I laid my bags down by the bed. 'Thanks, Mum.'

She nodded slightly, not convinced she'd done the right thing, but offered me tea and sandwiches, and by the time I joined her in the long kitchen they were on the table though she couldn't quite bring herself to sit with me as I ate.

She asked if I had 'made any progress today'.

'A little. We certainly didn't take any steps backwards.'

That small nod again. I was already becoming familiar with it. She excused herself then, saying that she must sit with my father a while. We said goodnight and I sat in the silent room, the sound of my own chewing echoing in my head. I thought again of the old days when it was I who'd lain in bed while my parents sat in the kitchen. When it was I who'd relied on them. For everything.

They'd failed me.

Would I fail them now?

Exeter Racecourse lay high on Haldon Hill where the weather was clear and sunny. I drove steadily down the main approach, weaving through the heavy pedestrian traffic, the usual herd of optimists moving confidently and excitedly towards the front lines to engage the bookies in the next battle of what was, for many, a lifelong war. Their demeanour on the trip back along this drive would be that of any casualty, light of pocket but leaden-footed.

When I entered the weighing room I realised I hadn't smiled so much for weeks. It was so good to be back among familiar faces, trusted people, friends. I had a very strong desire right then never to leave these guys again. I wished we could all form some full-time travelling band of companions, going from course to course, sticking close together, never having to face the outside world.

But if I'd have told any one of them how I felt they'd have taken the piss for the rest of my life. I settled for talking to and laughing with as many of them as possible throughout the day. The horse McGilvary had said would win skated in by ten lengths. His other one fell with me when going well, dealing me a neat kick in the ribs as he scrambled up, but I was okay although I accepted a lift back in the ambulance.

I picked up a spare ride which finished third and all in all had a bloody good day till the cloud of gloom those papers had created settled on me again. I was sitting in the weighing room just after the last, enjoying the banter as everyone packed up, thankful to be heading home still sound in the head, unbandaged and stitch-free. As I looked around I wondered what they'd all think of me if this story ever did get out.

A few of them were planning a drinking session at a local hotel. I'd been tempted but the depression that had crept in persuaded me to give it a miss despite much ribbing. I said my goodbyes and headed for the carpark.

As I approached my car I saw there was a bit of a party going on by the BMW parked next to me. Two tall young men in light suits were wielding champagne bottles by the neck and singing tunelessly. I smiled. I hoped they had a sober driver stashed away somewhere.

They were sitting on the bonnet, their backs to me as I opened my rear door and slung my kitbag inside. 'Beat the bookies?' I asked cheerfully. They both turned, smiling, holding their bottles towards me and moving in my direction remarkably quickly for drunks. They wore sunglasses. I recognised them too late. The darker one dropped his smile and his bottle and pushed me in through my half-open driver's door while the other one climbed in the passenger side. I glanced desperately around the carpark but there was no one near enough to cry out to.

Dark Hair got in behind me. I heard my kitbag squeak on the leather upholstery as he pushed it across the seat. 'Drive,' he said.

I drove.

Twenty-seven

He issued simple directions till we were heading south. I'd planned to go north but I wasn't too despondent. At least this was something, a further step. Anything was better than blundering around looking for unfindable clues.

Anything, Eddie. Death?

Maybe not.

When we were travelling at speed on the road he wanted, Dark Hair said, 'Should old acquaintance be forgot, Mr Malloy.'

'You've often been brought to mind,' I said.

'But not with sufficient nous on your part to want to avoid a resumption of that acquaintance.'

'You made such an impression on me,' I said, 'I just had to see you again.'

'Well, let's just see if we can consummate our relationship to your satisfaction this time. I'd hate to think you'd want to come back for more.'

At least that told me they didn't plan to kill me. I was scared but wasn't for showing it. I said, 'I just can't get enough of such riveting company.'

'Riveting. Now there's a thought. We're not too far from a shipyard, actually.'

The thought of a hot rivet gun against my flesh was enough to silence me for a while. In less than an hour we were on the South Devon coast, passing through villages which grew increasingly scattered and more sparsely populated the further we went. As the big orange sun began sinking Dark Hair directed me along a series of winding one-vehicle roads till suddenly we found ourselves heading directly towards the sea.

The further along the track I drove, the higher we climbed. The ocean lay far below as we drove across the grass now towards what could only be a cliff edge. I took heart from the fact that there

148

were two other cars parked within sight of where we stopped. The people I assumed were their owners strolled in silhouette against the pinkish sky and sea, following their dogs.

We stopped and I was told to switch off the engine. We sat in silence, all three of us, watching the dog-walkers, my companions with growing impatience, me with the fervent wish they were on a sponsored cliff-top walking marathon.

But they weren't. Within minutes of each other they led their pets back to the cars and drove away, the smell of their exhausts wafting through my half-opened window.

When the sound of the departing cars faded to silence the tension in the car increased. None of us spoke. After maybe fifteen minutes the gulls, up till now riding silently on the air currents over the cliffs, swept towards us and began crying for the show to begin.

Still they waited. The sun was huge, dropping slowly now behind the glassy horizon like an enormous orange coin into a wide slot. And I realised that what they'd been holding off for was dusk.

Dark Hair got out and opened my door while his friend sat close beside me. With the door just halfway open I'd already decided to kick out and slam it against Dark Hair's legs. Before I moved my foot an inch the guy beside me hit me hard and fast on the point of my chin and I felt my legs buckle and my eyes water at the same time as Dark Hair dragged me out on to the grass.

They both pulled me to my feet and half-dragged me towards the cliff edge as I fought desperately to regain my full senses. The blow had taken me completely by surprise. I'd been dazed often enough in my riding life, concussed a few times, but somehow this was different. Falling from a horse at speed can be bone-crunching but that split second of warning is often enough to prepare yourself mentally and, to some extent, physically for what's coming. Being hit in the face by a professional was another matter.

By the time we reached the edge my brain had stopped rattling in my skull though my legs remained weak. Dark Hair gripped the back of my neck with his big left hand and pushed me forward.

The sea was calm. Low tide. Dusk and distance softened the rocks hundreds of feet below till they looked no more threatening than chocolates lying haphazardly in a box. The ozone-rich air rose in currents off the cliff face, sharpening my senses now – and my fear.

Dark Hair said, 'Ready? There'll be top points for artistic impression depending on the degree of difficulty.'

Smart answers didn't seem so clever any more. I thought of my mother and felt the strongest pang of regret that my plans to be a proper son again would never be realised.

Dark Hair said, 'Goodbye, Mr Malloy.' Then he pushed me over the edge. I fought to keep my balance in what seemed an absurd slow-motion replay of those hundreds of cartoon characters windmilling wildly with their arms and pedalling furiously at fresh air but there was no Hanna Barbera storyboard to keep me upright and I went over, head plunging downwards.

Then I stopped. I threw out my hands to stop my nose hitting rock as I swung in towards the cliff face. They had me by the ankles.

Suspended.

Suspended belief.

Renewed hope.

They lowered me slowly. My fingers scrabbled for a hold, a crack, in case they dropped me now. I felt damp vegetation, scratched it, releasing a rich smell. They held me there, panting. I saw the rocks way below. Nothing between them and my eyes. I closed them. Sweat prickled.

Then, very slowly, my tormentors hauled me back up. They tried to make me stand but shock had triped my leg muscles. They laid me flat out in the grass and I went from staring at earth and sea to gazing lovingly at a darkening sky.

Dark Hair leaned over me, looked into my eyes. 'Stop following people. Stay out of this. Go back to riding horses for a living. Next time we'll drop you.'

Then they went away. I heard my car start up but didn't turn my head to watch them leave. I just lay there staring at the sky till it was black and sparkling with stars.

It was after midnight by the time I reached a garage. I called my mother and told her not to worry about me, and she said she had been a bit worried which cheered me. My next call was to Johnny Westmead, a jock I'd spoken to that day at Exeter. I knew he lived in Torquay which, the kid in the garage assured me, was only half an hour away by car.

Sleepy as he was, Johnny agreed right away to come and pick me up and give me a bed for the night. I spun him a tale about meeting a girl at the races and bringing her back here to make love on the clifftop, only to have her steal my car while I was dozing in the grass. He laughed and I knew he'd get plenty of mileage out of it whenever my name came up in future years.

Next morning I rang the police and reported that my car had been stolen from Exeter races. They asked why I hadn't reported it yesterday and I told them I'd left it there overnight when I'd gone for a drink. They then told me it had been found abandoned on the slip road exit of Taunton Deane services on the M5 and that my keys and kitbag were in the possession of the Taunton police.

Johnny agreed to drive me there and after completing a surprisingly small amount of paperwork I was heading north-east, back towards Newmarket. On the long journey I had plenty to occupy my mind.

Whoever Dark Hair and his friend were working for, and I didn't doubt they were just employees, was being extremely patient with me. Okay, last night had been scary but that was all. Was the cliffhanging episode really engineered by the same guy who'd had Brian Kincaid and, quite probably, Alex Dunn, killed? If so, then why go easy on me?

More interestingly, why hadn't they used the much more potent threat of publication? Could it be that my father's hopeful guess had been right, and that Dunn had indeed kept the story to himself?

No, that didn't make sense, not if he'd been killed. In that case the killer had laid the envelope out for me to find, knowing I was going to be there to meet Dunn. The killer must have known Dunn personally or he wouldn't have had that information.

Even if it had been suicide, Dunn also knew I'd be the only one on the scene. If he'd never meant to expose the secret to anyone then why leave it for me, somebody who already knew every detail, to find?

Someone else had to know, and if it was the person controlling Dark Hair and partner, then why hadn't he simply used it? A phone call would have been all that was needed rather than a day trip to the Devon coast.

It made no sense.

Unless the person in charge specifically didn't want me hurt, in which case he or she probably knew me and knew me well enough to have some feelings for me. The only lead I had on these guys, apart from my first meeting with them at Dunn's place, was seeing Dark Hair with Candy at Sandown. Now I'd like to have thought that Candy felt something for me as a friend, we'd been pretty good mates in his riding days. I knew him well and that was the trouble: I just couldn't see him being involved in mayhem and murder.

I worked on it all the way back to Newmarket and knew there was something there. Even though they were still fragmented in my head, there were enough pieces of the picture to tell me something solid, I just needed them to fall into place.

As the noon news came on the radio I was ten miles along the M4. My mobile rang. I punched the off button on the radio and answered the phone. It was Martin.

'Eddie! I need to see you! We're in bad trouble!'

He sounded panic-stricken. 'Martin, calm down. What's wrong?'

'Eddie! Eddie . . .' He broke down, sobbing.

'Martin! Listen, are you at home?'

Incoherent noises in reply.

'Hold on, Martin. I'll be with you soon.'

I had to assume he was at the stud. I reckoned I was less than an hour away.

Twenty-eight

I sped along the M4 at over a hundred miles an hour and it was frustrating having to slow down for the speed bumps along the driveway to the stud which saw me roll quietly up to the bungalow rather than arrive in a cloud of dust and burning rubber.

As I hurried towards the front step I heard raised voices through the open door. Fiona first. 'It won't do you any good, you know that! You admitted it yourself!'

Then Martin. 'Look, fuck off and leave me alone!'

'They won't have to kill you, Martin, you're killing yourself!'

I stood listening.

'Leave me alone, you bitch!'

Fiona started sobbing. 'Martin, please, for God's sake!' Her voice was softer now, trying not to upset him further. She said, 'Tell Malloy, he'll help us. Tell him about Dunn. Let me tell him.'

'No. Tell him nothing. I'm out of this now, he can do it on his own. He can have the stud. And he can have you! And Caroline! He can have the whole fucking lot of you!'

I heard breaking glass, furniture moving, then Martin came blundering out carrying a half-full bottle, almost knocking me over. He stank of whisky. He was clean-shaven for once but a fresh bruise was rising on his right cheek and on his lower left jawbone was a crescent-shaped ridge of weeping blisters.

He stared at me, anger draining from his eyes as he seemed to realise I might have heard what he'd just said. Fiona appeared in the doorway, red-faced and sullen in a plum-coloured smock. When she saw us, she turned and went back in. Martin's hangdog expression drew the last of the anger from him and he sat down on the step and swigged from the bottle.

I sat beside him. 'What's happened?'

He was washing the whisky around his mouth, staring at the

153

clear sky. He swallowed it and, without looking at me, said, 'Some-body came and took the pictures off me. And the cameras.'

'The pictures we shot at Ascot?'

He nodded.

'When?'

'Early this morning.' He drank again. 'He caught me as I went down to feed the horses.'

He swallowed a lump in his throat. I noticed a tear at the corner of his left eye. I waited a few seconds before asking any more questions. Between swigs and tears and nervous swallows, Martin told me that a man with a gun had demanded the pictures and nega-tives he'd had developed yesterday. Then he'd taken Martin to the forge, made him fire it up, heated a horseshoe and branded him lightly on the jaw, threatening the full treatment if he didn't 'stop following people around'. That was virtually the same message I'd had from Dark Hair, but I bore no scars. Martin's description of the guy didn't match either of the heavies I'd driven to the seaside.

Before leaving, the man had knocked him unconscious and locked him in the forge which was in a small building well away from the main yard. Fiona only heard his shouts because she was actually out looking for him.

When he finished his story he sat staring at the ground, his bottle now two-thirds empty. 'Was that full when you started?' I asked.

He nodded. I said nothing. Still gazing at the ground he said quietly, 'I'm finished, Eddie.'

I watched him.

'I'm scared,' he said, voice breaking.

I moved closer to him and put an arm around his shoulder and he slumped against me and started crying, softly at first then the floodgates opened and Fiona came and helped me get him inside and into bed. He lay, eyes closed, gripping her hand as she dried his glistening cheeks. Gradually his breathing levelled out and I left them together and went to the kitchen.

Ten minutes later Fiona came in alone. She filled the kettle and washed two mugs. 'He's asleep,' she said calmly. I was revising my opinion of her. For all Martin's problems, and booze now looked a serious one, she'd stood by him. He was nothing more than a child inside and here was she, more than twenty-five years younger, looking after him, carrying his baby.

She brought mugs of coffee to the table and, businesslike, unfolded the *Racing Post*. There was a big colour picture of Alex Dunn above a story about the coroner's report whose verdict was suicide by self-administration of approximately 5ccs of prostaglandin.

Fiona said, 'I'm sure Dunn came here about two weeks before Town Crier started firing blanks.'

'Go on.'

She smoothed the paper. 'He came here one day when Martin was out. I recognised him from this picture. He told me he was an RSPCA man come to check the horses.'

'And did he?'

She nodded.

'Did he say what he expected to find?'

'He said someone had reported that they weren't being fed properly.'

'And did he check them all?'

'Yes.'

She looked slightly doubtful. 'Did you go round with him?' I asked.

'Most of them.'

'What did he do?'

She shrugged. 'I don't know. Took a few tests, temperature, blood, that sort of thing.'

'Did he show you any ID?'

'He showed me a card or something, I think.'

'You sure it was him?' I indicated Dunn's picture.

'Almost sure. I think it was.'

'Apart from his looks, is there anything else you remember about him?'

'He was tall. Very tall and thin.'

'Did you tell Martin at the time?'

'I think I did but he was probably drunk. It didn't seem all that important.'

So, Dunn had been here, he'd had pretty much free access at my parents' place . . . Fiona found the list Martin had compiled of the other studs where we suspected one of their stallions was suffering from the same loss of fertility as Town Crier and my father's Heraklion. We had to try and find out if Dunn had been to these studs too. Fiona watched me pondering. I came close to asking her to help me further but she had enough on her plate. And it would only cause more friction with Martin whose heart was obviously no longer in it. I told her to look after him and not to worry. I said I'd make sure he was kept out of it in future and gave her my telephone numbers, making her promise to call me if she needed help.

She looked surprised when I kissed her goodbye.

On my journey home I wondered if my mother would agree to ring round the five studs posing as an RSPCA employee and saying something like, 'We've heard that a bogus vet is visiting studs, and wanted to warn you and to check with you in case he's actually been.'

It was worth a try.

Mother was in the kitchen making tuna and mayonnaise and chopping salad vegetables. A pungent mixture of smells filtered down the hall. She turned to look at me but couldn't quite manage a smile. 'You haven't shaved.'

'I know. Things were a bit hectic this morning.'

She sliced carrot lengthwise with smooth sweeps. 'When men reach a certain age they should never miss shaving. And they should always wear a tie.'

I smiled. 'And you think I've reached that age?'

'Yes, I do.'

'Okay.'

'Don't humour me.'

'I'm not. I mean it.'

We were quiet for a while, listening to the rhythm of the knife on the chopping board. 'How's Father?' I asked.

'Still unwell. Quite ill, I'm afraid.'

Sick of facing the world and his responsibilities, I thought. 'We need to talk later,' I said, 'all three of us.'

'We'll see.'

'It'll move us another step forward, Mum.'

She turned slowly to look at me. 'We'll see.'

I left her and went and lay for half an hour in a hot bath, noting the renewed colour in the old bruises on my ribs like a part-refilled artist's palette. Gazing at the steam-sheened brass taps, I turned over the new developments in my mind.

Our trailing of Candy and Capshaw at Ascot must have activated the visits from the heavy mob but why had Martin been assaulted?

Because he'd been the one with the pictures? How had they known that? Why hadn't Dark Hair mentioned pictures to me when dangling me over that cliff?

Whatever the answers, at least we now knew we were on the right track. Pity Martin had taken it so badly. Terror could be tough to deal with. I couldn't condemn him for wanting out.

The news of Dunn's RSPCA venture also added a very strong flavour. Again there came that terribly frustrating feeling of just having to shake everything up the right way for things to fall into place. I knew it wasn't far away.

That evening I ate alone again. My parents took their meals in Father's bedroom and I realised that I was still just a stranger in their house.

Next morning, after much canvassing by my mother, Father agreed to grant me another audience. I told them both about Dunn's deception in posing as an RSPCA man. Mother checked back through the stud diary and found that Heraklion's fertility had started failing a fortnight after one of Dunn's visits.

Most mares stay on at stud after being covered and are scanned within a few days of the mating to see if an egg has been fertilised.

Mother sat by the bed, the book open in her lap, and glanced at my father whose face looked pale in the curtained gloom. His chest wheezed each time he breathed out but there was some brightness in his eyes as he turned to me. 'Do you think Alex was doing something to those stallions?'

'It seems very likely.' I was wary of condemning Dunn immediately, feeling that my father still felt some friendship for him or his memory. 'I think he was being forced into it somehow, possibly blackmailed.'

Father looked puzzled. 'Why? Who profits from knocking half a dozen small studs out of business?'

I shrugged. 'I don't think that's the objective. If these people had something against the studs in particular, then why not just burn the buggers down?'

At the word 'buggers' my mother glanced up sharply at me as though I were still seven. I smiled but it didn't soften her expression. Father said, 'Then why are they doing it, and who are they?'

'The sixty-four-thousand-dollar question,' I said. 'But if we can find the answer then we'll have the people who left those papers by Alex Dunn's body.' Father's mouth straightened to a thin line as he clenched his jaw. Mother reached for his hand again. All three of us spent the next twenty minutes discussing what Dunn could have done to the stallions. If he'd been responsible for their fertility loss, how had he done it, why, and how could we cure them?

Father brooded throughout most of it, throwing in only the occasional remark, but Mother had been anxious to grasp the lifeline, to explore any option. But there were few and the room was soon silent again.

Father shifted uncomfortably and tried to clear his throat which brought on a coughing fit. Mother propped him up on his pillows and he reached to squeeze her hand, the first time I'd noticed him initiate any affection. She knew he was going to speak. He looked at me and said, 'When I first met Alex Dunn, I remember he was very enthusiastic about something he called chemical castration.'

Two words that came together like scissor blades cutting through all the supposition and speculation. My senses were suddenly sharp. I waited for more. He said, 'Alex was convinced that colts could be made much easier to handle when still in training by injecting something on a regular basis.'

'Something temporary?' I asked.

He nodded. 'When they were finished racing and were ready for stud, the injections would be discontinued.'

I almost held my breath before asking, 'What was the chemical? Do you know?'

He shook his head slowly and I thought I saw just a trace of satisfaction in his eyes, a glimmer of spiteful pleasure that I was still going to have to work very hard to save this. But maybe it was the poor light.

We talked a while longer then Father glanced at Mother and closed his eyes, effectively dismissing me. She looked up and mouthed the words, 'He's tired.' I nodded. Before leaving, I said goodbye to him. He raised both eyebrows slightly but didn't open his eyes and didn't speak.

I went to my room and found Martin's list of studs. When Mother came back I explained what I needed and she sat down immediately to start making calls. I felt like making a few myself but was constantly conscious now of the risk of exposing myself, especially after the events of last night. How did they fit into the puzzle?

The more I thought about it, the more it bugged me. It just didn't make sense. Why hadn't they simply threatened me with publishing those papers? I sat on the bed, Dunn's betting records spread out in front of me. I doodled lightly in pencil in the narrow margin of one of the printouts.

What had Dark Hair said to me? 'Stop following people. Stay out of this.' The message to Martin had been the same, albeit more forcefully delivered. Capshaw and Candy. Candy again cropping up with Dark Hair, his Sandown travelling companion.

Okay, assumption time. No hard evidence to hand so time for some assumptions.

Candy sent the heavies after us. The first time, back at Dunn's place, it was with a friendly violence-free warning. The second it was to scare the shit out of me but otherwise leave me relatively unhurt. Martin hadn't had the protection of an old friendship to rely on, or maybe they had to scare him more as they had no psychological hold over him like they did me with those papers.

Could it be Candy was taking a similarly 'sympathetic' view with the papers, knowing what publication would do to me and my parents? Possibly, but that shouldn't have stopped him using them as a threat.

So did someone else have the papers? Were we up against two different sets of people? What was Candy's interest in Dunn's activities? Supposing he knew Dunn had been scuppering those stallions. Supposing he knew about Dunn's interest in chemical castration. But what would that be to Candy? His boss had the best vets money could buy, the best of everything for his horses. What would . . .

Wait, Eddie.

There was something in the back of my mind. Something that hadn't rung true with me . . . Candy's party at Ascot the other day. How strained they'd all looked, from the Sheikh downwards. Candy, in particular, had looked under pressure. The same Candy who'd reacted just slightly oddly, just a little out of character, when I'd met him in Newmarket and told him about the stallion fertility problem.

The Sheikh.

What makes a fabulously rich, high-powered businessman unhappy?

A poorly performing business?

The Sheikh's racing empire was huge, probably the biggest in the world. What had started ten years ago as a hobby had developed into an obsession, some said, a desire to dominate racing the world over. The building blocks for that, the very foundations, were the Sheikh's luxurious studs, the biggest of which was in Newmarket. He had most of the top stallions and many of the best mares. Although that didn't guarantee success it went a long way towards seriously reducing the odds against failure.

His worst nightmare would have to be losing his stallions. Or the stallions losing their fertility. Maybe, just maybe, Alex Dunn's stallion-sabotaging programme hadn't been confined to small studs.

Jesus! No wonder Candy didn't want me blowing it wide open. If Martin Corish was petrified of breeders getting to know about Town Crier's infertility, how must the Sheikh feel if some of his stallions, among the best in the world, were also infertile?

I stared down at some of the dozen or so small doodles I'd created as I tried to comprehend the enormity of what might be happening. The Sheikh was well forward in his ambition to create the most powerful racing empire on earth. If he ended up with infertile stallions he had nothing. It would be like seeing Rome three-quarters built then watching the foundations crumble in front of your eyes.

I put down the pencil and sat back, trying to focus again, trying to pull away from the global implications and figure out the hows and whys. It was the equivalent of industrial sabotage in a multi-billion pound business. Who was behind it and what was the motive? Why mess around with a few two-bit stallions in tiny studs as well as the cream?

Was someone else involved 'on the ground'? Had Dunn just been covering the small studs? Was someone else still operating in the Sheikh's studs? If so, how? Security there must be tighter than Fort Knox.

I sighed and got to my feet. I had to slow things down, remind myself that all this had stemmed from a couple of assumptions. I was going to have to speak to Candy.

The door opened. Mother came in, still wearing her reading

glasses and carrying the list of studs. She looked quietly pleased. Of the seven calls she'd made four studs told her that they'd had a visit from the potentially bogus RSPCA man in the previous six months. One couldn't recall what he looked like, the other three gave a good description of Alex Dunn.

'Excellent,' I said. 'Have you told Father?'

'He's asleep. I'll tell him later.'

I looked at her. Outwardly calm. Turmoil inside. I wanted to tell her not to worry so much about Father but suspected the advice would be neither appreciated nor heeded.

'Is there anything else I can do just now?' she asked.

I smiled. 'No, thanks, Mum. You've done well.'

That slightly surprised look again then a trace of a smile before she turned to leave. Quietly I moved to the open door and watched her walk wearily away along the hall. Her straight shoulders drooped now that she thought no one was watching and her feet seemed to drag as she took a break from constantly bearing up for the sake of others. She seemed old and broken and when she stopped and almost slumped against the wall I had to hold back from hurrying towards her. But realising she wouldn't appreciate an audience when her guard was down, I stepped quietly backwards into my room.

That decided it. I would contact Candy. I knew of no other way that wouldn't take weeks, maybe months, while the pressure of possible exposure slowly squeezed the life out of my father and therefore my mother.

If my assumptions were correct I was taking the chance that Candy would finally be forced to do something to shut me up for good. The flipside was that he might back me and provide support, which would make a hell of a difference.

I got my diary and found the number of The Gulf Stud where Candy had a house which went with the job. He wasn't there. A secretary gave me his mobile number. It rang seven times then he answered and I concentrated acutely on his reaction as I said, 'Candy, Eddie Malloy.'

A moment's hesitation, then, 'Eddie, nice to hear from you! How are you?'

'Still full of health-giving ozone after yesterday's trip to the coast.'

Another moment's silence then his voice tightened noticeably. 'You, er, been taking a bit of a holiday?'

'Well, you might say that. Just hanging around by the sea for a while.'

There was a long silence now as we both realised the stage we'd reached.

I said, 'Remember I told you I was working for that small stud on a stallion fertility problem?'

'Uhuh?'

'I think I found the answer.'

Another long pause then he said, 'Have you told anyone else?'

'You're my first call.'

More silence. 'I think we should meet,' he said, 'but not in Newmarket.'

Twenty-nine

We met at a garage about fifteen miles from town. I followed Candy for a further two miles, speculating as I watched his head through the rear window whether Dark Hair and his friend were hiding in the back. He pulled off the road and down a slope into a long lay-by concealed by trees. I was relieved to see him get out of the car alone and walk towards me. He got in beside me and managed a grim smile.

I laid everything out as he watched me intently.

'Well,' I asked, 'am I right?'

He stared at me, unsure if I was saviour or executioner, then nodded slowly and told me the story. All eight stallions which had retired to the Sheikh's Newmarket stud in the past eighteen months had completely lost fertility within weeks of taking up stud duties.

'Was Alex Dunn your vet back then?'

Candy ran a hand through his thick chestnut hair. 'Alex Dunn's never set foot inside the place.'

'Well, one of his deputies then.'

Candy shook his head. 'We've checked every single person who's crossed the threshold in the past two years. All employees are thoroughly vetted as a matter of course, every visitor has to go through a security point where a Polaroid is taken and logged on file. We've gone back on everyone right down to the newspaper delivery boys, put private investigators on to many of them. The budget for this just topped a third of a million and climbing.'

'How much are you paying to keep it out of the papers?'

'Nothing. That's one thing we've been terrified of. No more than half a dozen people know about the problem.'

'What about the private investigators?'

He shook his head again, shiny hair swinging. 'They were given a specific brief on each individual, that's all.'

'It was your boys who warned me off at Dunn's place and took me to the seaside yesterday?'

He made an apologetic face. ''Fraid so.'

'I wondered why they'd been so soft on me.'

'Told them not to hurt you.'

'You're too kind, considering I was on your side.'

He shrugged. 'Sorry, Eddie, we simply couldn't risk you stumbling on what had been happening at The Gulf.'

'Why the strong-arm stuff on Martin Corish, then? Was it just for the pictures?'

'What?' He looked genuinely baffled.

'You sent someone else to the Corish Stud yesterday to get those pictures we took at Ascot.'

'What pictures? I haven't a clue what you're talking about.'

I watched him closely, trying to figure out why he'd lie about it. I couldn't think of a reason. 'Do you know Martin Corish?'

'I know of him.'

I explained about our partnership. Candy said whoever called on Martin wasn't sent by him. That narrowed the field. Capshaw was in a one-horse race. I didn't dwell on it with Candy. I wanted time to assemble my thoughts.

He said, 'Can you keep this quiet, Eddie? It'll be worth a lot of money to you.'

'I'd rather find out who killed Brian Kincaid. And Alex Dunn.'

'I'm sure we can do that in time.'

'How much time?'

'As long as it takes to find a cure for these stallions and mares.'

I sat forward. 'Mares?'

Candy rubbed his handsome face again, nodding slowly as he did so. 'Of the mares we've managed to get in foal, seventy-three percent have aborted within days of the pregnancy being confirmed.'

'Seventy-three percent?'

That weary nod again. 'They're still losing them, it's gone on right through the season.'

'Jesus, no wonder you look like shit!'

He let out a huge sigh. 'I've never felt so under pressure in my life, Eddie. Picked exactly the wrong time to saddle myself with a mortgage that would choke a Clydesdale. Bought a holiday home in Barbados just after New Year. Now the boss is looking around at us and all I can see in his eyes is my P45.'

'Spelt in Arabic?'

He found another smile and I admired him for it. I knew I needn't ask about the quality of the veterinary care the horses would have had. The Sheikh could afford the best in the world and that was what had been brought in, or rather the horses had been given false names and taken to the vets in small groups to avoid raising suspicion in the mind of any individual vet. No reason for the infertility had been found, let alone a possible antidote.

If the Arab stallions were suffering from the same affliction as Town Crier and the others, I was in no doubt that the clue to any antidote lay among Dunn's papers and lab samples which had to be somewhere. Whoever was behind this wouldn't want to stop at eight of the Sheikh's stallions.

We talked about Dunn who, until now, hadn't entered Candy's equation. He'd concentrated solely on people who'd had access to The Gulf Stud. He accepted now that there had to be a very strong chance that Dunn or his secret serum had to be involved but the lack of motive troubled him.

'He had close links with Capshaw, didn't he?' I said.

'So?'

'Didn't the Sheikh take all his horses away from Capshaw?'

'That was three years ago.'

'Revenge is a dish best savoured cold, as they say, Candy.'

'Nah, he's not the type – Capshaw's not the type. He knew there was no malice in the horses being taken away.'

'What was behind it?'

He shrugged. 'Simple, the Sheikh was experimenting further in having some of his horses trained in the Middle East. We'd seen definite improvement in the best we'd taken there and the Sheikh wanted to see what would happen by taking a full batch of horses of mixed ability at exactly the same time and preferably from the same stable. The idea was that they should, theoretically, show the same level of improvement.'

'And did they?'

'A large percentage did, quite a few.'

'And you don't think Capshaw would have held a grudge?'

'I know him quite well, Eddie, he was philosophical. We never ruled out sending some horses back to him.'

'And did you?'

'Not so far.'

I looked at him. 'Don't you think he might just have run out of patience?'

Candy sighed. 'Even if we assume he did, do you really think he'd go to all this trouble to stick one up the Sheikh, for the sake of twenty lost training fees? Also, believe me, Alex Dunn has not been near those horses. Thirdly, what about the mares? Was Dunn giving them some sort of serum, too? And if he was, why are ours still aborting after his death?'

I didn't have any answers. Candy looked even more tired and depressed. His brown eyes seemed to have grown duller, as if steadily leaking hope.

'Do you want my help on this?' I asked.

'What I want, what I need more than anything else, Eddie, is for you to keep it quiet. I'm running out of options but I know that the only thing keeping me in a job is the fact that this hasn't got out yet.'

'You've got my word on it.'

He nodded, almost managed a tired smile.

I said, 'Come on, the show ain't over till the fat lady sings.'

He looked at me. 'I think she's doing her final warm-up in the dressing room.'

We talked some more and agreed that it wouldn't be wise for me to be seen at The Gulf Stud. We arranged to meet again next morning and Candy promised to have a full brief with him that would tell me everything they'd done so far.

I expanded on my theory that Dunn hadn't killed himself then asked Candy, 'Can you find out exactly what effect five ccs of prostaglandin would have on a man? I mean, chapter and verse: how it would actually kill him, how long he'd take to die, that sort of stuff.'

'Okay.' He noted it in a small leatherbound book. 'I'll speak to one of the vets and see you back here at noon tomorrow.' I nodded. As he turned to get out I asked about his two henchmen and how much they knew.

'Very little. They don't ask questions.' He grinned.

'What's so funny?' I asked.

'Their names are Phil and Don. I call them the Heaverly Brothers.'

'Most amusing. They were a big hit with me.'

'Sorry, Eddie.' But the grin grew wider and when he left I even managed to find a smile myself.

I drove back at speed, boosted by renewed enthusiasm and relief at no longer having to face cracking this alone. All I needed to find was the link between Dunn and The Gulf Stud, that was the next step. I also felt considerably easier knowing Phil and Don wouldn't be paying me another visit. At least I hoped they wouldn't.

Knowing Candy wasn't the bad guy brought considerable relief and a strong confidence boost. It had to be Capshaw or someone close to him. My only reservation now was Candy's obvious conviction that Capshaw simply wasn't the type. Was the trainer being controlled in the same way Dunn had been?

One thing was certain: someone connected to Capshaw had those blackmail papers. And they had to know that I'd been doing the same as Martin at Ascot, so why no threat to publish still? Maybe the brand they'd left on Martin was meant to scare me off too. And maybe I'd be best pretending for the moment that it had done just that.

Thirty

Back home I told Mother that things looked a good deal brighter. She didn't ask for details, just made her way steadily upstairs to tell Father, offer this dose of psychological medicine. I just wished stocks of it were much higher.

I called Charlie Harris, the racecourse photographer, who agreed to send me copies of all the pictures he'd taken at Ascot the day we'd been there. Then, still convinced that Dunn was a key figure, I spent the rest of the day and long into the night with his betting records. The bets were broken down between those placed 'live' on course by Dunn and those placed by phone. By the time I met Candy again next day I had an extensive chart showing which courses Dunn had attended on which days over the past ten months.

Candy, informal for once in yellow polo shirt and cream trousers, stared at the hand-written columns stretching over pages and pages. 'What's the point?' he asked.

'Those eight stallions. I need to see their racing records.'

'Why?'

'Because if you're convinced that security hasn't been breached at The Gulf by Dunn or an accomplice, then Dunn must have got at those stallions on the racecourse.'

'Impossible.'

'Why? Each of the stallions had to be in the racecourse stables. Dunn would have been one of the few people with legitimate access.'

'To do what? Every one of those stallions was tested for fertility before retirement and just afterwards. Every single one was satisfactory at the least. If anything was administered to them it would have to have been after they'd finished racing.'

'But you've already said it was impossible for anyone to get at them once they'd entered the stud. You can't have it both ways, Candy. Now let me follow this hunch. Get me those racing records.'

He stared at me as though he wasn't sure he trusted my judgement.

I said, 'Come on, you've been negative for too long.'

His expression softened. 'Okay. Fair enough. You'll have them tomorrow.'

'Today. Ring me with them later.'

'No, it's not safe to talk on the phone.'

'Ring me from a call box.'

'I'll think about it. You'd better have a look at this first.' He opened his black briefcase and pulled out a grey laptop computer. He punched a series of buttons, eased the screen back to a reading angle and sat the computer on my lap. 'When you're ready to start reading hit that button, but as soon as the text starts scrolling up you have to concentrate hard to take everything in. You can't go back to something you've missed because as each line moves up the screen it's deleted. No copies of it can be printed out and it's a real pain setting it up to run again. It's a complete record of what has happened and what steps we've taken.'

I nodded, bemused, then hit the start button and concentrated like a man with a DIY vasectomy kit.

Most of it was unabsorbable: dates, times and results of veterinary tests on horses with annoyingly similar Arab names, employee biographies including some fairly detailed sexual histories and one sudden death, monies paid out to various 'contractors', including Phil and Don. And all the time the words disappeared off the top of the screen as though some invisible harvester was scything them line by line. After God knows how long I was left with just a blank grey void.

Bug-eyed and brain fizzing, I asked Candy who was supposed to benefit from this blizzard of information.

'I told you, it's a complete record.'

'But what use is it?'

'It logs everything that's happened, everything we've done.'

'Oh, I must have missed that part, the bit about what you've done. If this is it, Candy, you've done nothing. You're no further forward. No wonder the old Sheikh's spitting sand. If you can't blind them with science, baffle them with bullshit. Is that the principle?'

He looked miffed. 'The principle is to keep the whole thing under wraps, and that's what we've achieved.'

I sighed and leaned back in my seat. 'My old mum found out more yesterday morning than you guys have in all the months this covers. You should have brought someone in ages ago, someone who knew what they were doing.'

'Eddie, it's too sensitive and you know it.'

He was getting really huffy now but I was angry that all this money had been spent on vets and tests and badly briefed private investigators. Angry that I was still pretty much where I'd been two days ago. I'd expected Candy to have some serious stuff offering good leads. He reached across and snapped the lid closed on the computer then took it from my lap and stuffed it back into the case.

We sat in silence, giving each other time to cool off. Candy's window was open. I rolled mine down and the car sucked in a breeze that ruffled Candy's thick hair. He pushed it back into place and stared out at the trees.

One coldly reported fact that had scrolled past my eyes was the death of another vet. It stuck in my mind. I said, 'The vet who died, did they do a post mortem?'

'Heart attack so far as we know.'

'How old was he? What was his name again?'

'Simon Nish. He was thirty-four.'

'And he specialised in mares?'

'Uhuh. He was good.'

'But he didn't know what was making them abort?'

'No. It got him down badly.'

'Did he have a history of heart trouble?'

'Not that I know of. Why?'

'I don't know. It's young for a heart attack.'

'Not these days. I'm due about three myself.'

I looked across and smiled. Candy did too and that eased the tension. We talked some more about Simon Nish who'd been found dead in bed at home just over two weeks ago. 'Definitely natural causes? No question of suicide?'

'Nope. Poor bugger probably died of exhaustion. He tested those mares to distraction, had his arm inside so many of them in was unusual to see him without a mare's arse attached to his shoulder.'

Blood Ties

'And he had nothing to do with the stallions?'
'Nothing.'
'Never went near them?'
'What difference would it make if he did? He was trusted. He'd been with us for years.'
'I'm not slagging him off, Candy, I'm just trying to eliminate the possibility of him having been killed off as Dunn was.'
'He had absolutely no connection with Dunn.'
'Can you double check that?'
'I don't need to!'
'Candy, we're all on the one side here. Please just double check it. Today if you can, and tell me tonight when you're confirming those stallion racing records.'
He bit his lip then nodded. Much more used to giving orders than obeying them, he was finding the adjustment tough. 'Did you get the details on the prostaglandin injection?' I asked.
He looked baffled.
'The thing that killed Dunn,' I said.
'Oh, yes. I spoke to one of our vets this morning.' He produced a black Dictaphone and pressed the rewind button then clicked to play, releasing the tinny voices. Candy first: 'How would an injection of five ccs of prostaglandin affect a human being?'
A slightly effeminate voice in which I could almost hear the flinch replied: 'Pretty grimly, I should think. Death would come from internal suffocation. First you would feel sick, sweat heavily . . . the skin would turn very white as the shock effect hit the body. The chest, abdominal, and all other smooth muscle groups would contract, causing bronchial spasms then severe vomiting and diarrhoea. As intense pressure built, the heart rate would increase rapidly and the system would quickly suffocate and cease functioning.'
'Painful.'
'Agonising, I would guess.'
'How long before he'd die?'
'Three, maybe five, minutes.'
'Not the way you'd choose to go?'
'As the saying goes, I'll settle for being caught in bed with a young woman at the age of eighty-seven, shot by her jealous husband.'

171

Candy clicked it off. I looked at him. 'Still think Dunn wasn't deeply involved in this?'

'I'm coming round. We just need something more solid.'

'Call me as soon as you can with those racing records, that's the next step.'

He rang from a call box just before 7 that evening and I noted the information on the racecourse appearances of the eight infertile stallions.

'What about the dead vet, Simon Nish? Definitely no links with Dunn?'

'Absolutely none.'

We agreed to meet in the lay-by next morning at 8.15.

Thirty-one

A thick bright mist rolled over the flatlands. I drove through it, slowing automatically even though it reached only to the bonnet, making the car look like some air-cushioned vehicle in a sci-fi movie.

I was ten minutes early but Candy was in the lay-by waiting. I got in his car and smiled. 'We can't keep meeting like this,' I said.

'You're cheery.'

'For good reason, my friend.'

He waited, anticipation in his eyes. I said, 'Your horses had a total of thirty-nine runs in the past eighteen months. Alex Dunn was at the course on every occasion.'

'In an official capacity?'

'I don't know but he was definitely there.'

'But if he wasn't officiating, how would he have got access to the stables?'

'Come on, Candy, the security guys have known him for years. He'd walk into the stables without a question being asked.'

'Mmm. I suppose that's possible. But I still think you're up against it statistically. The guy's job was on the racecourse, he must have been at the races more times than not. I'd have thought it would have been more unusual if he *hadn't* been there the thirty-nine times those horses ran.'

'But . . .'

'*And*, bear in mind that if we're now assuming those colts were got at before they were retired to stud, we're talking about investigating their different trainers, hundreds of stable staff, all the visitors to those yards including other vets . . . It's a fucking nightmare, Eddie!'

I was annoyed. I'd travelled here feeling very positive after working late and hard. I said, 'That doesn't mean you can ignore it. You can't just keep building up reams of facts and

173

figures, Candy. At some point you're actually going to have to take some action.'

'And how do we keep the damn' thing out of the papers then?' He was almost shouting but it was end-of-the-tether stuff rather than anger at me. 'How do we work our way through, our *detailed* way through, all those people and not alert anybody?'

'That's why I'm saying, try it my way first. Believe me, Dunn is a very strong link, we've just got to build on it.'

'How?'

'We need to try and find out for sure if he visited the stables on each of those racedays. You know Peter McCarthy, Jockey Club Security, he'd be able to get the records checked. Every visitor should be logged.'

Candy looked nervous. He said, 'I can't risk making McCarthy suspicious.'

I thought for a minute then suggested he get one of the Sheikh's trainers to request the list. 'Tell him to tell Mac it's for an industrial tribunal hearing against a sacked lad or something. Ask for an additional few days outside those thirty-nine if you like, that'll help throw him off the scent if he does become suspicious.'

He looked at me as though I was crazy. 'Then the *trainer* would be suspicious!'

I sighed with frustration. 'Candy, this is the reason you've got nowhere on this so far. At some point you're going to have to take a calculated risk.'

'It's not mine to take! Can't I make you understand that?'

'Somebody's going to have to bite the bullet. What about the Sheikh himself?'

'No way!'

'Why not? If nobody can make a proper decision without his approval then you're going to have to put it to him.'

He sat staring wide-eyed out of the window as the prospect sank home. I pressed the point. 'Candy, if you don't you'll be sitting here next year with maybe eighteen bloody stallions firing blanks and you no further forward. Believe me!'

He turned to me. 'Why can't *you* ask McCarthy? You know him. I'll make sure you get well paid if you can handle this side of things discreetly.'

'I told you before, I need to keep a very low profile on this. I can't tell you exactly why just now but I do. I'm willing to do anything you need behind the scenes, I'll direct the whole damn' show if you want, but you're going to have to put a degree of trust in some people.'

He was shaking his head slowly. I said. 'Speak to the Sheikh. You can't tell what his reaction is going to be but if you give him an honest summary of where you've got to he will have to accept that something more has to be done, that some risk has to be taken.'

Candy rested his elbow on the car window and chewed at his thumbnail. All that his expression told me was that he wanted the world to go away. I touched his elbow. He turned slowly towards me, handsome face frowning, thumbnail still between his lips.

'Listen,' I said, 'you're fucked anyway, not to put too fine a point on it. Your boss ain't going to put up with this much longer, you admitted that yourself. The worst that can happen is that you bring things forward a month or two.'

I watched his eyes change as it seemed to dawn on him that I was right. The frown faded and something of the old Candy came back with his smile. 'You're right, Eddie. What the hell? The job's not worth it anyway. I can do without it. I'll always work.'

'Of course you will, but don't admit defeat just yet. We can crack this if the Sheikh will give you a bit more of a free hand. When can you speak to him?'

'Tonight. I speak to him every night.'

'Good. Will you call me when you've talked?'

'Sure.'

I spent the rest of the day in my room trying to make a more detailed analysis of each horse's run, looking for some sort of pattern. If my theory was right and Dunn was treating these horses in advance of their retirement to stud then whatever he was using had to be bloody powerful stuff. I found one colt who went ten months between his last appearance on a racecourse and the announcement of his retirement. How the hell could Dunn's serum or whatever it was remain effective so long? And why were the horses showing up so positively in fertility tests well after Dunn must have got at them?

The more I had to confront these facts, the shakier became my belief that I was right. As night fell and weariness set in I began losing my taste for the whole bloody business. I took a break and rang Martin to see how he was. Fiona answered and

175

told me he hadn't been sober since I'd left. I tried to reassure her. 'He'll come round, it's just his way of dealing with things.'

'He's killing himself,' she said flatly.

'I'll come and see him soon.'

'Don't, you'll just scare him. The thought of seeing you scares him. He told me that.'

I sighed. 'Okay, just keep me in touch with how he is.'

'All right.'

'You haven't had any more . . . er . . . visits?'

'No. Have you?'

'Not yet. Maybe they're assuming I'll learn from Martin's experience.'

'And will you?'

'What do you think, Fiona?'

'I think you've got a death wish.'

'That's reassuring.'

She said nothing. I said goodnight and wondered what went on in the girl's mind.

Just after ten Candy rang and what he told me picked me up again. Sheikh Ahmad Saad had agreed to give him a much freer hand and had even volunteered to take a more active part himself. The Sheikh was a Jockey Club member and rather than having to ask McCarthy for that list of stable visitors, the Sheikh was going to request it himself via McCarthy's boss. No one would dream of asking the Sheikh for a reason so confidentiality would be maintained.

Candy reckoned they'd have the list by tomorrow afternoon.

Thirty-two

He had it before 11.30 and brought it with him for our daily meeting. I could tell by the satisfied look on his face as I sat beside him in the car that he'd come up with something. He handed me the list of stable visitors. On every one of the thirty-nine the name Alex Dunn appeared, gleaming in a broad yellow stroke of highlighting ink.

We smiled widely at each other and he reached over to shake my hand. 'Well done.'

'All in a day's work,' I said.

'What next?'

'That depends on your priorities. We need to find out what Dunn did to those colts, and we need to find out who was behind it.'

'How do you know he wasn't acting alone?'

'Well, what do you think? The guy couldn't even control his gambling habit. How's he supposed to plan something like this? I mean what we're talking about is the virtual destruction of the Sheikh's empire.'

'You think that was the objective?'

'It seems favourite. We've got this far pretty much on assumptions so let's assume that it is.'

'Fine, but there's a difference between objective and motive. *Why* would anyone want to bring the Sheikh down? Hah! I could answer my own question, I suppose. If those who are jealous of the Arabs qualify as suspects there's enough of them out there to cover Newmarket Heath. Six deep.'

'I think we're talking hatred rather than jealousy here.'

'Okay, three deep.'

'Is it really that bad?'

'Almost. They were all quick enough to welcome the Arabs ten years ago when the poor sods didn't have much of a clue about the game. The trough was suddenly full of snouts and there was a long waiting list. Now that the Sheikh and the others have wised up and taken control of their own businesses, and their own money, suddenly they're the worst thing that ever happened to racing. They're killing it. The Press are against them, trainers, bloodstock agents, sales companies, superstar jockeys now retainerless . . . but when they were getting a million a year they thought the sun shone out of the Sheikh's djellaba.'

'Trainers,' I said. 'Capshaw. He's got to be the next logical step. Dunn did a lot of work for Capshaw and as far as I know spent time at his place. He also spent a lot of his money backing Capshaw's runners and maybe that was part of the deal. Maybe Capshaw gave him information in exchange for damaging those horses.'

'You honestly think Dunn would try to destroy a multi-million pound business for the sake of a few tips from a trainer?'

'Don't underestimate the desperation of the compulsive gambler. I'm sure there would have been cash involved too but inside information would have meant a lot to Dunn.'

A big green van pulled into the lay-by and edged past our cars to park fifty yards in front. We both stopped talking and watched the driver's door. Nobody got out.

Candy said, 'Well, if you don't think Dunn had the ability to organise this campaign then I'm telling you that Capshaw didn't either. I know him well, he's not up to it.'

I shrugged. 'Fine, so someone else is. But that still makes Capshaw the next link in the chain. It was after we followed him at Ascot that Martin was attacked and the pictures taken from him. Now if Capshaw or some of his cronies didn't set that up, who did? We've got to find out more about him, more about his personal life, his past history.' I made a mental note to chase Charlie Harris for those pictures.

'Okay, I'll get someone on to it this morning. Anything else we should be doing?'

'What about Dunn? This chemical castration idea he first had years ago, he must have discussed it with other vets, surely?'

'Maybe.'

'If we could even find out the basis of it, the particular chemical he had in mind back then, it might help us solve the second problem more quickly – the main problem I suppose, when you think about it. Even if we never catch the people behind this, at least with an antidote the stallions would be back to normal.'

'If only.'

We sat in silence for a while then I said, 'Bear in mind that if this is someone who hates the Sheikh enough he probably hasn't finished yet. Maybe he's already got somebody else out there. If not, he's probably looking to recruit a replacement for Dunn.'

Candy nodded, looking grim as the implications sunk in.

I said, 'Get a man on Dunn's past too if you can. And maybe somebody could check with removal companies to see if any of them picked up stuff from his place out at Six Mile Bottom. It would be nice to know where all his lab kit and papers are now. That would cut through a hell of a lot of the crap.'

'Leave it with me.' Candy noted it in his little leather book then said, 'What are you doing for the rest of the day?'

'I'm going back to bed to try and give my brain a rest. I haven't had a decent sleep for weeks. Then I'm going to go for a long sweaty run in the hope that a few more pieces get jogged into place. Can you give me a call this evening if there's anything to report on Capshaw and Dunn?'

'It'll be a bit early.'

'Let me know anyway, even if it's something that seems insignificant.'

'Okay.'

Back at the stud I rang Charlie Harris, got his answerphone, and asked him to send those Ascot shots as soon as possible.

I lay in bed in that small quiet room and tried to get my mind to rest. I felt badly in need of even an hour's peaceful dreamless sleep but none came. Just a constant barrage of thoughts and fears and strange emotions as I waited for that feeling of being at home in my parents' house. Instead I felt more alienated, more alone, than when I'd lived by myself.

The strong sun found each chink in the curtains and I watched the rays reach towards me till I felt like a corpse laid out in a funeral parlour. Sighing heavily, I got up and put on my running gear. Leaving by the back door I headed across the fields into the woods, building up a steady head of steam till I was travelling at a pace I knew I could maintain for miles.

And I started yet again to dissect the scraps of information in my mind. I had the niggling feeling that I'd overlooked something or misinterpreted it so I mentally broke down the structure I'd built and tried to look again at each of the individual pieces. The steady rhythm of my feet on the forest floor seemed to help the process.

Most of my discussions with Candy had been centred on the conspiracy against the stallions and the potential commercial fallout. The deaths of Brian Kincaid and Alex Dunn had somehow faded into the background. My guess now was that Brian had simply been unlucky that I'd approached him for help with Town Crier.

Dunn had been his mentor to a large extent and Brian would have known of Dunn's interest in chemical castration and sought his help to solve Town Crier's problem. Recalling Dunn's frightened reaction the day I confronted him at Newmarket, Brian's sudden approach must have panicked him completely. If Dunn had blabbed about Brian to whoever was running this, the decision to kill him must have been taken quickly.

What effect that would have had on Dunn I didn't know. He must have had some affection for Brian and maybe at first believed the sauna death was an accident. What if he later came to a different conclusion? Would he have been horrified at Brian's murder? Terrified? Would he have planned to go to the police? Was that why he disappeared so suddenly? Was he removed from the equation, kept alive for as long as he was useful then killed off like Brian?

Towards the southern edge of the forest long shafts of sunlight found their way through the tall trees, slicing my moving shadow into fragments.

Brian Kincaid. Whoever was running things hadn't killed him personally. He had hired someone to do it. I'd been so blinkered about Tranter, so convinced he'd been the killer, I'd never really given the matter any objective thought. As I did so now I realised how stupid I'd been. The fact that Brian had died in a sauna in the weighing room narrowed down the potential murderers dramatically.

Whoever killed him must have been fairly well known on the racecourse. At Stratford at the very least but more probably around the other courses too. Jockeys and valets, trainers and racecourse officials, were the only ones entitled to use the weighing room area. The changing room itself was restricted to jockeys and their valets though the sauna at Stratford was in the main body of the building itself, or had been until someone, probably Brian's killer, burned it down.

So, if it wasn't Tranter which, because of his alibi with a senior Steward, I had to accept, then it was another jockey, trainer, valet or official. A simple check back on the newspapers or racecard for that day would tell me almost every one of the above who'd been at Stratford. Valets would be difficult but if pushed I could probably come up with most of their names from memory.

I decided to cut the run short but made up for it by a sharp increase in pace as I turned to head back again, keen to check that Stratford card.

Such a modern contraption as a shower was unheard of in my parents' house and I had to settle for a cool bath before changing into jeans and a white T-shirt. I called Candy but got his answerphone. I left a message then drove into town to find a betting shop.

The manager agreed to dig through his file copies of the *Sporting Life* till he found the one from Stratford that day. I took it to the local library, photocopied the section I needed then returned it. I had no inclination to do any more work in that small cell of a room back at the stud so I set off for the library again where I settled in the reading room to study the Stratford card from that day.

Working through the list of trainers and jockeys, I tried the simple method of rejecting those I considered incapable of murder. It didn't take long to go through the card without ticking even one suspect. I then tried going through again and awarding points in a sort of Man Most Likely To Murder game, nobody notched up more than three.

Next I did racecourse officials but apart from the two who scored very highly on boring people to death I came up almost empty again. Valets were about the only ones whose names weren't published so, using pen and pad, I worked through a list in my head. I came up with the names of six valets, all of whom I'd known for years. I'd have bet my life none would have killed a cat, never mind Brian Kincaid.

And yet somebody among all the people I'd just discounted must have killed him. A stranger may have been able to gain access to the weighing room for a few minutes before being rumbled but no way would he have been able to get to the sauna and, indeed, spend some time inside as he must have done with Brian.

But wait, Brian would have gone in there after the last race. People would be packing up and heading home, rushing around. Maybe a stranger would have got further than usual at that time. The valets would be the guys to talk to. Their duties made it almost certain that they were the last to leave the weighing room on every racecourse. I made a list of the names and resolved to get contact numbers for them as soon as possible.

That too would have to be done through Candy as I still couldn't risk putting my head above the parapet. Outside the library I tried him again on my mobile. Still on answerphone. I tried to reach Candy ten times over the next two hours without success and after hearing the start of his answerphone message yet again, I shouted out in rage and frustration and threw my mobile phone into the small metal waste bin in my room.

This reliance on someone else was really beginning to piss me off. I was finding it very tough to handle the fact that I couldn't simply ring up someone I wanted to ask a question of or jump in the car and go to the races and speak to whoever I wanted.

Candy finally contacted me that evening with nothing new to report. Still annoyed at him, I complained that I hadn't been able to reach him all day and he got spiky, saying he still had a business to run and couldn't sit around waiting for me. It developed, as I'd known it would, into a childish argument fuelled solely by my frustration. In the end I apologised and explained why I was so wound up.

Candy said, 'Don't worry, I can get one of my guys to speak to all the valets that were at Stratford, see what they remember.'

'Which guy?'

'One of the investigators who's been working for me.'

'Racing man?'

'Well, no, but he knows his stuff.'

'Come on, Candy, you know what its like. Valets are hardly going to be falling over themselves to tell him what they know. And not just valets, everyone else. Shit, you know how secretive racing people can be!'

'Well, just what else do you suggest? Why don't *you* go and do it?'

'I've told you, I *can't* fucking do it!' Bitter frustration again. I apologised immediately.

'Forget it, Eddie. I know you're under pressure.'

'I'm sorry, Candy. I'll tell you about it when this is all over.'

'Eddie, promise me it's nothing that will affect your confidentiality on this?'

'I promise. Don't worry, I promise.'

There was a long pause then Candy said quietly, 'You okay?'

'Yeah.' I didn't sound okay and I knew it. 'I'll call you tomorrow.'

I flipped the phone closed and laid it down on the peach-coloured quilt then sat rocking back and forth till I ended up elbows on knees, head in hands, almost crying with frustration in this big silent loveless house, feeling my life dry up, feeling this place and my parents sucking the life from my every pore, killing me slowly but just as surely as that terrible sauna had done to Brian Kincaid.

Unable to face the night in this place I shoved a few things in an overnight bag and left, stopping only briefly at the bottom of the stairs to consider invading the sanctuary of my father's room. My father's world . . . that's what it had become since I'd moved in. His own little planet that imprisoned my mother now, making sure I was kept circumnavigating it forever, cut off from all affection. Lost in space.

I drove into Newmarket, booked a hotel room, went on a pub crawl, got as drunk as ten men and opened my eyes in the morning with a blank mind and a major headache.

Unable to stomach breakfast, I paid my bill and left to take a long walk up on to the gallops to try and clear my head. It was one of those hangovers where your brain is two seconds behind everything else that's happening to you and after an hour I decided that the best place for me was back in bed.

Praying I wouldn't be stopped and breathalysed, I drove back to my parents' place. As I approached the stud I became aware of a flashing blue light through the trees. When I was a hundred yards from the drive an ambulance pulled out from it and, light still flashing, accelerated away towards Cambridge. I swung fast and hard into the drive, jumped out and ran towards the house, cursing my shaking hands as I tried to separate the front door key from the others.

I leaned hard on the bell with my shoulder as I fought to find the key. Finally inside I ran upstairs. My father's room was empty, the door open, bedcovers pulled back. If he was gone, Mother would be with him. I rushed downstairs and back outside, pulling the door behind me to slam hard against the jamb.

Within five minutes I'd caught up with the ambulance. I trailed it all the way to Cambridge Hospital.

Thirty-three

Pneumonia, they said. Almost certainly pneumonia but they'd have to run a few tests before offering a prognosis. We sat in the waiting room. Mother looked as though she'd aged ten years. Distraught but silent she stared at the wall, deaf to whatever words of comfort I offered. After a while I just sat in silence beside her, suffering an appalling thirst and a burning headache and a scorched conscience for not being there when I was needed. Ashamed too that I was sitting with my mother, at this time of the morning, unkempt and unshaven and stinking of booze.

But even at my lowest ebb I couldn't find any real sorrow or sympathy for my father, nor any guilt that they were missing. It crossed my mind that he might die and that caused me no dismay whatever, the opposite in fact, which did make me feel a twinge of coldness. But no guilt.

After more than two hours a doctor invited us into a small office and told us that Father would have to stay in hospital for a considerable length of time.

'How long?' I asked.

'Six weeks, maybe more. He is very weak. His lungs are badly infected.'

'Will he die?' Mother asked. I looked at her to see if she was really prepared for the answer. She was staring at the young doctor with intense concentration.

'If he responds to treatment he has an excellent chance of returning to full health.'

'Is there any reason he shouldn't respond to treatment?' she asked.

'Occasionally it happens.'

'When will we know?'

He smiled. 'Within a week or so.'

Mother straightened in her chair. 'I'd like to stay with him.'

185

'I'm afraid that would be difficult, certainly in the early stages. Your husband will be treated in ICU – sorry, the Intensive Care Unit. We simply don't have the staff to cope with twenty-four-hour visiting.'

'When would normal visiting hours be?' I asked.

'Two till three in the afternoon, six-thirty till seven-thirty in the evening, though that would be dependent on the patient's condition.'

I looked at Mother who was staring past him now, into the distance, the future, her eyes clouding with misery. I thanked the doctor and helped her out. Dazed, she leant heavily on me all the way back to the car. I took her home, promising to bring her back as soon as she'd packed what she needed. I told her I'd find her a room in a hotel close to the hospital so that she could spend as much time with Father as the hospital would allow.

This financially rash promise brought to mind the image of my irate bank manager rushing from the little cupboard, hands on hips, staring at me like I was a lunatic. Six, eight, ten weeks of hotel bills. Whatever fee Candy was going to pay would have to be good.

My mother spoke little, just moved silently around the house looking at things, touching small ornaments, gazing through the back window across the fields. It was almost as if she expected this to be the last time she'd ever see this place. Eventually she wandered upstairs and I heard her go into my father's room. I knew then what I had to do.

After ten minutes I walked into the room to find her sitting in her usual chair, staring at the bed. I put my hand on her shoulder. She didn't acknowledge me. I said, 'Come on, Mum, I've made some tea. We have to talk.' I led her gently to the kitchen and sat her down at the big beech table.

I stirred sugar into her tea and pushed it across to her. She stared into the swirling liquid. 'Drink some,' I said. 'It'll help.'

She lifted the cup and sipped mechanically. After another silent minute she looked at me and said, 'It's the pressure of this that's killing him.' We both knew what 'this' meant. And although she added nothing it was implicit in her eyes that she thought I should somehow have done something to prevent it, to catch the people who might expose us, to make the future safe.

I said, 'I know, Mum. I have to find whoever's doing this.'

She nodded slowly, robotically, and sipped tea again, and I decided that when we got back to the hospital I'd ask that she be checked for shock. I drank some tea then said, 'Listen, Mum, the way we decided to do this, to lie low, make it look as if we'd pulled out – it's not going to work.'

She raised her tired eyes again to watch me almost like a disinterested observer.

I said, 'It's causing too many complications, taking too long. It could drag on for months and months and . . . and I'm not sure Father can stand it that long. I think I'm going to have to go for these people, all out. Now. That way we either stop them quickly or at least we get the painful part over with as soon as possible.'

Her look changed to one I recognised, one which said, *You don't understand, do you?*

She spoke. 'It will never be over with, Edward, not if it gets out. People will never let it be over with. It would kill your father.'

I leaned towards her, badly wanting to take her hand, squeeze some reassurance into it. 'Mum, it's killing him now, slowly and painfully. The waiting's killing him. The tension.'

I could see by her face she knew I was right, and followed up. 'I'm sure I've got enough to go on now to crack this in a couple of weeks at the most.'

That was a lie but one I could live with. She said. 'Would we have to tell him?'

That was for her to answer. I said, 'If we didn't, and the news did get out, could you live with it if he thought you'd . . .' deceived was the wrong word '. . . kept it from him?'

She gave the smallest of shrugs and her expression changed. She was trying to convey something with her eyes but I just couldn't read it. She spelt it out. 'Maybe he would think you'd kept it from both of us.'

My heart sank. I said, 'Will there ever be a point in my life where you'll want him to see me in a fair light? Is it always going to be me that's to blame for everything that's gone wrong in this family?'

She just stared stony-faced at me and I knew that so long as he was alive my father would be all that mattered to her. So I resolved then to do it with or without their approval, knowing full well that the whipping boy was on another hiding to nothing.

As I left I saw that the Ascot pictures had come in the post. I picked up the thick envelope and took it with me.

Thirty-four

I found a small hotel within a five-minute taxi ride of the hospital, booked my mother in, wrote the wide-eyed proprietor a cheque for a thousand pounds, and promised Mother I'd ring every night at the very least and try to make the visiting hours whenever I could. She said no more about our earlier conversation but I could tell she knew I was now going for broke.

I'd cleaned myself up before leaving the stud and although my hangover still simmered, the prospect of action started the adrenalin pumping again. I felt good. Nervous but good. I called Candy, got him first time.

'I'm coming out of the closet,' I said.

'Meaning?'

'You've got yourself another private dick.'

'No comment.'

I smiled. 'Candy, can you arrange an advance on my fee for this?'

'Sure. How much?'

'Five grand.'

'Is that the advance or the fee?'

'The advance.'

'You don't work cheap.'

'I don't think it'll make too much of a dent in the third of a million you've already spent on this.'

'True. Very true.'

'Can you transfer it direct to my bank today? I'd like it to catch a cheque that's about to drop from a great height.'

'Give me your bank details.'

I called McCarthy next. 'Thought you'd died,' he said when he heard my voice.

'Felt like it when I woke up this morning.'

'Mr Booze?'

'That's the man.'

'Well, you should be sleeping it off so why are you calling me?'

'I'm back on the Brian Kincaid case.'

He sighed. 'Eddie, the case is that the police could find no evidence of suspicious circumstances.'

'On account of that evidence being reduced to a very fine grey ash.'

'Maybe, but what were they supposed to do next?'

'What I'm about to do, if you can give me a little help?'

'A little or a lot?'

'I need the names of all the valets working at Stratford that day, just by way of a double check.'

'Why?'

'Because I want to speak to them.'

'Why?'

'Because I think one of them, at least, might to able to tell me something.'

'You're in one of your determined moods again, aren't you?'

'Make a bulldog look meek.'

That sigh again, of resignation this time, and he promised to get back to me within a couple of hours. It took a bit longer but by early-evening I had eight names, six of whom I knew well. I reckoned at least four of the eight would be at Uttoxeter next day. I decided against calling any of them to check. I'd turn up at the track tomorrow and see how they reacted to a few informal questions.

I'd packed an overnight bag and decided to head back to Shropshire and stay overnight at the flat. High time I checked in with Charles Tunney. He had been due back from Alaska yesterday though I knew he planned to bring the horses back in just two or three at a time. We wouldn't have any runners for weeks.

I headed north, stopping only to call my mother at the hotel. She still sounded dazed. Father was no better, no worse. I promised to call tomorrow.

There was just a tinge of pink left in the western sky as I rolled into the yard and it was good to see lights glowing, yellow and welcoming, in the big house again. Charles was in his usual chair by the inglenook fireplace when I went in, a half glass of whisky in his fist and a few more pounds of fat around his waist. His beloved

Mahler was playing softly in the background and his face told me that the current drink wasn't his first.

His eyes seemed to twinkle when he saw me and he lurched forward, pushing himself out of the big comfy chair with some difficulty. 'My dear Eddie! How good to see you! How the hell've you been?'

I reached to shake the offered hand, grasped it more warmly than I thought I would have. 'Good to see you too, Charles. You're looking very well.'

He slapped his belly. 'Too well.'

'I guess they sell chips and burgers in Alaska too.'

He laughed and flopped back into his chair. 'Great food but some bloody ugly women. Fix yourself a drink and I'll tell you about them.'

I fixed it and he did.

I don't think I can remember going to Uttoxeter on a dry day. The rainclouds must see my car coming from a long way off and hurry over to the course to guarantee me the usual wet welcome. Today was no different though trainers and owners travelling in the same direction would have no complaints about the weather. It had been a long dry summer with firm ground the rule rather than the exception.

Most trainers preferred good or soft going before risking their horses. Galloping and jumping on jarring ground can damage a horse's legs for months.

As I pulled into the carpark I glanced around at the back seat to check that I had indeed brought my riding gear. I'd nothing booked but it sometimes paid to come prepared. There were still two hours before the first and most of the valets would be fairly relaxed.

It is their job to look after a jockey's kit, make sure it's kept clean, that saddles, girths and stirrups are safe, that the correct amount of weight is loaded into the saddle 'cloths' if necessary.

They also act as friends, confessors, marriage guidance counsellors, hairdressers, denture finders, bankers, and God knows what else. The camaraderie in the changing room can be as addictive as the most powerful drug. Many valets are ex-jockeys, still as hooked as they will be all their lives.

Half a dozen of them were already there making preparations. Two of them had been at Stratford. I filled three Styrofoam cups from the tea urn and went to join them in the corner.

We chatted amicably for a few minutes then I steered the conversation round to Brian Kincaid's death. They were happy to talk about that day at Stratford and answered my questions openly but neither had seen anything they'd have called suspicious; no strangers hanging around, no odd behaviour from any of the other jocks. And neither could remember any particular racecourse official showing his face, though that was asking a bit much of them.

While we were talking two of the other valets who'd been at Stratford turned up and I managed to grab five minutes with each of them though I learnt nothing new. Before leaving I spoke to all four again, asking which of them had been the last to leave the racecourse that day. Pete Crilly, who was my valet, said the only person still in the weighing room when he'd left had been Ken Rossington, also known as Oz.

I didn't know Rossington as well as the others. He'd been a valet for just over a year after arriving in Britain from Australia. He was a bit of a practical joker, always looking to create a laugh at someone's expense, but he seemed a nice enough guy. Crilly said that Rossington had told him on Monday he was having a few days off but that he was fairly sure he'd be at Bangor on Saturday. This was Thursday. Nobody could give me his phone number.

Something about Rossington came back to me. That day at Stratford when Brian had moved aside to let Tranter past, he'd stood on Rossington's foot and the valet had made a considerable song and dance of it. If Rossington had been that close there was every chance he would have heard Brian say he was planning to use the sauna after racing.

I picked up a spare in the fifth which finished nowhere but jumped well enough for me to enjoy the ride round. The riding fee more than paid my expenses for the day and the rain stayed off during the race only to resume as I drove home, wipers swishing at double speed and still not coping.

Ten minutes from the yard my mobile rang. It was Candy. He had the reports on both Capshaw and Dunn. 'Anything interesting?' I asked.

'Not really, unless you can see something I haven't spotted.'

'Are the reports actually in written form?'
'All neatly typed. Six pages on each.'
'I'll be at the yard shortly, can you fax them to me?'
'Is that safe?'
'If you make sure you dial the right number it will be.'
'Okay, what is it?'
I told him.

Thirty-five

The reports were hanging from the fax machine when I got back and I started reading while the kettle boiled. Candy had been right. Nothing that was new in the reports was of any real interest, just gossip, mostly about Capshaw. Dunn seemed to have led a solitary life. His father had also been a compulsive gambler who had achieved the impossible by quitting for good after a major win. Dunn hadn't been so lucky.

I called Candy back.

'Well?' he asked.

'Dross.'

'I thought so. What next?'

'Good old-fashioned legwork.' I told him about Rossington the valet and that I was planning to see him at Bangor. Then I talked again about my gut feeling that Capshaw was the key to the way forward. I'd been putting a scheme together in my mind over the last twenty-four hours. I told Candy what it was and asked him to start preparing for it. He said, 'You know how to make a bloke nervous, Eddie.'

'All in a good cause. Start practising. And listen, I need you to look through some pictures of the people Capshaw was with at Ascot, see if you can identify any of them.'

'Fine, whenever you're ready.'

I couldn't wait for Saturday's Bangor declarations on Teletext. Crilly had told me the jockeys that Rossington looked after. Enough of them were engaged at Bangor to make it almost certain that Rossington would be there.

That night I gave the whisky a miss and rose early next morning to run five miles through the mist-covered fields. At 11 I set off through north Shropshire, heading for Bangor-on-Dee Racecourse. I was there in less than an hour and found Rossington

193

already in the weighing room, spit-polishing a boot slipped over his arm.

'Hi,' I said.

'Hi, Eddie, how are you?'

'I'm okay. You?'

'Good fettle.' He swiped a shine into the long black boot with the red-banded top. 'Don't know why they don't make these buggers all the one colour, you know, it would make life a damn' sight easier for us guys.' He stopped polishing, leaned forward, his sandy-coloured fringe dropping into his eyes as he winked at me. 'Not that I'm complainin', Eddie, know what I mean?'

I wasn't quite sure that I did but I let it go. 'Did you have a good break?' I asked. He looked puzzled. 'Pete Crilly told me you were taking a few days off.' For just a microsecond I thought anger sparked in his eyes though I couldn't be certain. He polished harder. 'Just caught up on my kip,' he said. 'Too many late nights, early mornings and long trips. To racecourses, I mean.'

I hadn't thought he meant anything else. Rossington seemed nervous talking to me. It was the first time I'd really said more than hello or goodbye to him and I simply didn't know whether he was always like this when the lads weren't around to be entertained or if he was actually hiding something.

I pressed on and asked him about Stratford and Brian Kincaid. He polished harder, his voice flat as though he had to make a conscious effort to keep it steady. And he wouldn't meet my eyes.

After a minute talking about Brian he seemed to settle again, become calmer.

'Did you see him go into the sauna?' I asked.

'Can't say as I did, I'm afraid.'

'Were you around quite late that day?'

'Not that I can remember, no later than usual.'

'Weren't you the last to leave?'

'No, definitely not. Pete Crilly was still there when I left, I'm sure he was.'

That wasn't what Pete had said but I didn't contradict him. Rossington still wouldn't look at me. He knew something. I thanked him and left to call Candy but got his answerphone. I hung around the weighing room for a while, saw Pete Crilly and briefly considered asking him if he was sure Rossington was the last man left at Stratford.

But he'd been certain on Thursday or he wouldn't have said it and I didn't want him asking Rossington to confirm it. The Australian seemed nervous enough.

The sun shone at Bangor and they got their usual big good-natured crowd. Some courses will always have dedicated horseracing fans, mostly country people, and Bangor is one of them.

I strayed out on to the track to watch the handicap 'chase and refresh my memory on what it felt like to stand by those big black fences as hoofbeats thundered towards you, building up to launch point, to smack and crackle through the top of the birch then land and race away, long bodies stretching, quarters bunching, muscles straining, then gradually silence. My view of the field fading into the distance reminded me of how it felt to fall in a race. As you watched your comrades leave you behind there were always mixed feelings: frustration at having come off, relief at being fit to stand and watch them gallop away.

Candy rang. I told him about Rossington and asked him to find out what he could about the guy, not forgetting he'd spent most of his life in Australia. 'That might take a while.' Candy said.

'I ain't doing anything else in the meantime.'

'Okay.'

'What about our other cunning little plan, have you spoken to the boss?'

'He's given the go ahead.'

'Good, I thought he might. When do we start?'

'Monday. Windsor. I'm not looking forward to it.'

'Into every life a little rain must fall.'

'Except that this time every other bastard's going to be under cover watching me get wet.'

'Pack your shampoo, you can wash that lovely hair of yours.'

'Very funny. It's not you who's going to be humiliated.'

'For me that makes a change, believe me. Call me if you learn anything, especially about Rossington. I'll be back in Cambridge this evening to see my father.'

'How is he?'

'No change. A very long-standing diagnosis.'

'Pardon?'

'Nothing. Maybe we can meet for breakfast tomorrow.'

'Call me this evening when you reach Cambridge and we'll arrange a definite time.'

'Fine.'

I stayed till the fifth then left to beat the traffic. No spare rides but the more I thought about Rossington's reaction, the surer I became that the journey had been worthwhile.

Thirty-six

Only twenty minutes remained of the visiting period when I reached the hospital which didn't dismay me unduly.

Father was sitting up, eyes closed but breathing on his own, albeit through lungs that sounded like decayed organ pipes. Mother was in her customary position by the bed, holding his thin jaundiced-looking hand. She looked more contented than when I'd last seen her. We nodded to each other and I gently placed the fruit I'd brought on the white bedside cabinet.

I mouthed the words, 'How is he?' Mother nodded slowly and quietly but mouthed nothing in return. It was only when we got outside that she told me there had been no real change. She'd decided to treat this as positive news. I offered to take her to dinner but she said she'd rather go back to the hotel to be by the telephone. I took her there then headed back to the stud to spend the night.

Candy didn't think it advisable for us to be seen having breakfast together. We met in our old reliable lay-by where he told me that the feelers were still out on Rossington and that it might be midweek before he'd have any news on him.

It was a warm morning. We rolled the windows down and sat looking through the pictures Charlie Harris had sent me. Most of the shots had been taken either in the parade ring before each race or in the winner's enclosure afterwards. Capshaw's party in the last race featured in nineteen shots, a mixture from the same general pool in each.

Most of the pictures featured the celebrations after the Guterson's Gloves-sponsored race that the company had won with its own horse, trained by Capshaw. Candy pointed to the smiling face of Bob Guterson. 'I've seen him around.'

'Bob Guterson. Owned the winner. Got three others in training with Capshaw.'

He nodded, scanned the other pictures then stopped and held one up to the light. 'See the guy in the corner, grey hair, dark suit?'

I looked. The face was indistinct in the background, slightly out of focus. 'Uhuh?'

'I think that's Simeon Prior. What on earth would he be doing with that lot?'

'Who's Simeon Prior when he's at home?'

'He's the Chairman of one of the biggest sales companies in Europe.'

'Sales?'

'Bloodstock sales. An outfit called Triplecrown.' He squinted closer. 'Could you get this one blown up?'

'Sure. Do you think there's any significance in Prior's being there?'

'They're just not his type, Capshaw and this Guterson, a plastic glove-maker.'

I looked again at the picture. 'Are you sure he is with them? He's standing well away from the main team.'

Candy shrugged. 'I don't know. It just seems odd. He seldom goes racing.'

'You know him well?'

'Not really, met him a couple of times, said hello.'

'I'll get an enlargement done.'

Candy flicked through three more and stopped at one in the parade ring. He smiled and pointed to an attractive blonde woman presenting what I assumed was the prize to the lad for the Best Turned Out Horse in the Guterson's Gloves race. 'Know who that is?' he asked.

I looked. The face was vaguely familiar but I couldn't name her.

'Jean Kerman,' Candy said. 'Mean Jean.'

Kerman was the vicious gossip columnist who specialised in racing exposés. She'd been the one Spindari had threatened us with. 'Is that her?' I asked in surprise.

'She's all right, isn't she?' Candy said. 'Doesn't look poisonous from here.'

'What the hell's she doing presenting the prize?'

'Maybe Mr Guterson just had a right old hooley to celebrate his sponsorship. They normally invite press and celebs, these corporate people.'

Candy was right. Almost every race sponsor has a private box and makes a major day out of it, inviting business contacts and sometimes paying celebrities to come and mix with their guests. The only reason for my suspicion was that Capshaw was in there somewhere. Everyone else in these pictures might well be completely innocent but Capshaw was in deep.

We got out of the car and walked the three hundred or so yards of the lay-by then back again. Candy wore an immaculate fawn suit, pale blue shirt and very expensive-looking shoes. Despite his year-round tan he looked drawn.

'You're not looking forward to tomorrow, are you?' I asked.

'Not in the least.'

'It's for the best, Candy.'

'I know it is.'

'What's the plan?'

'Jidda runs in the first at Windsor. He cost us two point two million, bought on my advice. Wherever he finishes the Sheikh is going to tell the Press he feels he was badly advised, that he paid too much.'

'Even if he wins easily?'

'Yes. He'll do it another two or three times in the coming week till the Press are in no doubt that I'm not flavour of the month.'

'Then the word will spread that you're on your way out.'

He nodded.

'It'll be an interesting experiment, finding out who your friends are, if nothing else.'

'A very clinical summary, Eddie. I wonder if you'd be quite so nonchalant about it if you were the guinea pig?'

'Maybe not. I'm sorry, I didn't mean to make it sound like nothing at all. But everything will be put right once we catch these people. The Sheikh will tell the Press then about the whole plot, won't he?'

'I don't know. I just hope he tells them enough to recover my reputation. What's left of it.'

'Don't worry.'

'Two of the easiest used words in the English language, always spoken by people who have no worries themselves.'

I looked across at him as we walked. His face was grim.

Thirty-seven

By the end of the following week everybody in racing knew that Candy was for the chop. The Racing Press are too protective of their own people to break a story like this but one of the tabloid gossip columns featured a paragraph about the 'unrest', as they put it, between the Sheikh and his Racing Manager, confirming also that Candy had almost three years of a five-year contract to run.

Nothing else happened that week that helped us. Rossington, the Australian valet, came up cleaner than bones from an acid bath, which set me on a path I found distasteful. Using Candy's private investigators to compile personal histories of people had already become a lazy habit. I gave Candy the names of all the racecourse officials and the other valets at Stratford that day and asked for a report on each.

If nothing came of them I wondered how long I'd be able to resist betraying my fellow jockeys in the same way. But Brian's murder was seldom out of my mind now. Unless I accepted that a stranger had somehow not only gained access to the weighing room but had known, one, that Brian would definitely be there after the others had gone and, two, that he'd be in the sauna, the odds were just too long for me to accept such a triple coincidence. It had to be someone who knew him.

I'd called Mac again and pressed him about Tranter's alibi with the Steward and the car crash. I wanted to be absolutely certain that he was out of the picture. Mac assured me he'd had word straight from the mouth of the Steward concerned. He could think of no reason in the world why the man in question would simply have concocted that sort of story.

I suggested that Tranter might have had something on him. Mac said if he did then it hadn't affected the Steward's judgement a week before when he'd stood Tranter down for what some had thought was a minor offence. Fair point.

That brought me back full circle to the conclusion that someone in the weighing room that afternoon killed Brian Kincaid. The alternative was the 'tragic accident' theory but too much had happened before and since for me ever to swallow that. My mind returned to how nervous Rossington had seemed when I first questioned him, and towards the end of what was probably the worst week of Candy's life I met him at the lay-by again and prodded him to get a double check done on the Australian.

'Why do you want another report? We've already done one?'

'A gut feeling. He was uncomfortable when I was questioning him.'

'Eddie, he didn't kill anybody. He's got no history of crime or violence. He worked with sheep and horses in Australia. Came from Melbourne racetrack with good references.'

'Candy, he was nervous!'

'So maybe he's been smuggling fucking kangaroos or something! For Christ's sake, Eddie, gimme a break with these fucking personal profiles! They're costing more than the horses!'

I shut up for a while to let him cool down. Finally he said, 'Sorry Eddie. I didn't mean to blow like that. It's been a bad week.'

'Yeah, my fault. I'm afraid I'm not the most sensitive guy in the world.'

'Look, leave Rossington with me, I'll ask them to have another look.'

'No, it's okay. Just get me the name and number of the guy who compiled that profile. Maybe he can tell me something or give me a few of his sources.'

'It would be best if I had him call you.'

'Fine, give him my mobile number.'

We walked in silence for a while. 'I'm going to see Capshaw tonight,' he said.

'Have you spoken to him?'

'Met him at Sandown yesterday.'

'Does he know what you have in mind?'

'I very much doubt it.'

We got back in the car. Candy sat rigid in the seat for a few seconds then leant forward, elbows on steering wheel, face in his hands.

I said, 'You'll be okay, Candy. You'll pull it off.'

He continued rubbing his eyes and temples, then his hands went down and he sat back, leaning against the headrest and triggering a long sigh. 'You think everybody finds this sort of stuff as easy as you do, Eddie. Why? Why do you think everybody sees things the same way as you, thinks the same way?'

'I don't.'

He turned to me. 'You do. You ought to listen to yourself sometime, watch yourself performing.'

Performing?

I smiled. 'You're performing pretty well yourself this morning, going all prima donna-ish on me. I'm not asking you to play King Lear. Just go to Capshaw's and be convincing, which means being nervous and hesitant and insecure, all the things you're feeling just now anyway. That's what he'll expect, not a command performance. 'Cos you look like a big handsome actor doesn't mean that's what everyone expects you to be.'

He sighed again. Then smiled.

'What time are you seeing him?' I asked.

'Seven-thirty.'

'I'll be in the royal box, cheering you on.'

The plan was that Candy would approach Capshaw and offer him a three-year contract to train ten of the Sheikh's horses. Candy would say that he'd fallen out of favour with the Sheikh and that he thought his employer was going to get rid of him soon but that he still had the power to sign contracts which would have to be honoured or bought off for large amounts.

He'd say that, to take revenge on the Sheikh, he intended to approach five trainers offering this contract on the basis of a fifty-fifty cut from the compensation money when the Sheikh subsequently cancelled. Capshaw was to be the first trainer on his list.

The true purpose of the exercise was to try and flush out the lizards.

We reckoned that if they were still looking for a replacement for Alex Dunn, someone to carry on the sabotage at The Gulf Stud, then they would be sorely tempted to try and recruit Candy, an embittered member of staff with the power to do untold damage personally or else quietly put someone in place who could do it after he'd gone.

I wanted to see Candy as soon as I could after he left Capshaw's place but he was nervous about meeting twice in one day, especially if it meant coming back to the lay-by again. He reluctantly agreed to drive to a derelict farm we both knew within two miles of my parents' stud. I reminded him to take his Dictaphone to Capshaw's.

I'd been waiting at the farm since 8.30, parked behind a half-ruined greystone wall. I stood by the corner of it now and as twilight fell on the empty fields I watched the road half a mile away. By 9.45 I was getting worried about Candy. Maybe Capshaw had twigged the plan and called in the big guns. But how could he have known? There was no way.

The doubts nibbled at me till I saw a car slow and turn down the road towards the farm, headlights bouncing wildly on the uneven track. I waited till I was certain it was Candy before stepping out as he nosed along the weed-strewn drive.

He got out and as he came towards me I noticed how much more relaxed he seemed. The stiffness and tension of this morning had gone from his limbs and he moved like the natural athlete he was. No frown either. He looked pretty pleased with himself.

I smiled. 'It went well, obviously.'

His white teeth flashed in the dusk. 'Hook and line. Sinker maybe tomorrow or the next day.'

'Brilliant.'

We leant on the bonnet of my car and he replayed the tape on his Dictaphone. At first Capshaw had acted almost dumb about Candy's troubles with the Sheikh though I got the impression that his reaction was aimed at not embarrassing Candy. When he realised that the whole subject was the reason for Candy's visit he listened more and talked less. Until, of course, Candy offered him the horses; then he became very animated.

Capshaw cooled a bit as Candy revealed the full plan. He seemed more interested in having the Sheikh's horses back again than collecting a large compensation payment for breach of contract. I warmed to him a bit for that.

But Candy played it smart and said that although the Sheikh might want out of some of the contracts, he did need to place horses with new trainers and there might be a chance, bearing in mind how well Capshaw had taken the Sheikh's previous clearout of his stable, that the Sheikh would let him keep this batch for the full term.

Capshaw began asking about the actual horses Candy planned to give him, their breeding, cost at the sales, etc. Candy said he couldn't really give full details at this stage but promised that, since Capshaw was the first he'd approached, he'd let him have the pick of the bunch.

The trainer's enthusiasm increased a few notches then and it was some time before he seemed to realise that maybe someone else might have an interest in this, at which point he started cooling off. He told Candy he couldn't give him an answer right away. It might be tomorrow, it might be next week. Candy said, of course, don't worry, no problem, and generally left Capshaw with the impression that there wasn't a high degree of urgency. But he did say he couldn't wait longer than a week. Capshaw promised him a call next day.

Candy clicked the tape off and looked at me. 'What do you think?'

'I think that Mr William Capshaw is not the brightest guy in the world. He seemed far too open. I'd have thought he would have showed some suspicion at least. It only confirms to me that someone else is running things. I just wonder what hold they've got over him?'

'Me too.'

We never got to find out. Twenty-four hours later Capshaw was dead.

Thirty-eight

Next day the promised call from Capshaw never came and when we heard early on Wednesday morning of his death, the sense of dejection, almost despair, was palpable. I thought Candy was going to quit on the spot.

Through one of his contacts Candy got hold of a copy of the police report which said that Capshaw had received a call just before 10 on Tuesday night, and immediately told his wife that he had to go out. He gave no reason but promised to be back by midnight.

A police patrol found him dead under his car in the early hours of Wednesday on a straight stretch of road down by Six Mile Bottom. It seemed he'd been changing a punctured wheel on the offside rear when he'd been hit by a passing vehicle which hadn't stopped. The impact had shattered his pelvis, severed his spine and driven the jack out of its support, causing the car to collapse and crush Capshaw's head, pushing his eyes from their sockets and spraying brain matter the width of the road, on to the grass verge and some upwards, where it stuck to and cooked on the hot exhaust pipe.

The police had taken the unusual step of sparing Mrs Capshaw the ordeal of identifying the body and had accepted the head lad's assurance that the corpse was indeed Capshaw's.

The police said they were seeking a dark blue vehicle which very probably had bull bars fitted at the front though they did not think it had been a jeep.

We'd gone through the report back at our derelict farm, standing in the sunshine leaning against Candy's car. He folded the papers and threw them in disgust through the open back window on to the seat. He was angry too about Capshaw's death. He'd quite liked him.

'What now, Batman?' he asked.

'We find out who called Capshaw. Whoever it was must have arranged the rather convenient puncture and equally convenient hit and run vehicle.'

Candy stared and I could see he was baffled by my certainty. I said, 'Between you seeing Capshaw and last night, something obviously happened. Whether he took cold feet and wanted out or our Mr Big decided a wrong decision had been made in even talking to you, who knows, but Capshaw had obviously served his purpose. Whoever the guy is, Capshaw was obviously scared of him, scared enough to go dashing out as soon as he received the call.'

'So how do we find out who made it?'

'Why don't you ask your contact to get hold of the BT records? I'm sure the cops will have requested them already.'

Candy nodded thoughtfully then said, 'The guy's hardly going to be stupid enough to call from his own base.'

'Probably not but who knows?'

'What if this Mr Big, as you call him, approaches me direct now?'

'All the better, but I doubt it.'

We stood in silence for a while then Candy said, 'What if we can't trace the call?'

I shrugged. 'Rulers and pencils out and back to the drawing board.'

'Oh, fine! I feel I've been *pinned* to the drawing board this last week or so and half my fucking life's been erased!'

'No point in giving up now then, is there? Let's get you sketched back in again. We'll see if we can make a better job of you second time around.'

To his credit he managed a smile.

The BT records showed that the call to Capshaw came from a public telephone in Cambridge. Candy became very disheartened. I told him we must press on and try and find out who killed Brian Kincaid at Stratford. The candidates were relatively few and that offered us the best chance of success.

The guy who'd compiled the profile on Ken Rossington called me at Candy's request and we talked about his sources and what he'd found out. Rossington's persona in Australia – reserved, industrious, a private man – sounded quite different from the one he'd adopted when he'd stepped off the plane over a year ago. Unless Qantas had started dishing out personality changes along with the in-flight meals then Rossington had transformed himself virtually overnight into the ebullient practical joker who now inhabited the weighing room.

I knew Rossington had been at Stratford. I knew almost for certain that he was last to leave that day. I knew there was a strong chance he'd overheard Brian mention the sauna. And I knew he'd been distinctly nervous when I raised the subject of Stratford. There was a strong possibility that he knew something about Brian's death. Did he let a murderer have access to or, indeed, did he himself kill Brian?

I wondered where Rossington had been the day Alex Dunn died. I called McCarthy who came back fairly promptly with the information that Rossington had not been racing that day. So he could have been at my parents' stud injecting prostaglandin into Alex Dunn and tying me on to that mare.

Maybe a quiet spot of tailing Mr Rossington for a day or two might pay off. I pestered McCarthy again to find out where he would be next day. Mac was annoyed. 'What's this thing about Rossington, what are you up to now?'

'I'm trying to persuade the guy to admit he was the last man to see Brian Kincaid alive.'

Mac sighed. 'You know, Eddie, when you're an old man walking with a stick, you'll still be tottering around racecourses looking for the fictitious murderer of Kincaid.'

'I know. Tenacious, ain't I?'

'Tendentious, more like.'

'What does that mean?'

'It means partisan, biased, bloody stubborn.'

'I think I like tenacious better.'

Mac called me back within five minutes with the news that Rossington would be at Worcester races next day. 'So will I, then,' I said. 'So will I.'

There's a small public carpark just off the main road as you enter Worcester Racecourse. Most cars drive through it and over the sand crossing the track itself to park in the grassy centre of the course. But it could be a bitch getting back out and I needed to be close to Rossington when he left, so I got there early and found a space in the small carpark.

I saw him a few times throughout the day but did no more than say hello as I passed him. There was a mild degree of apprehension in his face then but I avoided looking at him for the rest of the afternoon, hoping he'd feel steadily more secure.

I never strayed far from the weighing room. If the Aussie came out I wanted to see where he was going. Sod's law was in operation that day and I was offered a ride in the last which I had to refuse as none of Rossington's jocks were in the race and there was every chance he'd leave before or during it.

He didn't, and was among the last to go. The horse I could have ridden got beaten half a length (I reckoned I'd have won on him) and Rossington hung around so long that there was no way I could safely tail him to the official carpark to see which car was his. I left before him and got to my own car where I watched through binoculars till I saw him come walking bow-legged towards his own car, a green Nissan Estate. He slung two obviously heavy bags in the back and seemed to have some trouble opening his driver's door.

Eventually he came trundling out and I had to let him get right on to the main road before following. Rossington lived near Bristol. If that was where he was headed I wouldn't lose him, we were only ten minutes from the M5 and a straight run south.

When we reached the motorway I tucked in a few vehicles behind on the inside lane but the Aussie made life difficult by staying below sixty miles an hour – the only person in racing who didn't drive everywhere at full tilt.

After twenty miles or so he began varying his speed and I wondered if he'd twigged me. I dropped further back but ten miles on the bastard pulled on to the hard shoulder, hazard lights flashing. I passed him on the outside of a truck so he wouldn't see my face but to pull my car over as well would have been too obvious.

I rolled off at the next junction about seven miles further on and took the chance of sitting at the roundabout on the top, waiting for the Aussie to come by. When he did I rejoined and tucked in again. Five minutes later he pulled the same stunt on the hard shoulder and I thought it safest to give up for the day. He was almost certainly on to me.

I drove back north with some degree of satisfaction. If Rossington was nervous of me he might make a mistake or force someone else to make one. When I reached the flat I made coffee and a sandwich and called Candy.

'Anything else on Capshaw?' I asked.

'Nothing.'

'How's old Sheikhy taking the setback?'

'Calm as ever on the surface but I think his patience is running out.'

'I'm not surprised.'

'And we've got another vet badly ill.'

'Who?'

'John Snell, the guy who took over from Simon.'

'Simon's the one found dead in bed?'

'That's right, Snell took over his duties. Now he's poorly too.'

'He's doing the mares now?'

'Uhuh, been doing loads of tests on the ones who lost foals.'

'Any findings?'

'Not a jot so far.'

'And what exactly is wrong with Snell?'

'The doctor doesn't know, they're still doing tests on him too. He thinks it might be exhaustion, which they say could have been a contributory factor in Simon Nish's heart attack.'

'Can't you tell these guys to slow down a bit?'

'The vets? Eddie, everyone's the same here! It's not just them. We're all under pressure, we want this sorted out. It's self-imposed!'

'Okay, okay, but they're only horses, for God's sake! It's just a job even if it does pay well. Are you going to kill yourself for it, too?'

'Listen to who's talking. The scrapes you've been in!'

'But I do it for the love of it, not the money.'

'Ha, bloody ha.'

'Keep laughing, Candy. I'm planning to up the stakes now and you'd better get yourself in gear too. I'm beginning to think that whoever's behind all this just might have twigged what we were trying to do through Capshaw.'

'Plant me in there, you mean?'

'That's right, and if they do suspect that then they know we're closing in a bit. Okay, we might not have them surrounded but they'll realise that we're on the right track. Also, Rossington's rattled, and if he is involved, I think we can expect some more action soon.'

'If you're right then I think Rossington will be more worried about his own health than doing us any damage.'

'Maybe, but they've got to stop killing their own people at some point.'

'And start killing us?'

'Start trying.'

Thirty-nine

Candy's man got me the names of three people in Australia who knew Ken Rossington. None of them was available to talk when I called though one, Clive Torpen, promised me a call back later if I could 'stay awake long enough'. I promised to have the phone by the bed and moved it on to the small bedside table. Then I settled down to lie on top of the bed with notepad and pen and a headful of theories.

I don't know what time I dozed off but the trill of the telephone woke me. Still in a daze I reached out and scooped up the receiver, trying to recall the name of the Aussie I was expecting a call from. But all I heard was a dial tone. A phone still ringing. Then a click and the sound of my fax machine working.

I rolled off the bed and went towards the machine. The digital clock on top of it read one minute past midnight. The paper spooled out. No first-page identification, just heavy dark print in a large typeface like a newspaper headline. The words below were laid out in newspaper-style columns and the content was a reproduction of the document I'd found beside Alex Dunn. The headline read 'Shameful Secret of Top Jockey'.

There were no details of who'd sent it.

I didn't think they'd given it to the Press. That was their ace and they wouldn't play it this early. Also whoever got the story would do the usual and ring me for my comments 'in the interests of fairness', which really meant in the interests of possibly getting some more salacious information.

Still, thinking about it kept me awake there on the bed, the light of the single lamp glowing on my scribbled notes on which I'd drawn boxes and arrows in the hope that some pattern would emerge to pull together damaged stallions, aborting mares and dead men.

At 2.10 my contact in Australia rang. Five minutes later I told

211

him how much I appreciated the call and how grateful I was he'd
taken the trouble to tell me about Ken Rossington.

'No trouble, mate, anytime.'

He didn't know just how helpful he'd been.

Come morning I'd had no more than three hours of troubled
sleep and promised myself I'd catch up by having an early night
tonight. Then, over breakfast, Charles reminded me of a dinner
date we both had in London.

'Shit, that's not tonight, is it?'

'Afraid so.'

'I thought that was next month.'

'Afraid not.' He was smiling, his chubby cheeks red from an
hour out walking the gallops, checking and planning. Six of our
horses were due back in tomorrow and Charles, as optimistic as
most other racing folk, was looking forward to a better season
than last when he'd trained so few winners.

I told him I'd have to call off from this charity dinner but
he reminded me that it was a 'three-line whip' from Gary Rice
who owned the property, the horses, and paid me a retainer
to ride for the stable. Gary had 'bought' a table for this high-
profile charity event at a cost of three grand. Charles and I
were to be two of his nine guests.

After breakfast I called Candy and told him what I'd discovered about Rossington, asking him to cancel any pending
enquiries about the Aussie for fear of alerting him. Then I
contacted McCarthy. I couldn't afford to tell him everything
about Rossington – he'd have gone all official on me which
I didn't need at this stage – but I said enough to convince
him he should carry on co-operating with me over Rossington's
past movements. I also arranged to take advantage of my trip to
London by having a meeting there with Mac next morning.

Neither Charles nor I liked driving in London so we decided
to take the train. At Euston the taxi rank was empty of cabs and
full of people. We took the tube then walked the remaining few
hundred yards to the Dorchester, skirting the edge of Hyde Park
and its dog-walkers, roller-bladers and tourists.

It was a fine sunny evening and we smiled and chatted as we
entered the pedestrian underpass to walk beneath Park Lane
– at which point our smiles faded as we saw the ragged rows

of homeless people already settled for the night in makeshift cardboard beds while chauffeur-driven limousines glided above their heads, carrying the lucky people of the world to their clubs and casinos and three-hundred-pound-a-night rooms.

My three-hundred-pound-a-head-dinner took some forcing down and I couldn't quite bring myself to join in the applause as egos fuelled by liquor paid crazy prices for sports memorabilia. It was for charity which made it palatable. But I wondered what charity would help those poor bastards sleeping in the basement of the world. Especially when the winter came.

By 11, the tables had been cleared, the lights were low, the orchestra played in the background and alcohol had draped its usual soft curtains around each party, making them think they were the only ones who really mattered. Nonsense was talked, boasts made, libidos stoked, promises sworn – till finally I decided to have a few more drinks and stop being so bloody judgemental.

Charles had been away from the seat beside me for about twenty minutes when it was quietly filled by a lady in a black dress, a string of pearls and a sweet haze of perfume. Early-forties, blonde shoulder-length hair, pale pink lipstick on narrow lips, grey-blue eyes wrinkled pleasantly by her smile, biggish nose but not unattractive given her strong bone structure. Her breasts were too heavy for whatever wire support was pushing them up, making little wrinkles either side of the tight line of cleavage. Over exposure to UVA rays made it look even worse – tanned in more ways than one.

She smiled at me as if I should know her and I did. I recognised her from that picture at Ascot. 'Eddie?' She held out her hand. 'Jean Kerman.'

The newspaper columnist. The gorgon of the gossip pages, destroyer of reputations, specialising in racing personalities the way a forensic pathologist specialises in bodies – the difference being the medic has the good grace to wait till you are dead.

I took her hand. 'Nice to meet you at last,' she said.

'Likewise,' I replied, not meaning it but wondering what she wanted.

A stalking waiter, eager to help seal what he obviously saw as a potential liaison, appeared and offered champagne. Kerman, without acknowledging the man himself, took two glasses and placed one in front of me. She drank half the other at a gulp. I left mine untouched.

We spent five minutes in small talk and I was finding it tough to hide my wariness of her. I was tempted to ask her if she shouldn't be moving around looking for someone to write about, but I had the uncomfortable feeling that was exactly what she'd been doing and I was the target.

She inched her chair closer and lit a cigarette, thin lips closing to a pencil line as she drew on it then tilted back her head to blow a stream of smoke from the corner of her mouth. Chin raised and eyes half-closed she thought she was posing sexily but the most striking part of the view was up her wide nostrils.

The band was doing some nice slow forties stuff and the floor was pretty full. Kerman stood up and asked if I wanted to dance. I didn't but didn't want to embarrass her either so I got up and she led me on to the floor, turned and moved in so close her breast wrinkles washed backwards like a big wave. Her high heels brought her to my height and she pulled my head forward, raising her shoulder to nudge me close to her neck.

'I never inspect ears on a first date,' I said.

She laughed, pulling back her head to look at me. I managed what I hoped was a reasonably pleasant expression with a hint of warning attached that I wasn't quite so keen on having sex on the dance floor of the Dorchester as she seemed to be.

She settled a bit then and we moved round the floor in a slow but rhythmic circle. She eased her pelvis closer to mine and I felt the softness of her stomach against me. Her perfume seemed muskier close up, her body warm. As the music came to an end I was still trying to figure her out when she raised her chin, putting her lips close to my ear. She said, 'You dance well. Did your mum teach you when you were a boy?' She drew her head back and looked at me, eyes much colder now. Then she said, 'Or were you too busy going out for walks in the bracing Cumbrian air? Walks by the river. Or maybe climbing trees? Maybe that was your favourite, Eddie, eh?'

And I wondered if, in the relative darkness, she could see the colour draining from me. A smile glinted hard and steely on her face before she turned and walked away.

Forty

I went out into the brightly lit busy streets and found a newspaper seller. Kerman's paper was called the *Examiner* and tomorrow's early edition would already be on the stands. It was and I scanned through quickly, knowing that if she'd run the story it would probably be over two full pages.

It wasn't there.

I leaned back against a lamp-post, trying to breathe deeply, feeling the tension pounding in my throat, realising quickly that the sense of relief I was feeling was false, that it would be followed very soon by another bout of fear, another steady winding of the tension spring as I waited for Friday's edition then Saturday's and so on.

The dinner suit suddenly felt tight, the wing collar choking. I reached up to loosen it. Sweat broke through on my forehead as I stared at the sky. I went back to my hotel room. It was after midnight, too late to call Mother and warn her. And what good would it do anyway? I'd goaded them, tempted them to come out, and they had. They'd given the story to Kerman and she'd teased and goaded me and I knew she would run the story soon. She had to, that was her job.

I spent another sleepless night which led into the longest day of my life. The next morning I met Mac at Jockey Club HQ, Portman Square.

He looked at my face as we sat down in his office and waited for some of the coffee whose rich smell permeated the place. He said, 'I can't tell whether it was a good night or a bloody bad one, but you look like you've been up for most of it.'

'I was, one way or another.'

He smiled. 'One of those, eh?'

'No, not one of *those*.'

He kept smiling stupidly till the coffee came. I hadn't planned to tell him about Rossington but Kerman had increased the pressure so much I was determined to get these people. I was going to suffer the consequences anyway, and if I could bring them down too it would help ease the pain.

I sipped some black coffee, savouring the long aftertaste, then said to Mac, 'Ken Rossington's not who he says he is.'

'He says he's Ken Rossington. His passport says he's Ken Rossington. His racecourse ID from Melbourne says he's Ken Rossington.'

'He's not.'

Mac settled back behind the big desk in that comfortable way I'd now grown used to. At first it used to be the opposite. Before he knew me properly or trusted my judgement he used to stiffen, sit straighter when I started setting out my theories. But experience had deflated the mild pomposity and quelled the doubts a bit. We'd been through a few things together, arguing and falling out along the way, but always building respect for each other.

Slowly he drank his coffee. Lifting my cup and holding his gaze, I mimicked his action. We both smiled. 'Go on,' he said.

'The Ken Rossington who worked at Melbourne was at least three inches shorter than our man and maybe twenty pounds lighter. He was quiet, reserved, industrious, a private man. Our guy behaves like CoCo the Clown half the time. His hair and eye colouring are the same and he has the same general facial shape but they are two different men.'

Mac shrugged. 'Maybe they are. Maybe it was us that got them confused.'

I shook my head. 'Rossington's CV lays claim to everything his Melbourne counterpart has done.'

'Okay, who is our man?'

'I don't know.'

'Why is he impersonating Rossington?'

'I don't know.'

'Where is the real Rossington?'

'You've just completed the hat-trick. I don't know. The real Ken Rossington left Melbourne on March the twelfth last year after the break-up of a long-term affair with a jockey.'

Mac sat forward slightly. 'A jockey? A female jockey?'

'No, the type with the hanging genitalia.'

Mac looked shocked. 'A homosexual jockey?'

'I certainly hope so or it must have been a touch unpleasant for him.'

He sat back again, slowly shaking his head. 'Why do you say "a homosexual jockey"?' I asked. 'Rossington was the other half, why don't you say, "a homosexual valet"?'

'I don't know. It just seems odd.'

'We're all human under those silks, you know.'

He nodded. 'Anyway, go on.'

'Rossington decided to make a new life for himself in England. He had dual nationality so didn't see a problem getting work in racing. The rumour is that an owner he knew out there, a guy who also had horses in England and France, promised to help him get started here.'

'Who was the owner?'

'I'm still waiting to find out. My man says he'll get back to me.'

'Well, when he does your problem is solved. If the owner knows Rossington well enough to offer him a job, then he'll be able to tell you if our man's an imposter.'

'Question is, how long can we afford to wait?'

Mac drummed on his thick blotting pad with a pen, finishing off with two pings on the edge of his coffee cup. 'Does this all lead back to Kincaid?'

I nodded. He smiled slowly, shaking his head.

'And maybe Alex Dunn.'

He stared at me.

'And William Capshaw,' I said.

I couldn't expand much on it and I'm not sure that was what Mac wanted at this stage anyway. Hard facts were his bread and butter and a good spread of evidence the jam. All I had at the moment were the basic ingredients. If I involved him too deeply, too soon, he'd feel ethically obliged to bring in the cops and I couldn't afford that, for my sake or for Candy's.

'If you could just do me a favour?' I asked. 'I know you've got friends in Melbourne. Whoever Rossington really is, he does seem to know about horses and jockeys. Can you get hold of a photo of Rossington and send a few prints to Melbourne, see if anyone recognises him?'

He made a note. 'Okay, I'll deal with it.' It looked like the potential implications were beginning to sink in. He agreed to do what he could on our usual understanding that if the shit hit the fan, he'd be free to claim he was never anywhere in the room.

I asked one more favour of him; to contact Ascot Racecourse and ask for a copy of Bob Guterson's guest list on the day he sponsored that race. He got me that by fax within minutes. It included the table plan for lunch. Kerman's name was there, seated between Guterson and Simeon Prior. There were nineteen more names on the list and Mac went through it with me but of the few he knew none gave him any reason for suspicion though he raised the same point Candy had: that Simeon Prior, the chairman of Triplecrown Bloodstock, seemed out of place in that company.

Why then had Prior accepted Guterson's invitation?

I left and went straight home to wait by the phone. Kerman had to run the story next day, Friday. I sat waiting for her call, waiting for the 'chance to comment'.

But the call never came and the story didn't run on Friday nor on Saturday. Sunday was their biggest circulation day; she had to print it then or risk losing it to a rival. Her informants wouldn't wait forever. She didn't. Nothing appeared and I began to wonder just what Jean Kerman's role was. Sitting on this must have been killing her.

Had she been invited to Ascot just so someone could plant the story about me in her mind? If so, how had they made her hold back from running it? Had they fed her just the small part she'd teased me with? No, that wouldn't have been acceptable to her.

And why had she taken such a personal line with me? Why not simply ring me up and tell me she knew and that she would have to publish? I recalled that cold hard look in her eyes as she'd left me on the dance floor, that cruel glint almost of revenge.

Was she involved with them? Could Kerman be in on it somehow?

I rang Candy. Although I couldn't tell him why I wanted it, he agreed to put someone straight to work on every destructive racing piece that Kerman had written in the past five years.

'How many men can you put on it?' I asked.

'How quickly do you want it?'

'Yesterday.'

'What's the big hurry?'

'I think the key to the next move, maybe something more, might be in there among those stories.'

He sighed. 'Let me speak to someone. I'll call you back.'

'Candy! While you're at it, see what you can find out about Bob Guterson.'

Within the hour he rang back to tell me that his man could get the *Examiner* on a computer CD Rom which meant he could search five years' worth and report within twenty-four hours.

I travelled south and went back to my parents' stud to wait for Candy's call next day. I spent a miserable evening visiting hour at the hospital, my small talk ricocheting off the almost tangible barrier my father had erected round himself and my mother, resenting my presence, glorying in my discomfort, drawing every moment of my mother's attention towards himself.

I sat there, elbows on the edge of the bed, feeling like a trapped audience of one to a terrible soap opera that would never be turned off. And I took cold-hearted wicked comfort in the fact that when the Kerman story broke he would know some of the suffering I'd endured.

I dropped my mother off at her hotel and drove back in a desolate mood. After re-establishing contact with her and moving into the house I'd held such hopes for the future, such plans for repairing all the hurt. Now I wished earnestly that the pneumonia would take vicious hold and kill him before all chance with my mother was gone.

Another night. More sleepless miserable hours in a cold bed in a lonely dark desperate house.

Roll on daybreak.

Forty-one

We got two results next day. My contact in Australia came back with the name of the owner who'd got Rossington the valet's job: Bob Guterson. Surprise, surprise.

Dunn, Capshaw, Rossington, Guterson . . . the links were steadily appearing. Did Kerman fit in somewhere? Candy arrived with her cuttings and I told him about Guterson fixing up Rossington, or whoever he was, with the job. Candy already had some information on the guy. Guterson had sixteen horses in training in Europe and Australia; not a very big string to be so thinly spread, but understandable perhaps when Candy told me he also did business on both continents.

He'd been in racing less than five years though his company had been involved on the perimeter through its business of supplying the veterinary industry with plastic gloves. Not a huge market but one that Guterson's company had virtually cornered with large sales all over Europe and Australia. The connection with Simeon Prior became clearer too: eighteen months ago Guterson had bought a 20 percent share in Triplecrown Bloodstock, an investment which had seemed particularly poorly timed as the company hadn't been performing well for some time. Nor had things improved since Guterson bought in.

We kicked things around for a while without coming to any conclusions. I could see Candy was anxious to start working through the cuttings on Kerman's past 'victims'. I made coffee and we settled down at the big kitchen table and worked through the night sifting, sorting, discussing. Kerman had already laid bare most of the lives of her victims but we dissected them all at length, including our own memories of them, and Candy showed how sharp an eye for detail he had by recalling small facts and anecdotes.

We found three people to be of particular interest, all of them speared by Kerman within the last fourteen months. The first was Ben Campbell who'd been the Sheikh's Racing Manager before Candy. Campbell had a heavy cocaine habit which was exposed by one of Kerman's 'reporters' who'd set the poor guy up.

The next to go was a guy called James Summerville, a respected bloodstock journalist and agent who was heavily pro-Arab in his writing. Summerville supported Sheikh Ahmad's attempts to establish his own superior thoroughbred blood lines, arguing that this was in essence the original intention behind thoroughbred breeding, which went back to the days of the Crusades.

Unfortunately it was proved that while wearing his agent's hat he'd accepted bribes to help inflate the prices of horses he'd been entrusted to buy. Again it seemed he'd been set up by one of Kerman's people.

The last guy to go, and maybe the most significant to us, was a top vet who'd been based at the Equine Fertility Unit in Newmarket. His name was Stephen Spenser and he was the top man in his field. Kerman had nailed him after discovering he'd conducted experiments on live ex-racehorses, two of which had died as a result of his research. Spenser had been struck off. Candy was certain he'd gone to America. He'd been one of the guys Candy had considered trying to recruit when the stallion problem blew up.

'You think he could have cracked it?' I asked, sipping tepid coffee.

'He would have had a better chance than most,' Candy said, 'and I'd have used him if I could have traced him in the States.'

'And if he was that good our friends may have known it and wanted him out of the picture before they started on those stallions.'

'Possibly,' Candy said absent-mindedly as he pulled the Ben Campbell page back under the lamp beam and stared at the picture, frowning. 'You know,' he said, 'I think Campbell was related somehow to Alex Dunn. Either related or his godson or something.'

'That would make sense. Dunn would probably have been very reluctant to damage Campbell's career. Whoever's behind this would know that so he simply took Campbell out of the equation before involving Dunn, knowing it would be highly unlikely that he would have any particular attachment to his successor. You.'

Candy sighed and shook his head. 'Shit, you could say all three of these affected our situation, directly or indirectly. You're talking about some pretty elaborate planning here.'

'I know. Not to mention three killings. Somehow I think we're dealing with a slightly stronger motive than a simple dislike of the Sheikh and his empire.'

We still knew neither motive nor method and were both getting too tired to think sensibly. We sat and stared at Campbell's smiling picture. Candy sighed, laid back his head and yawned, long and large as a hippo. Within seconds I followed. We laughed gently then I stood up. 'You get the coffee, I'll get the fresh air.' And I went and opened the kitchen door to let in the cold night, to brace us awake. I stood on the step looking up at the clear black-blue sky and diamond-sharp stars.

Candy moved around behind me, fixing more coffee. 'We're close to something here, Eddie,' he said. I listened. 'Those three pieces point to Kerman doing more than her journalistic duty. She's working for somebody other than the *Examiner*.'

I smiled up at the sky, knowing I couldn't tell him about her approach to me at the Dorchester but feeling more and more certain that she was in with these people. Because if she was, and we could bring her down with the rest of them, shame her, then there wouldn't be any *Examiner* story about Eddie Malloy and family. And maybe, just maybe, things would be all right again.

I turned to Candy as he poured hot water into a mug. 'I think it's time we got your personal profile man to work again. Let's see if the secrets of Jean Kerman's life can stand the test.'

Next morning Candy rang The Gulf Stud to tell them he'd be there later in the afternoon. He came off the phone looking serious. 'What's up?'

'John Snell's back in hospital.'

'Who?'

'Snell, the vet who took over from Simon Nish, remember? He came back to work three days ago, now he's back in hospital, very ill, showing signs of heart failure.'

'You shouldn't have let him come back so soon. I thought they said it was exhaustion?'

'He wanted to. He seemed okay.' Candy slumped down on a

hard kitchen chair and rubbed his tired eyes. 'Jesus Christ, when are we going to get a break?'

Heart failure. That's what Dunn ultimately had died of, and so had Simon Nish. Now Snell.

I sat down opposite Candy. 'Did he go straight back to working on mares?'

Candy nodded wearily.

I went to the phone and rang my mother at the hotel. She was surprised to hear from me so early in the day. 'Is anything wrong?' she asked.

'No, everything's okay. How's Father?'

She sighed quietly. 'Not much change.'

'Listen, Mum, did you have many mares abort this year in the early stages of pregnancy?'

She was quiet for a moment. 'Yes.'

'How many?'

'Quite a few.'

'More than usual?'

'Possibly three times as many. It was one of the reasons business was so bad.'

'Who treated all these mares?'

'Alex Dunn.'

I told her I'd call later and hung up. Candy was watching me. 'What are you on to?' he asked.

'Your vets, Snell and the dead man, Simon Nish . . . which brand of plastic gloves did they use for examinations?'

He looked bewildered. 'I don't know. Whatever we supplied them with at The Gulf, I suppose.'

I carried the phone to the table and handed him the receiver. 'Find out. Quickly.'

He dialled The Gulf Stud and asked the manager. Covering the mouthpiece, he said, 'Guterson's.'

'Tell him to stop using them immediately.'

He frowned at me.

'Go on!'

He told the manager to suspend all testing on mares then slowly put down the phone and waited for an explanation.

'Just a hunch,' I said, 'a wild hunch. What makes mares abort?'

He shrugged. 'A number of factors.'

'What do vets use to clear out the uterus?'

'Prostaglandin.'

'What killed Alex Dunn?'

'Prostaglandin.'

'What would continued exposure of the skin surface to prostaglandin do to a man?'

'Kill him, I suppose, if he got enough of it. Or make him very ill.'

'Like John Snell and Simon Nish?'

He looked puzzled. 'I still don't get it.'

'Guterson's Gloves. What if they were impregnated with prostaglandin? It's a naturally occurring substance in mares hence the reason that all the testing in the world wouldn't show up anything unusual. This way they get the mare and eventually the vet who's pulling on fifty gloves a day. What sort of prostaglandin dose does that add up to?'

He nodded silently, taking it in, then said, 'So why aren't mares aborting all over the country?'

'Because they're only impregnating selected batches. Dunn used Guterson's Gloves and he worked on my father's mares which also showed a high abortion rate. I saw boxes of the gloves at his place and couldn't figure out at the time why they were under lock and key. He must have been trying them out on Father's mares.'

'What about the risk to himself?'

'Insufficient numbers, or more likely he'd have worn skin protection when using them.'

Candy shook his head and a smile slowly warmed his face as he gave me an admiring look. I was chuffed. Candy went straight back to The Gulf Stud to arrange a quick analysis of Guterson's Gloves.

He rang me back within the hour, triumphant but angry. 'We've checked more than fifty gloves. Every one is saturated with prostaglandin. Let's get that bastard Guterson!'

Forty-two

If I'd learned anything since that day almost five years ago when I'd been forced into amateur detective work it was that cat-skinning could indeed be done in several ways. I persuaded Candy it was pointless to go waving glove samples at the cops, asking for Guterson to be arrested. Although it now looked likely that he was behind everything we needed more evidence, especially about what we were now convinced were the killings of Kincaid, Dunn, Capshaw and Nish.

Also it would have been nice to try and establish a motive behind this madness. I thought it was time to pull in Jockey Club Security officially and tried to persuade Candy we were close enough to cracking it to justify involving them. Maybe all I really wanted was an increased sense of security. At the moment it was still just Candy and me, and as the killings mounted it was getting to feel more and more like we were defending the Alamo.

Anyway, Candy put the blocks on me calling McCarthy. He was still fearful that things would drag on and that word about the Sheikh's stallions would get out. One thing we did agree on was that the man calling himself Rossington was now the weak link in the chain. Very strong circumstantial evidence pointed to him as Kincaid's killer, and if that was so there was reason enough to assume he'd been involved in the deaths of Dunn and Capshaw.

I thought back to Rossington's behaviour on the motorway and concluded he'd almost certainly known I was following him. The faxed mock-up of the newspaper article and Kerman's poorly veiled threat had come shortly after that. Rossington must have gone running straight back to tell them I'd been on his tail. I wondered just how wise that had been from his viewpoint. Once I'd latched on to Dunn and Capshaw they'd been killed. If the same policy was in force then Rossington must now be sleeping very uneasily in his bed.

But who would they get to hit the hitman?

I called Candy. 'Have you still got those two heavies working for you, the ones who were using me as a yo-yo at the seaside?'

'They're available.'

'We need to pick up Rossington.'

'What do you mean, pick up?'

'For his own protection.' I explained my thinking but Candy was nervous. I said, 'Look, until we can prove Guterson's involved, and maybe Kerman, we need to keep Rossington alive. The guy is scared. If he's got any brains he might welcome the chance of protection.'

It took a few more minutes but Candy finally agreed to try and have Rossington picked up by which time I was sure we'd know more about his real identity. Before hanging up I said, 'And, Candy, ask your guys to have a good look around Rossington's property for a blue vehicle with bull bars. Maybe we can implicate him in Capshaw's killing.'

I put the phone down and suddenly felt very tired. It was after 7. I'd missed visiting hour at the hospital which was one blessing. Heavy-footed, I trailed through to my room, lay on the bed and watched the late sunlight filter through the old curtains. It was a matter of waiting now. For Rossington, and for more information on Guterson and Kerman. There were still big gaps to be filled, like motive, Dunn's method . . .

The latter intrigued me. Whatever he'd done to the Sheikh's stallions he'd done it in the racecourse stables, I was sure of that. It was the only time he'd had access to them. But whatever he'd treated them with had only been activated once they'd retired from racing. What the hell had he done, planted some sort of radio transmitter that could be switched on remotely?

Nah . . . too ridiculous.

I crossed my ankles, linked my hands behind my head and let everything I knew about Dunn run through my mind again. He'd been keen on experimenting with chemical castration so we must assume he'd perfected something in that field that was undetectable. Then he'd had to test it which he did on my father's stallion and on maybe half a dozen others, including Town Crier, in small studs around England.

But why? Why take that risk, the posing as an RSPCA man, the visits to different places? If the stuff needed road testing, he could easily have used it on my father's other three stallions. He'd buggered his business almost completely so what difference would it have made to sterilise the other stallions? Whatever way I looked at it, I just couldn't figure it out.

I chanelled my thoughts into trying to summarise what evidence was hard fact. There were two definites: whatever he had used, he'd used it on Town Crier, and when he'd administered it Fiona had been with him.

I got up and rang the Corish Stud. Fiona answered. I asked how Martin was.

'Still drinking.'

'As much?'

'Almost, though he sleeps a lot now.' Her voice was flat, almost robotic.

'Are you all right?'

'Mmm.'

Suffering in silence. I asked her a few questions about Dunn's visit and told her I'd like to come and see her. She said she wasn't going anywhere.

I called Candy and told him he could get me on my mobile. By the time I reached the Corish Stud the sun was low in the sky and insects buzzed among the trees. I stopped at the bungalow and watched the round figure of Fiona gathering washing from the line.

She told me Martin was asleep, passed out. We went to Town Crier's box. Standing in the gloom, the big horse seemed happy to see Fiona but wary of my presence. I stood outside the door. Fiona went in and rubbed his nose, clapped his neck, looking as if she was taking more comfort from it than the stallion was.

I said, 'Fiona, think hard about the day Alex Dunn came here, the tall guy posing as the RSPCA man. I need you to try and picture everything he did when he was checking Town Crier over.'

She looked vacantly at me for a while then shrugged. 'Just what you'd expect; he checked his coat and his teeth, his eyes, legs, feet, ears. He had me walk him round the box a couple of times. He took a blood sample . . .' She hesitated, frowned slightly. 'That did seem odd, seemed to take him longer than normal. Usually they just whiz a syringe in under his neck and draw what they want. This seemed to take a few minutes and he worked on the other side of the horse, quite high up, for a sample.'

'What do you mean, the other side?'

'The side I couldn't see.'

'Were you holding him?'

'No. I suppose that was a bit strange too. He asked me to tie him up and stand by the door saying he might get a bit fractious.'

'Quite high up, you said.'

She nodded, frowning again. Town Crier looked down at her as if to enquire what was wrong. She rubbed his nose. 'He seemed to be working under his mane.'

I moved into the box. 'Can you hold him, Fiona?' She took a tighter hold on the halter. 'Which side?' I asked.

'Near side.'

I walked round, Town Crier's suspicious eyes following me, his muscles tensing slightly. Fiona tightened her grip again. I put both hands on his neck. He moved sideways. 'Whoah, boy. That's a good boy!' I said quietly, and kept talking horsetalk as I ran my hands softly over every inch of his neck under his mane till, high up, just below the ridge where the hard hair starts growing, my middle finger came to rest on a small bump, a node no larger than a TicTac mint.

I felt it, ran my finger over it. It gave slightly, like a small jelly capsule. We got the horse out into what was left of the daylight and Fiona held the tuft of mane away. I could see no incision or damage to the hair around the bump but that could easily have healed completely. I smiled and asked her to put the horse away and meet me back at the bungalow. By the time she returned Candy was already on his way to check under the manes of the Sheikh's stallions.

I sat on the edge of the kitchen table, smiling stupidly. Fiona looked confused. I smiled wider, luxuriating in the feeling of having guessed right once again. It was a sensation I rarely experienced. Right on cue, at the height of my self-congratulation, the phone rang.

'Every fucking one of them! Exact same spot!'

'Yeehaaa!'

Fiona stared at me as though considering leaving quickly.

I said to Candy, 'Get them out and get them analysed.'

'Already arranged! Results in under an hour!'

'You sound like an advert for Boots.'

'I feel like a glass of champagne.'

'Have one for me. I'll call you.'

Fiona stood open-mouthed. I smiled at her. 'You'd best close that before a fly gets in. Tomorrow I'm sending a vet to look at Town Crier. I'll let you know his name and I'll make sure he's carrying ID. If Martin sobers up sufficiently between now and then, tell him I think our problems are almost over.'

Forty-three

I left Wiltshire in the dusk and reached my parents' stud in the darkness. My heart sang for most of the trip. The thought that my luck was running kept entering my mind and I tried to blot it out. I'd long ago learned the folly of tempting fate. But I prayed all the same, prayed that it would hold just long enough to nail Kerman, to silence her, to save the secret.

Save the secret.

I didn't care about Guterson any more, or Rossington or Dunn or Capshaw. Or, to my shame, Brian Kincaid, not right at that moment. I was obsessed with my own ends. At my parents' place the phone was ringing as I turned the key in the lock. I ran inside. It was Candy. 'Can I come down there now?' he asked.

'Sure.'

'See you soon.'

It was almost midnight when he arrived but Candy looked bright-eyed and elated. He smelled of aftershave. 'You haven't just shaved, at this time of night?' I asked.

He smiled, strong teeth white against the tan. 'Second shave of the day. Got to keep up appearances.'

'God save me from vanity!'

'He will.'

We sat down with a full teapot and two mugs, neither of us really wanting to tempt fate with a premature celebratory drink. Candy pulled a notepad from the pocket of his yellow polo shirt, then dug in again to produce a small green capsule which he rolled towards me. I squeezed it between my fingers. It reminded me of a cod liver oil pill.

Candy said, 'Filled with a variant on methyl testosterone which Dunn must have concocted himself. They're still working on it but the early verdict is that the chemical would lie dormant until set off by a surge of sexual activity during which the increased testosterone levels play a dual part: they neutralise all traces of the drug in the system and they rapidly sterilise the sperm.'

'Hence the reason Dunn could pre-plant them in horses who were still racing, knowing they wouldn't take effect until the horse became sexually active.'

'Correct.'

'So yours were done in the racecourse stables as per the old list of visits, matey.' I smiled. Candy returned it. 'You're a right bloody clever dick, aren't you?'

'Now all we need is the motive.'

'And the perpetrators.'

I nodded.

'Speaking of which,' Candy said, 'our boys picked Rossington up at his home just after nine-thirty.'

'Where is he?'

'They're holding him at Dunn's old place at Six Mile Bottom.'

'Has he said anything?'

'They haven't asked him anything. We were sort of waiting for you.'

'Sort of?'

'Well, we were. I'm getting a wee bit nervous about it, to be honest. I think it's time we brought in the authorities.'

'The police?'

'Yes.'

'Not yet, Candy.'

'Why? We're in the clear.'

'You're in the clear, your stallions will be operational again. But all we've got is one of the mugs. We need to get Guterson and whoever else is involved.'

He waved the suggestion away. 'Nah, the cops can do that.'

'The cops might fuck it up, Candy, and I can't afford that!'

He looked surprised. 'Don't worry, Eddie. I'll make sure you're well paid.'

'I know you will but it's not the money. You *know* I've got another interest in this that I can't tell you about just now. You can't just dump everything because you've got a result!'

He lowered his eyes but I wasn't sure if the guilty expression was genuine. 'You're right. What do you want to do with Rossington?'

'I'll go and see him tomorrow. Will those profiles on Guterson and Jean Kerman be ready?'

'I'll chase them in the morning.'

'Okay.'

'Right.' He got up. 'Brilliant. Well done, Eddie.'

'Save it till the fat lady's done an encore, Candy, I'm due a turn of bad luck.'

I walked with him to the door and watched him go out into the darkness. I lay in bed bathing a while longer in the afterglow before settling down for what I hoped would be my first peaceful night's sleep in weeks.

Just after 3 a.m. the phone rang. Groggy with sleep, I didn't recognise McCarthy's voice at first. He had to introduce himself. 'I thought I'd best ring you straightaway. I've just been wakened by a call from Melbourne about your man Rossington.'

'Uhuh.' I was still trying to get my brain in gear.

'Remember, you gave me those pictures of him?'

'Yes, I remember.'

Mac told me what he'd learned and I extended the chain of early-morning alarm calls by ringing Candy, though I gave him more time to come to his senses than Mac had given me.

'According to McCarthy's contacts in Melbourne, our man Rossington is a ghost. His real name is Paul Cantrell and his body was found on a road near Melbourne Airport in March last year in a hit and run incident very similar to the one in which Capshaw was killed. I've asked Mac to try and find out how positive the identification of Cantrell's corpse was. What would you like to bet that his face was badly disfigured?'

'You think the real Rossington was the hit and run victim?'

'A very convenient way to exchange identities. Cantrell was wanted by the police when he "died".'

'What for?'

'Armed robbery.'

'Shit!'

'Are your guys contactable at Dunn's place?'

'On mobile.'

'I think you'd best call and warn them that Cantrell's a lot more dangerous than we thought.'

Forty-four

Exhaustion caught up with me and I slept late next morning, Candy's phone call rousing me just before 10. 'Kerman and Guterson. We've got a connection by the look of things.'

'Uhuh?' I was still half-asleep.

'Should I bring the reports?'

'Sure, yeah, sure. I'll have a bath,' I said stupidly.

He arrived while I was still soaking and shouted through the letterbox. Dripping, I wrapped a towel around me, let him in and told him to put the kettle on while I got dressed. He told me Rossington or Cantrell, whoever he was, was still securely locked up.

With my hair still wet, I sat at the table looking at the highlighted parts of the two reports Candy had brought.

Jean Kerman's maiden name was Prior. She was the daughter of Simeon Prior, the Triplecrown Chairman. Candy also had a breakdown on Triplecrown's business. They did everything from arranging matings to selling the subsequent foals, and in the past three years turnover and profit had been on the slide.

At the same time as Bob Guterson acquired his 20 percent stake in Triplecrown, Simeon Prior had bought a 25 percent share in Guterson's Gloves.

I read it through again. 'Motive?' I said.

'Let me try this time,' Candy said, beaming.

I waited. He said, 'Triplecrown Bloodstock rose to prominence in the years when the Arabs were buying from them. They made millions. But now the Arabs are spending less and less as they build up their own breeding operation. Not only that, they're starting to do everything in-house and offer their facilities to other breeders. So Triplecrown hasn't just lost the Arabs' custom – all their other customers now have the option of doing their business with the Arabs instead.

I nodded, smiling. Candy went on, 'Simple solution for Triplecrown: smother the Arab operation at source by taking out the stallions.'

I applauded softly and Candy looked chuffed. 'Now prove it,' I said.

'Rossington will grass to save his skin.'

'I doubt it. He's none to save. It's very likely he's killed three men, at least. No plea-bargain there.'

Candy looked flustered. 'Okay, but he won't take the rap on his own, he'll take the others with him.'

I smiled. ' "Take the rap?" You've been watching those old Edward G. Robinson films again, haven't you?'

'Well, you know what I mean.'

'I do, and you might be right, but we can't take the chance and the police won't just take his word for it anyway. We'll need something more concrete, something that definitely incriminates Guterson and Prior.'

'Surely there's enough circumstantial evidence?'

'Where? All you've laid out is based on assumption, pure theory. There isn't a single piece of solid evidence linking Guterson, Prior or Kerman.'

'It's obvious that Triplecrown would have the strongest of motives to . . .'

'And what about Town Crier and Heraklion and the other half-dozen stallions at the smaller studs? Where's Triplecrown's interest there?'

He shrugged, confused. 'Red herrings. Decoys set up for exactly this type of situation, so they can use it in their defence. You know how well they've planned this, Eddie!'

'I know! I'm only playing Devil's Advocate. You're probably right but how do we *prove* it?'

'We've got to get this guy Rossington, or whatever he's called, to talk.'

'But how?'

The phone rang. It was Martin. I was surprised. He sounded bright and sober. 'Fiona tells me we might be out of the woods,' he said.

'Not quite. We can see the edge of the trees.'

'How long do you reckon?'

'I don't know. Soon. A couple of days, maybe.'

'Anything I can do?'

The question provoked a sudden surge of anger in me. Martin had been unable to hack it when things got tough. Now here he was offering help because he thought it was almost over. I was tempted to concoct something dangerous and ask him to deal with it but I resisted. 'If there's anything I can think of, I'll call you. It might be best if you stay off the booze for a day or two in case I do need you.'

He laughed. 'Sure. Keep me informed, eh?'

'Okay.' I went back to the table. Candy had been thinking. 'Maybe it *is* just Guterson. Maybe it was his stake in the company that made him set this up.'

'So how come Prior's daughter so effectively removes three of the possible stumbling blocks to the success of the whole thing in Campbell, Summerville and the EFU vet guy . . . what do you call him?'

'Spenser.'

'Yeah.'

Candy looked thoughtful. 'Good point.'

'I know, but having said that you can bet your boots Prior's kept his own hands lily white. Jean Kerman and Guterson will have done the high-level dirty work and Rossington the basics.'

We sat around for an hour trying to figure some way to trap Guterson and the others. Martin's offer of help came back to me and sparked an idea. I called him. He'd gone to the pub. I spoke to Fiona. 'Do you remember that guy Spindari, the one we had you make a phone call to when he was trying to blackmail us?'

'I remember.'

'Do you still have his phone number?'

'I'm not sure. I can probably find it.'

'Good, here's what I want you to do.'

Fiona called back within half an hour. 'He'll be here at two-thirty.'

'Fine. We'll see you then.'

Forty-five

When Candy and I walked into the office at the Corish Stud, the tall, dark and handsome Simon Spindari seemed to lose some of his Latin colour, not to mention his composure. He turned on Fiona. 'You little bitch! You said you had a good story for me!'

Smiling, I said, 'We have, Simon, we have. Sit yourself down.'

Glowering, he sat down on the chair by the desk and swept the thick dark hair away from his eyes. 'Thanks, Fiona,' I said, and she left without looking at Spindari.

I explained that we knew everything about his blackmail attempt way back at the beginning and he agreed to co-operate if we promised not to tell the police what he'd been doing. He admitted having 'investigated' a couple of other cases for Jean Kerman and said she still contacted him from time to time.

I told him what we wanted him to do and watched him as he made the call to Kerman, telling her he had a brilliant story for her about a guy named Paul Cantrell who was impersonating a certain man on British racecourses, and that if Kerman wanted to know exactly who he was impersonating, she should meet Spindari in a pub in Newmarket and he'd take her to Cantrell.

'Incidentally,' he said, acting it out well. 'The guy he's impersonating is probably dead! How's that for an exclusive?'

As I'd expected, Kerman didn't ask too many questions. She agreed the time and place, a popular pub on a country road not far from Dunn's place at 7 this evening. Spindari said he'd meet her in the beer garden.

By 6.30 McCarthy, Candy and I were concealed in the trees overlooking the beer garden. Spindari sat at a white table sipping lager in the evening sunshine and reading a newspaper. At 6.50 a big blue BMW with smoked glass windows purred into the carpark of the pub. Jean Kerman, dressed in a black two-piece, got out of the back and walked towards Spindari's table. He saw her coming, got up, smiled and reached into the pocket of his jeans as though to go and buy her a drink. Kerman shook her head and spoke quite animatedly to him.

Spindari pointed to the half-full lager glass and sat down again. Kerman turned to look back at the car. The passenger door opened and a fat man in a dark grey suit hauled himself out and hurried towards the beer garden. He was completely bald. Mac turned to me and whispered, 'Guterson.' Candy and I smiled.

We crept backwards through the trees to where our car was parked then headed for Dunn's place.

Within ten minutes of our arrival we watched from inside the bungalow as the BMW slowed and pulled into the driveway. Each of us moved into position. I stood by the edge of the curtains at the side window, hidden, I hoped, from view.

Car doors clunked closed. 'Two heavies,' I warned everyone. In the corner Phil and Don grinned. I watched Spindari, still smiling and playing the fool a bit, chatting to them as he approached the porch door. He knocked loudly. McCarthy was behind it and opened it almost immediately.

We could hear his voice along the hall and I could see reactions on some of the faces: bafflement, shock. I heard Mac say, 'Mr Guterson, how nice to see you again.' And I watched Guterson offer a very tentative hand. Mac shook it and stepped aside. 'And Mrs Kerman, always the first on a hot story. Do come in.' Kerman turned and glared at Spindari who, for the first time, looked a bit sheepish.

The two heavies looked at each other. They'd seemed tense coming along the path and didn't seem sure any more if they should still be on red alert. All five filed in past Mac. 'This way,' he said, and led them right in among us in the living room. Kerman and Guterson looked around at me, Candy, Phil and Don, bewilderment giving way to anger then worry on both their faces.

Still smiling, Mac said, 'I think you both know Mr Malloy and Mr Loss. These other two gentlemen are from Cambridge CID.' Phil and Don smiled and nodded pleasantly. Kerman turned and looked at Guterson whose face and head were reddening by the second. He reached up to loosen his gaudy tie.

Mac said, 'Now maybe your chaps and Mr Spindari could go into the kitchen and have a nice cup of tea. Would you both like one?' Kerman and Guterson shook their heads in unison.

'Coffee?' Mac offered pleasantly. He was better at this than I'd expected.

'No, thanks!' Kerman said bitterly.

Phil and Don walked forward. 'We'll show you where the kitchen is.' Guterson turned to his guys and nodded. They left. A smiling Spindari followed. They went to the kitchen and closed the door behind them. A few moments later Phil and Don rejoined us. Mac said to Kerman and Guterson, 'There's one person you haven't met yet, if you'd like to come this way?' He moved along the hall towards the office door, saying, 'Well, you have met him but not today.' Candy and I followed.

Mac turned the key and eased the door open. Kerman and Guterson moved into the doorway to look. I watched their faces go pale as Mac said, 'Mr Ken Rossington, alias Paul Cantrell.'

He closed and locked the door again before anyone could speak and we all returned to the living room. Kerman sat down on a chair, straight-backed, knees clamped, looking defiant, but Guterson slumped on the sofa looking beaten and dejected.

Mac pulled some papers from his inside pocket. He looked at Guterson. 'Cantrell spent much of yesterday dictating this statement to our CID friends here.' Mac started reading everything Candy and I had put together, all the theories starting from Kerman's setting up of Ben Campbell, Summerville and Spenser through to the recruiting of Dunn and his methods of implanting the horses.

Every so often Kerman would splutter, 'Nonsense! Ridiculous!'

But when Mac actually started listing the dates that Dunn had visited the racecourse stables and implanted the Sheikh's horses she seemed finally to give up, physically to deflate as though the weight of evidence had crushed the fight out of her.

Shaking his head, Guterson said to no one in particular, 'Cantrell didn't know half of this. How the hell . . .'

'He was obviously a damn' sight smarter than you thought, you stupid bastard!' Kerman snarled.

Guterson was still shaking his head. 'But why? Why drop himself in it after what he's done?' He grunted then as he pushed himself to his feet, becoming more animated as the instinct for self-preservation took over. He went towards Phil and Don and said, 'Look, I don't know what else is in that statement but I was

238

only acting as an agent for Simeon Prior. He's the main man. He thought the whole thing up.'

'Shut up!' Kerman yelled. 'Shut up, you silly bastard!'

Guterson said, 'Ignore her, she's his daughter!'

Then began a long cursing argument, all of which was caught on tape along with everything else that had been said. Mac excused himself politely and went to call a police inspector he knew in Cambridge.

A proper one.

The police had to let Guterson's heavies go as they'd done nothing. When Guterson, Kerman and Cantrell were being led out, Kerman turned to me, spite contorting her face. 'You'll regret this for the rest of your life, Malloy!'

I smiled. 'I don't think that even the *Examiner* would publish your stuff any more, Mrs Kerman.'

'There'll be someone else, don't worry.'

And there was.

Forty-six

The *Examiner* made no announcement about the 'departure' of Jean Kerman. It simply trumpeted the arrival of the most 'exciting voice in investigative journalism: Cynthia Clarke. Look out for her debut story on Wednesday which will shock the racing world'.

Cynthia Clarke rang me on the Monday evening just after I'd returned from visiting my father who seemed coldly determined now to stay in hospital as long as he could. He'd been moved to a new ward and had effectively trained Mother into this new routine where she was with him for more than half the day, coming and going at his bidding.

Clarke was quiet-voiced, polite but unshakeable. She told me there was a story on file which she planned to run on Wednesday and she wanted to make sure I was aware of the contents, wanted to give me 'a chance to comment'.

She read it through to me and though I knew it word for word my heart seemed to sink a step closer to hell with every line she spoke. I told her that I thought that the *Examiner* was the last vehicle to be moralising, bearing in mind the charges its previous columnist now faced. But Clarke was unmoved. 'It's news, I'm afraid, Mr Malloy. If we don't run it, someone else will. Now can I speak to your father?'

'He's very ill. If this story runs it may kill him.'

'Is he in hospital?'

My hopes rose for a moment. 'Yes.'

'Which one?'

'Will you put a hold on the story?'

'I can't, but I must give him the chance to comment.'

'He won't have any comment to make. Doesn't it make any difference to you that this might kill him?'

'I'm only doing a job, Mr Malloy.'

'I'd rather shovel shit!' I said angrily, and banged the phone down, that familiar feeling of desolation engulfing me quickly. Filled with impotent rage, I drove at speed back to the hospital to warn my mother.

We sat in the coffee lounge. She looked completely worn out. 'Is there anything we can do?' she asked weakly.

I shook my head. She bowed hers, accepting defeat for the first time in her life, then unexpectedly her hand reached across the tabletop for mine. Gently I clasped the warm, wrinkled skin, the fragile bones, and squeezed softly. Her head was down and a tear dripped silently into her lap.

I arranged to be with her at the hospital when the paper came out on Wednesday morning. She warned Father about it and suddenly he decided he'd leave the hospital on Tuesday afternoon, the day before the *Examiner* hit the streets, and come back home.

He couldn't bear the thought of everyone at the hospital knowing.

First thing Wednesday I drove to a petrol station where nobody knew me and bought a copy of the newspaper. It was on the front page. I folded the paper and drove, for some reason, to the derelict farm Candy and I had used as a meeting place.

I got out of the car and went to lean against the ruined wall. The sun in a clear blue sky was beginning to warm the morning but inside I was cold as I opened the paper. There was a smiling picture of me under a banner headline:

Top Jockey 'Killed' His Brother
The father of top jump jockey Eddie Malloy believes Malloy killed his younger brother, Michael. When Malloy was just ten years old and living on a farm near Penrith, Cumbria, he was in charge of young Michael, six, when the child fell into a swollen river and was swept away.

Eddie Malloy, apparently unable to face his parents with the terrible news, returned home to tell them Michael had disappeared into the woods. It was two days before Malloy admitted to police and search parties what had happened.

Edward Malloy Snr. has always believed that had Eddie run home immediately to report his brother's fate, young Michael could have been saved before he drowned.

*　*　*

The story was continued on page two. Dry-mouthed and shaking, I turned to it with a picture in my mind of two million others doing the same thing this morning.

Malloy Snr.'s resentment of his eldest son led to the boy's becoming an outcast. He was cruelly banished from his parents' house and sent to live with the horses in the stableblock. For the next six years the young Malloy's bed was among straw bales and his only companions were the horses he came to love and trust.

His mother, Constance, brought him meals three times a day in a regime that was almost prison-like. But there was to be no remission for the frightened ten-year-old. Malloy Snr. effectively duped the local authorities into believing that his son was being educated at home.

But the only education Eddie received came from the racing books his mother smuggled out to him during the first two years of his 'imprisonment', a privilege that stopped the moment his father found out about it.

The boy's misery ended on his sixteenth birthday when he was finally banished permanently from the farm and sent out to make his own way in the world.

But the years of living so close to horses served Malloy well and maybe today he looks back with less resentment than some might expect. Within a week of leaving home he found a job with the late Peter Sample, a top jumps trainer in Lambourn, and less than five years later he was champion National Hunt Jockey.

Malloy's champagne life at the top lasted less than two years before he was embroiled in a horse-doping scandal which cost him his jockey's licence and a five-year warning off which disbarred him from setting foot on any property that was subject to Jockey Club rules.

Effectively Malloy had gone from riding the cream of the country's jumpers to being forbidden even to muck out the stable of the lowliest selling plater.

Malloy always proclaimed his innocence in the affair which also saw Jockey Club life bans for three other men, two of them known criminals.

The disgraced jockey found himself in more trouble when he was found guilty of inflicting grievous bodily harm on the man he claimed masterminded the horse-doping syndicate. Five years later the man was found dead, in suspicious circumstances, in the carpark at Stratford Racecourse.

Malloy served eighteen months of a two-year sentence and came out of prison the forgotten man of racing, ending up living in an old caravan, breaking horses for a dealer.

The ex-jockey's fortunes took an upturn once again when a Jockey Club Security Officer sought his help to crack a doping ring whose operation bore marked similarities to the one that had cost Malloy his career five years previously. Working under cover, he helped smash the ring and convict the culprits. Malloy's reward from the Jockey Club, though they deny he was offered this in advance, was the return of his jockey's licence.

Since then Malloy's career has never looked like reaching the heights he achieved as a young man though with an average of 288 rides a season since his comeback four years ago he could make a living at the jumping game for some time yet if he stays free from serious injury.

If he's looking for alternative employment this commentator believes that the Jockey Club Security Department could do much worse than welcome Malloy on their side of the racing fence. Poacher turned gamekeeper maybe but Malloy's inside knowledge would only be part of it. Since helping crack the dope ring, he has also tracked down the man responsible for the murders of two jockeys, a trainer and a vet.

Malloy's skills as a detective were further in evidence when he was instrumental in uncovering a huge insurance fraud which saw him gain a healthy financial reward from Silverdale, the major insurance company involved, a reward Malloy shared with wheelchair-bound friend and former jockey Kenny Hawkins.

Malloy's parents now run a small stud in Newmarket where they've lived for . . .

Clarke rambled on about my parents and how deep and damaging family rifts could be. Tell me about it, Cynthia.

Tell the whole world about it. You just have. But among all the summaries of the cases I'd worked on there was, predictably, no mention of the one involving Kerman.

I sat on the wall staring at the front-page headline, at the colour picture of me smiling and punching the air as I came in on Cragrock at Haydock, the first big race winner since my comeback.

There I was three years ago, jubilant, delirious.

Here I was now, ashamed, empty, desolate.

I stood staring into the distance. The sun was well up and drying the night's rain from the surrounding fields. There was a beautiful smell of freshness and newness. Away to my right the road stretched straight and tempting towards the horizon and I wished to God that I was in one of those old cowboy movies and could just get in the saddle and ride off to where nobody could ever find me.

Ride off to wherever our Michael was and tell him what I'd longed to tell him since that terrible day when I heard him shout and looked down through the thick branches of the tree I'd climbed and sat there in horror, rooted as surely as the tree itself, unable to move as his fair head bobbed on the surface, as his little hands reached and scrabbled at the morning air. I could hear him crying in panic and confusion as he wondered what was happening to him and why his big brother wasn't there to help him, to save him, to pull him out . . .

Sometimes he'd come to me in dreams and tell me it was all right, tell me he'd died quickly and quietly after a few minutes in the water, tell me that he didn't blame me for what I'd done, tell me that heaven was a great place for kids, tell me that he loved me, tell me that someday he'd see me again . . .

And I'd tell him I was sorry.

I'm sorry, Michael.

An animal-like howl rose from my chest and burst from my throat and my legs gave way as I slid slowly down the side of the wall to lie slumped and weeping uncontrollably by the front wheel of the car.

I don't know how long I lay there but somehow I hauled myself back into the car and drove, weak and shocked, back to my parents' place, carrying the newspaper into the house as though it was the corpse of our Michael himself.

The most heartening thing over the next week or so was the level of support everywhere from people I hardly knew. The warmth was unexpected and very welcome. My parents didn't fare quite so well. There were a number of terrible phone calls and poisonous letters, and no matter how much they'd tried to prepare themselves, the shock of it was nightmarish.

My father never recovered from it. His health deteriorated steadily throughout the autumn. On 2 December he died in that prison-like room of his. My mother and I were there, and my sister Louise came back, another home from exile, albeit self-imposed, scarred by what had happened all those years ago.

Guterson, Simeon Prior and Cantrell are on remand as I write though Jean Kerman was released on substantial bail. Brian Kincaid's widow, Judy, made a special trip to come and thank me personally for helping track down his killer.

Martin's been off the booze for over two months and tells me he can't wait for the birth of his baby. Candy's a new man, too. Alive again, happy, looking forward to the new breeding season as I guess his stallions are.

Things are going well for me. Charles's horses are back to their best. I've ridden 67 winners so far.

My mother is, at last, showing signs of becoming her own person. Louise and I have stayed with her since Father died. On Christmas Eve we travelled to Cumbria to visit our Michael's grave. Standing there in the early frost, I finally felt a sense of peace.

On Christmas Day we had our first family dinner since Louise and I were kids. We didn't talk much about Father and, cheered by a couple of sherries and the sight of a late but heavy snow-fall, my mother smiled warmly and talked of the wonderful Christmases we used to have.

I went outside and stood by the paddock rails watching Christmas Day fade to dusk, the yellow glow from the windows lighting the gently falling snowflakes. I heard a door open, slow footsteps crunching, then Louise was beside me, snow melting on her dark hair.

'Mum's asleep by the fire,' she said softly.

I nodded. She slipped her hand into mine and rested her head on my shoulder and I felt a warm contentment rising in me. An unfamiliar feeling. Louise said quietly, 'Maybe this is a new beginning for all of us, Eddie.'

'Maybe. I hope so.'

She raised her head and kissed me lightly on the cheek. 'Happy Christmas,' she whispered.

'Happy Christmas.'